THE MOREAU WITCHES

HELL HATH NO FURY LIKE WITCHES SCORNED

ALEXIS CHATEAU

I0592867

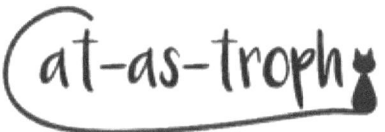

black CATastrophy

The Independent Author Division of Alexis Chateau PR, LLC

Atlanta

THE MOREAU WITCHES

BY

ALEXIS CHATEAU

Copyright © Alexis Chateau

Book Cover Design
Marina Aivazian, *TheNightmareZone*
Alyssa Williams, *Alexis Chateau PR*

Book Editing
Shadow the PR Cat, *black CATastrophy*
Elizabeth Slaughter, *Saved by Words*
Rosetta Yorke, *Turtlewriters*
Tristan O'Bryan, *Alexis Chateau PR*

ISBN: 978-0-692-19823-0

The Moreau Witches is a work of historical fiction. References have been made to historical figures, events, and locales to lend credence to the novel. However, the Moreau women and all other non-historical characters in the book are drawn from the author's imagination and are used fictitiously. Any resemblance of non-historical characters and events to actual ones is entirely coincidental. Contact the author for more information.

COMMENDATIONS

Praise for the original *The Moreau Witches* short story series written by Alexis Chateau, on which this novel is based.

Not only is this gripping but it contains such valuable life lessons.

I love this – "A true leader must find their own way of inspiring loyalty and trust in the people around them." I wish all employers knew this.

And this – "Superior in station and prestige," Madeleine answered honestly, "but never in intellect or skill, or worthiness of fair treatment." If I had the hard copy, I'd be highlighting. Have you ever seen a fiction with highlights?

I really, really, really love your work!

—Anna Jailene Aguilar, *Editor of Cinderella Reimagined*

"Great writing! Brings to mind Anne Rice."

—George F, *Anonymous Author at Unknown*

"I'm really loving this series! I need to see it on screen. I can literally picture the characters."

—Tikeetha Thomas, *Blogger at A Thomas Point of View*

"It's a delight to read. I especially enjoy coming to the end of an installment and thinking, "Uh-oh!"

—Vanessa Baca, *Owner of Food In Books*

Table of Contents

AUTHOR'S NOTE

This novel is written in Victorian English and includes themes of melodrama and Gothic symbolism, in keeping with the era in which it is set.

Beginning in 1700s Saint-Domingue—now known as Haiti—and ending in post-revolutionary France, the novel features European and West Indian characters. Together, they occupy a wide spectrum from White to Mulatto to Black.

Due to the varying nationalities and native tongues of these characters, except for the names of people and places, all non-English words are italicised even when they bear a close resemblance to English. Additionally, all titles of nobility begin with capital letters, when they double as forms of address. Please see glossary at the end of the novel for definitions, translations, historical references, and additional information. A character list has also been included at the start of the novel to help you keep track of the characters.

While I do hope everyone who reads this story comes to love it, it was admittedly not written with every reader in mind. It may be difficult to follow for those unfamiliar with West Indian culture, slave history, the French Revolution, and Victorian era Britain.

May *Bondye* light your way on the witches' tale.

~ALEXIS~

CHARACTER LIST

Archie: An English bartender and retired sailor in France. Friend to Sir Jacob and husband to Esther.

Basile Dubois-Moreau (self-styled *Marquis de Lamoreaux)*: A former poor tradesman who marries a noblewoman. He is the legal husband of Charlotte and father of Madeleine.

Betha: A Haitian servant of the Moreau Family, head of staff at the London house, and the best friend of Charlotte.

Charlotte Moreau (also the Lady Moreau, *Madame* Moreau): A French noblewoman, naturalised British citizen, and renowned playwright. The estranged wife of Basile, mother of Madeleine, and daughter of Mamie.

Chief Inspector Brown: Head of the Scotland Yard investigation to find Charlotte and prosecute Basile.

Countess of Lovelace (also Ada Lovelace): See glossary.

Dr. Frederik: A physician in Barfleur.

Earl of Lovelace (also Lord Lovelace): See glossary.

Eli Bernard (also Élian Bernard, Elijah Bernard): A Creole Frenchman from Haiti who manages Charlotte's theatre in London. The romantic interest of Gaëlle and nephew of Regina.

Esther: A former Jamaican slave who was bought and freed by her husband, Archie. She is a Myal Priestess and friend to Sir Jacob.

Father Castello: A parish priest in France who died under suspicious circumstances.

Father Colombo: An Italian priest.

Gaëlle (also Ellie): Servant to the Moreau Family, the best friend of Madeleine, and the romantic interest of Eli.

George Walker: An English journalist and the much younger romantic interest of Charlotte.

Giu: Italian servant of Severina, father of Ines, and husband to Wilma.

Ines: Daughter of Giu and Wilma, the Italian servants of Severina.

Inspector Garland: Scotland Yard Inspector in the West End, England.

Inspector Laurent: French Inspector who leads the investigation to find Charlotte and prosecute Basile.

Jeanne-Louise: A *mambo asogwe* on the Les Moreaux plantation in Saint-Domingue, during the Haitian Revolution. Sister to Regina, lover of the master of the plantation, and mother to Eli.

John: A drunkard Englishman who is friend to Eli.

Madeleine Moreau (also Lady Madeleine, *Mademoiselle* Moreau, Maddie): The youngest of the Moreau Matriarchy, heir to the family fortune and titles, daughter of Charlotte, and granddaughter of Mamie.

***Mademoiselle* Dubois (also Miss Dubois):** The deceased mother of Basile.

Mamie (also *Marquise de Lamoreaux*; formerly *Seigneuresse* Moreau, *Seigneuresse de Lamoreaux*): A talented healer, alleged witch, and noblewoman. Mother of Charlotte and grandmother of Madeleine.

***Marchesa del Schiavone*:** A wealthy Italian noblewoman and widowed aunt of Sir Jacob.

Maria: A *mambo si pwen* (Haitian Vodou Junior Priestess) and daughter of Olga in 1700s Saint-Domingue.

Monsieur **Popescu:** Wallachian paramour of Mamie.

Olga: Enslaved *mambo asogwe* (Haitian Vodou High Priestess) in 1700s Saint-Domingue.

Pierre Anglais (also Lord Anglais, *Monsieur* Pierre Anglais): The baron at Château d'Anglais in Barfleur. Husband to Severina.

Pierre Moreau (also *Seigneur* Pierre Moreau, *Seigneur de Lamoreaux,*): The father of the Moreau Matriarchy and the first *Seigneur de Lamoreaux.*

Professor Rámon (also *Monsieur* Rámon): An aristocrat and retired doctor of medicine who instructs Madeleine against her father's wishes.

Regina (also Reggie): A Haitian Servant of the Moreau Family, head of staff at the Barfleur Estate. Friend to Gaëlle, Madeleine, and Mamie. Aunt to Eli.

Sarah Harper (also Miss Harper): The only White servant at the Barfleur Estate, and special attendant to Basile.

Seigneur **Bernard-Moreau:** The deceased father of Charlotte and late husband of Mamie.

Seigneur **Boucher:** French planter in 1700s Saint-Domingue who lynched Olga.

Severina Anglais (also *Madame* Anglais, *Signora* Anglais, Rina): The Italian wife of the French baron, *Monsieur* Pierre Anglais, and lover of Basile Dubois-Moreau.

Sir Jacob Andrews (also Jake, Jack): The second-son of an English baron, nephew of an Italian marchioness, a knighted soldier, and Madeleine's suitor.

Stanley (also Stan): A mysterious assassin well known to John and Sir Jacob.

Thibaut & Olivier: Twin sons of a wealthy merchant. Students at the *Université de Paris.*

William Scott IV: An English attorney who represents the Moreau Family.

Wilma: Italian servant of Severina, mother of Ines, and wife to Giu.

"Shall anything saucier be found

than united woman!"

—"Mr. Sphinks" in *Under the Greenwood Tree*
by Thomas Hardy

PROLOGUE

The Black Abyss

So, this was grief.

She could feel the cold, alien fingers taking hold of her. Squeezing. Choking. The very air seemed impossible to breathe. She dropped to her knees, her white dress of silk and cotton now ruined by mud and blood.

Overhead, the creaking of the rope against the wood grew louder and louder as the body swayed back and forth. Summoning her last bit of strength, she forced herself to look up at the corpse that had once been her mother—now blooded, bruised, and hanged.

"Get up!" he commanded her.

She stood, her eyes never leaving the lifeless form before her, still swaying in the island breeze. Tears brimmed in her eyes, but she would not look away. She wanted to remember, to engrave every small detail into her mind: the swollen eyelids; the bleeding scalp, where chestnut curls had been ruthlessly torn out at the roots; the back torn open by the indelicate touch of leather to flesh; the bare, dirt-caked feet.

"Betray me, and you'll be next," he warned. "That witch isn't here to protect you now. And your father wouldn't dare cross me!" The bottle of rum he had emptied fell with an impotent thud into the mud, and the whip after it.

She clenched her fists, holding them stiffly at her sides. If someone could but put a sword in her hand, she would run him clear through with it, come what may. He was drunk, unsteady on his feet; his speech slurred. What defence could he possibly muster against her?

"Maria." A much gentler voice said her name, long after her mother's murderer had gone.

She felt his touch upon her hand, usually welcome, but now like a curse burning into her skin. She drew away from him, hearing the hurt of her rejection in his prolonged silence.

"I'm sorry."

His words only roused her rage. "You watched it happen and did nothing! And coward that you are, you did not even summon me until the black deed was done."

"He is my father, Maria."

She rounded on him, the anger lighting a flame in her eyes he had never seen before. "And *she* is my mother! When it is *my* turn, when *I* am next, will you just watch then, too? Will you come to my grave after the lynching to tell me you are *sorry?*" She spat at his feet and brushed past him in a whirlwind of pain and anger.

Her dirtied white dress seemed to glow beneath the full moon glaring down from overhead, but, in time, she was swallowed by the darkness and the trees.

Her mother had built her hut deep in the woods, on a quarter acre of land bordering Les Bouchers and La Guinaudée. Here, Olga had lived in peace, growing her herbs for medicine, for healing. Maria knew them all by name and sight and scent, though she had never before given any serious thought to the life of a *mambo*.

The door was scarcely upon its hinges when she arrived. The one large room inside told of a struggle. To her left, the two beds upon which they had lain their heads many a night—Maria telling of her exploits and Olga tsking away—were overturned. To her right, the fire in the hearth had died out, and the meal they should have shared was seeping into the clay earth.

Drops of blood spattered across the dirt floor and wooden furniture told of the violence with which they had overpowered her mother. An elderly woman who had never lifted a finger against them. A *mambo asogwe.* An indispensable and honoured member of the coloured and White community, long before *Seigneur* Boucher ever set foot on Saint-Domingue.

The weight of Maria's loss now fell heavily upon her. How could she ever again think of her mother without visions of her body dangling from a rope by a broken neck? Her lips tainted with the blue of death. Her skin paler than it had ever been in life. And all while *Seigneur* Boucher walked free, protected by the privilege of plantocracy.

But there was one power yet which knew no race or colour or class. The memory of this gave her new strength, new purpose. No, she could not give in to despair! There was work to be done and a life to claim.

She tossed wood onto the fire, lit a few candles, and retrieved a book from beneath the pile of overturned bottles that had once contained cures for everything from headaches to unwanted children. The *Sekrè*, as her mother had called it, was a collection of spells and potions written by Olga's mother, the book of choice when Olga had first taught Maria how to read.

"Literacy is a magic of sorts," she had insisted, when her only child showed obvious disinterest in her letters.

What good were adventures in books when she could live adventures of her own? Even at a young age, Maria had been cursed with a nose for trouble, and she much preferred to sniff around the slave huts, causing the occasional fuss with the slave children.

As she grew older, she learned that the frightening howls in the night, not long after she received a mere harsh word or two from her planter father, were those of the slave children who had accompanied her on her rendezvous. Thereafter, she spent more time at home in the company of her mother, sulking all the while, and consenting to the boring adventure of pursuing letters.

One day, the troublesome combination of disobedience and clumsiness had sent the *Sekrè* tumbling to the floor. When she picked it up, it was opened to a chapter she had never seen before. Almost leaping from the pages was a half-goat, half-man with red-rimmed eyes, dancing in a barren land. The words *Liv Lanmò* were written in red below his hoofed feet, in the elegant hand of her grandmother.

"It is the Book of Death: the final chapter of the *Sekrè*," Olga had said in response to her questioning gaze.

Maria's curiosity was instantly piqued, but Olga said but little more of it. "Let us first focus on all the good we can do," she insisted. "When you are older, you may learn the rest. Not now."

At sixteen, "older" had come. Only then did Olga finally teach her the power of the dark side of *Vodou*, and the responsibility that came with the work of a *caplata*. "When nothing else will save you and those you love, but never otherwise," she had cautioned. "There is always a price for black magic."

"What price?" had been young Maria's eager question, failing even then to grasp the gravity of her mother's words.

"Your legacy," Olga had answered. "Your line will always have a hole in their soul, so the darkness can creep in.

"But sometimes a dark hole is a good thing, for it provides a window to the other side. Never forget, however, that when we look into that black abyss, it stares right back into us."

Maria now threw the *Sekrè* open and found the exact passage her mother had shown her, so many years before. She had memorised it in her sixteenth year when she had been ordained a *mambo si pwen*, but, like her mother, and hers before her, she had never found cause to use it.

Not until tonight.

Tonight, she would make no mistakes. She would not say the words with half-hearted interest, as though they were foreign to her. Tonight, she believed. And tonight, she would call on all the powers of Darkness to do her bidding.

CHAPTER I

A Bitter Quarrel

Madeleine crouched low at the end of the corridor, listening as the voices carried through the open door in a heated exchange. She could hear the growl of her father's anger and the high pitch of her mother's frustration, but could not make out the words.

As her very future rode upon the wings of this conversation, she was determined to hear every word. She tiptoed down the hallway as carefully as ever, but the old manor had fallen into some disrepair of late. Halfway to the door, a floorboard loudly heralded the presence of trespassing feet. She held her breath, waiting to be discovered, but her parents were so absorbed in their disagreement that neither seemed to notice.

"And why *shouldn't* she go?" Charlotte challenged her husband.

"In neither England nor France will you find a college that would permit her attendance."

"Then she can learn in the comfort of our home, just as I did. Until times change. Until sex is no longer a pitiful requirement for genius."

"She will not be taught any further under my roof. Education is for boys, for *men!*" her father shouted, though he had himself married an educated woman.

Madeleine peeked through the open door. She could see her mother's expression change from annoyance to bitter amusement; her eyebrows arched and her lips curled almost into a snarl. "Perchance, is that why *you* went to school, husband?" she shot back at him.

Madeleine's heart lurched in her chest at the slap that cut through the air. Charlotte tumbled backwards onto her writing desk and then to the floor, with her husband's hand emblazoned in red upon her cheek.

He grabbed her by the hair, lifting her up, his eyes wild with fury. "Women should know their place! You have ventured far from yours for long enough."

"Father!" Madeleine shouted from the doorway.

"Back to your room!" Charlotte cried, her voice breaking, but Madeleine would not budge.

Basile released his wife and marched up to his daughter, with the threat of violence still lingering in his eyes. A purple vein pulsated in his forehead as though at any second it would burst. Madeleine looked up at him unflinchingly, though her heart drummed out the beat of panic in her chest.

"Madeleine, go!" Charlotte begged her.

"I will not!" Madeleine insisted, stomping her foot on the wooden floor in open defiance, her eyes never leaving her father.

Basile looked her up and down as if sizing her up for a beating, but seemed to think better of his plan and stormed from the room. Madeleine then rushed to her mother's side as three servants came stampeding down the hall. No doubt they had heard the shouting and the crash of inkwells, steel pens, and heavy books to the floor.

Betha rushed to her mistress and helped Madeleine lift her to her feet. Regina tried to clear up the mess, cursing all the while in *Kreyol*. Gaëlle, of a more delicate constitution, stood crying in the doorway.

"This will need to be dressed," Betha insisted. "I will call for the doctor."

"You will do no such thing," Charlotte replied, touching the base of her neck. The edge of the desk had torn into her skin and already it had turned purple. "To call the doctor is to risk scandal. I assure you, I am well."

"Is this not the final straw now, Mother? Will you not leave him?" Madeleine asked. "He is a horrid, horrid little man!"

Charlotte turned to face her, hurt and anger welling up in her eyes. Yet, they softened at the look on her daughter's face. "I want to," she said, "but I cannot. Not yet. In the meantime, your education will continue. And I... well, I think I shall go to the London house and let Basile cool off for a moment. You will come with me; yes?"

Madeleine did not hesitate to give her assent. There were few things she looked forward to as much as a trip with her mother to the London flat, such trips taken almost invariably after Basile had one of his episodes. As he was known to be a hot-tempered husband, this happened often enough. Even so, this was the first time he had struck his wife.

There were times when Madeleine remembered quieter years, long gone, when her parents had been in love, she supposed. Yet, even those had been littered by heated arguments, usually about the same thing: Charlotte allegedly forgetting her place as a woman or saying or doing some small thing which made her husband feel less of a man.

As she grew older, the fights had become louder, more frequent, and now, more violent. Madeleine was certain if her mother remained, the next blow would make the first appear as little more than child's play.

"I don't understand why women marry."

Gaëlle leaned over and carefully added warm water to Madeleine's bath. Her mistress's head was against the back of the tub, her dark hair hanging over the sides, her brows knitted together in a frown. Her eyes were shut tight, as though if she didn't look, she could change her present predicament.

There were days when Gaëlle would have given anything to be in Madeleine's place. To be beautiful, rich, White, and a Lady; today wasn't one of them. She knew how Madeleine agonised over her parents' marriage, and how much she blamed herself, for all the household knew Charlotte remained only for the sake of her daughter.

"Some women do it for love," Gaëlle told her. "And some for station. Your mother already had station, a title, a legacy, so she married your father for love."

"Who can love such a man?"

"Love is blind, and men do change—oft' for the worst."

Madeleine sighed, and sank further into the bath, the water now coming up to her chin. Some splashed along the sides and onto the floor. Gaëlle rushed to dry it up.

Madeleine opened her eyes and looked over at the mess she had caused. "Oh, don't fret about that, Gaëlle. I am sorry. I did not realise there was this much water in the bath."

Gaëlle's cheeks burned red. "I am a servant, Madeleine," she reminded her. "It is my duty to see to your comforts, not you to mine."

"You are my friend," Madeleine insisted.

"Yes, but first, your servant," Gaëlle answered, good-naturedly. She dried the floor, and then took her usual seat on a chair a few feet away from her mistress. She held a robe on her lap, waiting patiently for Madeleine to leave the bath.

In truth, she enjoyed these quiet moments together, where they could talk and laugh without listening ears. Sometimes, Regina joined them to tell a naughty tale or two, or to share some rich kitchen gossip, but more often than not, it was just the two of them.

"Please, don't ever marry, Gaëlle," Madeleine said, sinking into the tub again. "I could not bear to lose you. You are as dear to me as a sister."

Gaëlle's heart quickened in her chest. "You flatter me, Madeleine."

"Good," she replied. "Someone should."

When half a dozen trunks appeared in the anteroom the following day, it became clear this was no ordinary trip to London. Charlotte was leaving, and she hadn't the slightest intention of coming back anytime soon.

"I will send for you in a week," she said to Madeleine. "I will need to find a larger flat and get settled. Gaëlle, you must join us, as well. I know Eli will be delighted to see you."

"Really, *Madame!* I could not refuse such an invitation!"

Madeleine laced her fingers through Gaëlle's, her spirits lifted. "What a holiday we shall have in London!"

"What is the meaning of all this?" Basile demanded. He had evidently just awoken, his hair not yet combed, his moustache yet uncurled.

"I'm going to London," Charlotte answered, her gaze cold and uncaring, the fresh print of his palm still marring the delicate flesh of her cheek.

"And you need all this?" Basile replied, growing sheepish.

"It will be a rather long trip, I'm afraid."

Basile stared at her for a moment, and then looked to Madeleine, who still clung happily to Gaëlle. "Get away from my daughter! Do not propose to make yourself familiar with your betters."

Gaëlle tried to pull her hand free, but Madeleine held it, firmly. "It was I who made myself familiar, Father," she spoke up. "And I find Gaëlle is far better company than many of the ladies you presume to force upon me." She turned away, taking Gaëlle with her. "Mother, I will be back in a moment. Please, wait for me."

"You will be next, if you continue to speak to your father in such a manner," Gaëlle warned, though her heart warmed at Madeleine's defensiveness.

"I am not my mother," Madeleine replied. "If he raises a hand against me, he may not live to regret it."

The sharpness of her tone pricked fear in Gaëlle's heart. "I will end him, if he hurts you; I swear it."

"You will do no such thing," Madeleine replied. "I am quite capable of fending for myself. Can you please ask Regina to fix me my favourite this morning? I find I may need a bit of cheering up. Mother's leaving, though long overdue, is nonetheless bittersweet."

Gaëlle bowed her head in assent and then left her in the hallway. When Madeleine returned to the anteroom, Basile was storming by her in the opposite direction. He stopped as though to issue a threat or warning, but could not seem to find the words, and strode off.

"Are you truly leaving him, Mother?"

"Geographically," Charlotte answered. Seeing the light fade from her daughter's eyes, she added, "Madeleine, it is not possible for a French-woman to divorce her husband." When Madeleine's lips parted in protest, she raised a gloved hand to silence her. With her trap waiting just beyond the door, there was little time for revisiting an argument they had shared many a time before.

"We have more pressing matters, my dear; let me speak," she said, not unkindly. "It appears Basile is not alone in his prejudices against our sex. The only professor I could find willing to instruct you is here in Barfleur. I will do my best to sway him, but already he has made it clear he cannot abide London, would never suffer the company of country folk in Lamoreaux, and, in short, will not leave Barfleur.

"You are a woman now, Madeleine, and as your mother, it is ever my pleasure to provide you with every opportunity at my disposal. You know my hopes for you, and you know how I loathe to be far from you, but you must think hard upon this and make the decision which best suits your purpose.

"If you come with me to London, you may be free of your father. But, if two years of searching has only brought us Professor Rámon, I do not foresee another will step forward. You would then need to give up your ambitions of an education in medicine, until France or England come to their senses, or until another professor is willing to risk the scandal of a female student.

"Yet, if you remain—if you should stay here with this foul creature I took to my heart and my bed—I know he will stop at nothing to make himself a constant obstacle in the path of all your best ambitions." Pausing as though to search Madeleine's eyes for a hint of which direction she would take, she then added, "You needn't decide now; we may discuss it further when you join me in London."

But already, the wheels of Madeleine's mind had gone to turning. She saw immediately the fire and frying pan before her: the danger of remaining beneath her father's roof in Barfleur, the crushing blow if she allowed her ambitions to be thwarted. And so, already, she knew what her answer would be—*must* be.

"It will break my heart to be separated from you, Mother," she said, "but I did not make the sacrifices I have, nor suffer the ridicule of boys and men and chasten my heart against courting and love, to then set aside my greatest aspirations for fear of my father's displeasure. If I must remain here to be instructed, then here I shall be.

"I know you worry for me, but it is time you sought your own happiness, for I know you grow ever more miserable here. You have suffered long enough on my account. Besides, we both know he is almost always all bark and no bite. And was it not you who told me strong women do not become thus by being coddled by their mothers?"

Charlotte had not expected otherwise, and yet she had hoped, perhaps selfishly, that Madeleine would flee Barfleur with her. She blinked away the sting of tears. "How can I leave you here with him, Madeleine? At eighteen, I myself rarely strayed far from the hem of my mother's dress. Maybe—maybe in another year, the laws will have changed and you may yet be educated at Oxford or Cambridge."

"Perhaps they will," Madeleine agreed, forcing her own tears to remain at bay, for she knew one tear from her eyes would release a dam from her mother's. "Until then, this is where I remain. But you: you must go. Oh, the guilt I have suffered, Mother, to know you stayed here because of me!"

"And I would stay longer still if you wished it," Charlotte avowed.

"I do not wish it, Mother. I wish you away from this place, which has brought you such pain, however well you may hide it."

Charlotte's hands trembled as she set them to her daughter's face. "You will forgive me for saying so, Madeleine, but you have inherited your father's fiery temper. Please do not incite his own in my absence. I know he vexes you, but you must take care with your words. I cannot bear the thought of him laying his hands upon you."

"He may lose his hands if he does such a thing."

Charlotte's lips broke into a sad smile. "You are a Little Mamie, I see. But I would prefer it not come to that; promise me."

"I will do my best, Mother." After a moment's hesitation, she asked, "Whom will you take with you? Will you take Regina?"

"There would be chaos in this house without Regina. I will take Betha."

"Your Gaëlle," Madeleine noted. "I am not much surprised. I will miss you both."

Charlotte took her in her arms and kissed both her cheeks. "Take care my feisty feline. I shall see you in a week's time. Rein in those claws."

Three months went by without Charlotte setting foot in the manor again. And then it was six. And then it was a year. And then it seemed to fade from memory when last she had visited.

For a time, Basile was glad for her absence. There was no one to challenge him, to curb his spending, or drinking, or whoring. And as her fame grew in London, so his notoriety grew in Barfleur. People began to whisper; his conduct seemed to imply it was his own doing that had caused *Madame* Moreau to seek refuge in London. It was then, almost a year later, that he thought it fit to spend more time abroad, visiting with his estranged wife.

When he travelled to London, so did Madeleine, but she took many more trips without his dark shadow cast upon it. Indeed, it was a wonder why he ever visited at all. Charlotte was ever occupied with organising charity balls, speaking at events, and debating with learned men in coffee houses. As a well-respected French socialite in London, she was never short of invitations to show her face in high society or amongst fellow intellectuals.

Often entertained in her West End home were other women Basile believed had lost sight of their place, like Mary Shelley and the Countess of Lovelace. The occasional presence of the famous Charles Dickens did not bring him cheer either, for Dickens often encouraged Charlotte's independence and took obvious delight in picking her brains on everything from the management of wealth to the plight of the poor.

In all this, Madeleine was a constant presence at her mother's side when visiting London: well-loved and well-sought after by many an Englishman of title and wealth. She was ever the attentive scholar in Barfleur, but, in London, she set aside her books for the intrigue of noble society and the world of fiction. She read everything from the penny dreadfuls, much loved by the poor of East End, to Dickens's *Pickwick Papers*.

Meanwhile Basile, who did not speak a word of English, often remained locked away in his bedchamber. This only made him more jealous, more drunk, more violent. The arguing continued, but as Charlotte's theatre manager never strayed far from her side, Basile learned to cast only words in his wife's direction, while fuming at the Creole Frenchman's constant presence. Unfortunately for him, as a wordsmith, Charlotte always had better words to return. And so, in due time, he would pack his things and storm back to Barfleur, leaving Madeleine behind.

In spite of these disruptions, Charlotte was happy in London. Her husband's infrequent appearances barely cast a shadow upon her life. Little did she know that while she smiled, he plotted; while she slept, he dreamed of her demise; while she basked in the glory of admiration, there was a storm brewing that would threaten the legacy Maria Moreau had risked so much to build.

CHAPTER II

A Shrew Untamed

"So hot..." she muttered, through cracked lips.

Gaëlle crossed the room and threw the windows open. The chilly air rolling in put a tremor in her hands, but already Madeleine seemed to be in better spirits. Outside, fiery foliage fell from the trees by the window and into the gardens below. In floated the sweet scent of light rain and the laughter of children.

"Water."

Gaëlle tied the curtains back, and then rushed to fill her glass with the cool water Regina had just brought up from the spring. Madeleine drank it greedily, droplets mingling with the sticky sweat that glued her clothes and hair to her skin.

"Better?" Gaëlle asked.

Madeleine nodded weakly, and then settled down to sleep again. It had been two days since she had last been herself. The sickness had come on suddenly after a routine evening stroll through the garden, and she had been confined to bed since. Twice, Dr. Frederik had come and gone, declaring he hadn't a clue what had befallen her.

"You said if you had not improved by today, we could send for Mamie," Gaëlle ventured.

Madeleine waved the suggestion away, her movements as faint as they were the day before. "I am only tired now, Gaëlle. No need to trouble Mamie. I would be long recovered by the time she made the day's ride from Lamoreaux. Only let me rest a bit and I shall come right down for dinner."

Gaëlle did not think it at all likely, but sure enough, when her mistress woke, she was as right as rain. She was able to take a bath on her own, dressed without complaint of pain, and was at the table within minutes of Regina bringing out her meal.

"I hear you dining downstairs, tonight," Regina greeted her in *Kreyol*, as she set the dishes before her. "You look almost better. How you feeling?"

"Starved," Madeleine admitted. "I am sure I shall be better, after I have eaten."

"Good. I make your favourite tonight," Regina announced, as she set down a plate of rice and beans. To the left, she placed a bowl of Creole chicken sauce and another of *sos pwa* bean sauce. To the right was a plate of sweet fritters she called *dous beniyè* and a glass of wine.

Basile's face twitched with anger, but he said not a word. He had specifically asked to be served by the only White servant in the house and absolutely refused to touch anything the Blacks gave him, especially their Haitian food, so spicy he could feel his eyes already watering from a distance. Even so, he took it as a grave insult that his daughter should be served before him.

When Sarah brought his food out a few minutes later, he did not neglect to chastise her for her tardiness. A young and sensitive girl, she fled the room in tears. Basile looked after her in disgust, before digging into his meal.

"The maid says you have not been well."

"I have not," Madeleine confirmed.

"Your servants called for the doctor twice, without my leave."

"I am sure they had only my best interest at heart."

"And can they afford to pay me back for that interest? I would very much like my pockets to be refilled for the unexpected expense."

"I will apply to Mother, post-haste."

It had the desired effect. "You will do no such thing!" After a time, he added, "One would almost think this the residence of a commoner.

The house has been in constant disarray, while you lazed about in bed, probably of some woman's complaint, as if the whole lot of you are not moody enough already."

Madeleine met his gaze across the table. "Perchance father, is it a 'woman's complaint' that keeps you in such a foul mood for days at a time?"

Dishes clattered and one glass smashed on the floor as he rose from the table and stalked towards her.

Madeleine rose from her chair as well, with slow and measured movements, her skirts gathered in her hands. "Take care, Father. If you lay a hand on me, I will give Sir Jacob Andrews mine own in marriage, in exchange for your head. You will find this shrew is not so easily tamed or beaten. Do not give in to folly."

Her threat gave him pause. The British soldier had made his bid for Madeleine's hand no secret. His contempt for Basile was no secret either, though the two exchanged polite smiles in public and maintained a healthy distance.

"Gaëlle!" Madeleine called, her eyes still fixed upon her father, who now stood but a foot away from her. "I will be finishing my meal in my bedchamber. Please inform the others."

Gaëlle did not move until she saw Madeleine turn and head for the archway. She hurried after her, making her way to the kitchen, while Madeleine disappeared up the stairs.

"Sarah!" Basile bellowed. "Clean up this mess! Immediately!"

Time seemed to stretch on forever, before she heard the familiar and anxious footsteps of Gaëlle, accompanied by the more self-assured steps of Regina. The former threw the door open as though expecting some horror would await her. The latter waltzed in and shut the door with a slight sway of her hips, and a press of her derrière to the door.

"Madeleine, you mustn't tempt your father so. You know how he is," Gaëlle cautioned.

Regina chuckled as she set the tray of food down on Madeleine's secondary work desk. The young heiress had already undressed and was brushing out her hair.

"I always told Charlotte, you your grandmother's child," Regina said in *Kreyol*, as she removed Madeleine's meal from the silver tray. When Gaëlle did not move to help, she snapped her fingers and gestured to the empty cup.

Gaëlle filled it with shaking hands.

"What I would *give* to have seen his face, Maddie."

"Don't encourage her!" Gaëlle snapped in a sharp whisper.

Regina fanned her off and perched at the edge of the desk. "You did well, Maddie. Don't let anyone put you down, not even your good-for-nothing sorry excuse of a father."

"Regina!" Perspiration appeared on Gaëlle's forehead.

"What? Everyone know he about as useful as a lump of wet flour."

A small laugh escaped Madeleine for the first time in days, followed almost immediately by a dry cough.

"See? A little bit of humour. That's what she needed. You may be her confidant, Gaëlle, but I bring the comedy!" Despite her cheerful words, she looked at Madeleine with some concern. She noticed a sickly paleness had crept into her skin, reminiscent of her earlier illness. "Are you well, Miss?"

"Quite well, Reggie. Thank you." She coughed again, but her appetite was still with her, and that gave reason for hope.

"He's poisoned her!" Gaëlle all but collapsed onto the bed.

Another chuckle and another cough from Madeleine.

"You should have never spoken to him like that. You know how he is... what he has done."

It was Regina's turn to laugh. "You worry too much, Gaëlle!" But in her heart, she cherished a secret fear that Gaëlle's paranoia was not unfounded.

More than once, she had found Sarah getting closer than was necessary to Madeleine's meals in the kitchen. The last time, she had confronted the girl, and the conversation that followed was not one she was like to forget. In the end, Sarah had left the room as docile as ever, but had impressed upon Regina that she knew more than she let on, and was perhaps not so foolish as she appeared to be. Regina had cast a watchful eye in her direction ever since.

She stood, now. "Gaëlle, I'm sure you won't mind keeping an eye on things for the rest of the evening. I have an errand to run before the hour grows late."

"Where will you go?" Madeleine enquired.

"To gather some supplies to brew you a special tea that will bring some colour back to those lovely cheeks."

"Regina, the last time you promised me a special tea, it tasted like horse filth."

"So, it did! And, so might this one." She headed for the door. "Gaëlle?" she added as calmly as possible. "Do keep an eye on Sarah, as well. She seems a little shaken after that incident with the *Monsieur*."

"Yes, yes, of course," Gaëlle assured her.

After she had gone, Madeleine ate quietly, her mind wandering. Was it too much to ask, for a father who appreciated her intellect, in spite of her sex? Irrespective of her sex, even? Too much to ask for him to care? To love?

"I am sure he was a better man once, or your mother would never have married him," Gaëlle said, guessing at her train of thoughts. "Wealth and power changes people, and not always for the better. You should see what happens to many of my own kind, and how we treat each other when we are made or born free. Not everyone has the gift of empathy. Not everyone is like you and *Madame* Charlotte."

"I suppose not," Madeleine answered, sipping her wine. "The world can be an ugly place for a woman."

"It can be an ugly place for anyone," Gaëlle replied, "but there is beauty if you choose to see it. You need only look."

It was almost midnight when Regina returned. By then, Madeleine had taken to bed again with sweat upon her forehead, fading in and out of either sleep or unconsciousness.

"I fear for the worst, Reggie," Gaëlle said when she entered.

"As you always do," Regina quipped. "Help her sit up."

"But, she sleeps."

"Then, wake her."

Gaëlle grabbed some pillows to put behind Madeleine's back, and helped raise her up, while Regina pulled a curious bottle from her pockets. It was small, and the liquid inside looked black and vile.

"What is that?" Madeleine enquired, her words slurred by sleep and sickness.

"Horse filth," Regina answered. "Now, open up."

Madeleine made a face, but did as she was told. She gagged as she swallowed the thick and insipid liquid. Regina pinched her nose and clamped her hand to her mouth, forcing her to keep it all down or suffocate. Madeleine chose the latter, but then broke into a fit of coughing that so exhausted her, she fell back into a deep sleep.

"What that?" Gaëlle asked in *Kreyol*, helping Madeleine to settle in again.

"She'll be alright in the morning," was all Regina said in answer. "Sarah feeling any better?"

"She came to check on Madeleine earlier, offered her some wine, but Madeleine was already asleep." Gaëlle gestured to the cup sitting untouched on the dressing table. "She retired to bed after that."

"And the others?"

"Everything is cleaned up, and everyone eat and gone to bed. Only I am awake. I heard *Monsieur* outside the door earlier, but he didn't come in, thank God."

Regina acknowledged her report with a brief nod. "Will you be able to stay up with her?"

"Yes, all night."

"I will relieve you before dawn," Regina assured her. She took the wine Sarah had set down for Madeleine and then left the room.

CHAPTER III

A Dead Pup

When Madeleine threw the curtains back, the sunlight burst into the room with the vengeance of a thousand suns.

Gaëlle bolted up from the armchair where she had kept vigil the night before, the weight of languor heavy on her eyelids. *"Mademoiselle,* why did you not ask me to open them for you, if that was your wish?" she said, with obvious embarrassment.

Madeleine laughed. "Oh, Gaëlle! Am I truly as helpless as you and Regina make me out to be? I think not. I believe I can open a few windows and tie a few curtains without causing injury to myself."

Gaëlle stifled a yawn against the back of her hand and looked about the room as she shrugged off the last clutches of sleep. The sunlight brightened the white bed linen, and the spotless floor of the attic apartment Mamie reserved for her granddaughter at the Château de Lamoreaux. At all other times, it was shut up: dusty and musty and neglected.

"'Tis such a beautiful day! Let us go for a walk in the gardens."

Already, Gaëlle was grasping clumsily for excuses, while Madeleine hurried to the door. "But Maddie, you are not dressed!" she finally managed, lagging behind.

"Gaëlle, Mamie isn't concerned with such things. I would be rather surprised if even *she* was dressed. Come!" She stretched a hand out to her friend, who now looked longingly at *Le Capitaine Pamphile,* which she had evidently hoped to finish. Still, Gaëlle could not resist Madeleine's smiling face. And so, the two made their way down the steps and the hallways, arm in arm.

By then, Madeleine's newfound cheerfulness had infected her companion. And so, Gaëlle was now just as enamoured by the last of the summer sunshine lighting the house through the large windows, shining from floor to ceiling. The brightly coloured birds against the equally bright leaves that had only just begun to turn to their fiery autumn shades. The whistle of the wind, which now carried them away.

"Pray, let me enquire about breakfast before we go into the gardens," Gaëlle pleaded.

Madeleine released her and went to the back door of the kitchen, while the servants gossiped and chopped and laughed behind her. The wind came in through the open door, sending invisible fingers through her hair. It whipped the skirts of her nightgown into a wild cadence about her feet, while the sun kissed her skin.

Suddenly, her blissful autumn reverie was interrupted by the sound of a scuffle beyond the compost Mamie kept for her garden. Her curiosity piqued, she hurried out to see what was amiss. She found herself the sole audience of two beautiful Pyrenean Mountain pups, perhaps no more than six months old. The two played happily together for a time, but the female pup was stronger, and the male pup became increasingly frustrated at how easily she pinned him to the ground.

The third time that she easily swatted him over onto his back, he bared his teeth at her and growled. Confused, she jumped back from him, staring as though unsure of what her next move should be. The male advanced slowly, and then with one swift movement, lunged at her.

He tore at her throat, and Madeleine watched in horror as her coat went from snow white and gold to a ghastly shade of red—the red of death. The red of murder. An impotent scream seemed to fill her throat. Try as she might, she could not get it out. And all the while, the dog tore and ate his playmate as though she were meat from the kitchens.

The dog then turned to face her, fangs bared, growl deepening, blood dripping into the earth below him.

He lunged at her.

It rang throughout the Barfleur Manor like a high-pitched death knell, raising goose bumps on the arms of all who heard it, and striking fear into their hearts. Gaëlle, who had only just nodded off, jumped up from the armchair as she had done in Madeleine's dream, knocking her book to the floor.

"Madeleine!" she cried, rushing to her mistress. "Are you well? What is amiss? 'Tis only a dream, Madeleine. Please, wake up!"

Madeleine sat upright in bed, her chest rising and falling rapidly as she caught her breath. She stared at Gaëlle with half parts relief and fear.

"What is it, Madeleine?" Gaëlle pressed her. "Have you... have you *seen* something?"

The door was flung open wide as Regina came rushing in, the key to the door still in her hand. Relief washed over her when she saw her worst fears had not come true. She crossed herself and then hurried to her side.

Some of the other servants hovered outside the door, peering in and whispering, but unwilling to cross the threshold into Madeleine's bed-chamber. Though they counted themselves lucky to have a mistress as kind as Madeleine; hitherto, only Regina, Gaëlle, and Betha had the privilege of claiming familiarity with her.

"What is all this fuss?" a loud voice boomed from behind. "Step aside! Back to work! The whole lot of you!"

The crowd dispersed almost immediately, though Sarah lingered behind, long after Basile had stepped into the room. Regina did not fail to notice as Sarah's watchful green eyes searched the room with obvious purpose, no doubt looking for the cup of wine she had left for Madeleine the night before.

"Did you not hear me? Get back to work!" Basile shouted.

Regina stood and bowed. "With all due respect, *Monsieur,* our orders come from Madeleine, and we had arrangements for me to sit with her this morning. Gaëlle has been with her all night, and must be tired, I am sure."

"Thank you for sitting up with me, Gaëlle," Madeleine said to her friend, squeezing her hand. "Please, get some rest."

She nodded and left the room, passing Sarah in the doorway.

"Regina, I am thirsty and a little hungry, but quite well now. Would you be so kind as to fetch me some breakfast, and a bit of water, before you sit with me? I am still tired, and do not foresee my leaving the bed until evening."

Regina nodded. "Yes, Maddie. I'll only be a moment."

"Her name is Madeleine, slave."

"And her name is Regina," Madeleine cut in. "She is no slave, Father. She is a free woman and my friend."

"Thank you, *Madeleine,*" Regina said with great emphasis and then she left the room.

"You must end this familiarity with these *négres.* Servants serve their betters, not those they believe to be their equals." When Madeleine did not reply, he sat in the armchair next to her bed and looked about her room with a curiosity that spoke of their own unfamiliarity with each other. "You are well now; I trust?"

"Quite so, Father, but I'll remain in bed a while longer."

"Yes; that is for the best. I suspect we have no need of the doctor again?"

"None at all."

"Hmm..." He stood. "Good. I will be leaving shortly, but wanted to see that you were well, especially after that scream. Whatever was that for?"

"Bad dreams, Father."

He looked with distaste at the medical books on her work desk. "Yes; perhaps your grotesque studies are proving a bit too much for your delicate female constitution?" He stood then, and straightened his golden-embroidered swallowtail coat and his matching golden cravat. "We have our differences, you and I, Madeleine, but I am not the enemy. I am your father, after all. I have only your best interest at heart."

"Of course, Father."

He seemed to want to say more but could not find the words. When he could stand no more of the awkward silence, he turned to leave the room. He found Sarah still standing in the doorway, a faraway look upon her face. "Do I pay you to daydream, girl? Get back to work!"

Roused from her ruminations, she strung together a stutter of words, making little sense, if any, and then fled the room.

Regina stood rooted to the spot, lost in thought. There was only one person in the household who would ever want to hurt Madeleine. But would he really go to cowardly lengths to do it? And what could he hope to gain from such wickedness against his own child?

The clatter of a clumsy mistake roused her from thought. She reprimanded the servant and hurried back to Madeleine's room with breakfast. To her dismay, the room was empty—empty after Basile had only just been left alone with her.

Regina set the food down and walked to the open window. All was still outside. Not a leaf stirred, nor a dog barked. But more importantly, there was no broken body on the flowerbed below.

She fled the bedroom then and hurried back into the hall, debating on whether or not it was prudent to call aloud. Settling on stealth, she went from door to door, checking the bedrooms, the library, even Charlotte's study.

Her hands trembled as she found the keys for Basile's office, but when she touched the door it opened before her. Madeleine spun around to face her, frightened.

"Madeleine, what in Heaven's name you doing in here?"

"Father is up to something. I know he is."

"He will be furious if he finds you here."

"He has a family seal," Madeleine continued as though she hadn't heard her. "And look here: a letter from Mother about her recent trip to Italy. I have not even seen it yet, and here he has it in his office, opened, with this counterfeit seal beside it. There is only one true seal and Mother has it in London. Mamie passed it to her last year, since she no longer handles the family's official business."

"He been reading your letters?" Regina said, incredulously. "But—but he can't."

"He must have help. Maybe Sarah?"

Regina hissed the way only a West Indian woman could: long, melodious, menacing. "She can't read worth a fig. That girl would see her name on bread and eat it."

"Or so she lets us think," Madeleine conjectured. "I also found this." She handed the envelope to Regina. "It is an account of Mother and Eli's movements in London, and even as far as Italy. She is being watched, and rather closely."

Regina handed them back to her. "Do you think he knows about Eli?"

"I don't believe so; no. Mother has never referred to Eli in her letters as anything but his name. And anyway, our letters are all written in Old Romani. Even if Sarah could read it, I don't think she could understand it."

Regina fixed Madeleine with a calculating gaze. "What brought you in here? Why did you come? Did you *see* something?"

Madeleine looked away and began to replace all she had disturbed on the desk. "I suppose I shall have my letter soon enough."

"Madeleine," Regina pressed.

"There is no such thing as magic, Regina."

"And yet you in here."

"And yet, I am here. Come now. I have seen all I need to see. Let us hurry back before we are found out. It should not end well for us if we were."

CHAPTER IV

The Pet Snake

"It is good to see you well again," Gaëlle confessed, as she braided Madeleine's dark curls into one long plait. "I quite missed our walks in the garden. These four walls do seem to close in on you when you stay here for long, don't they? It has been three days! Whate'er could have left you indisposed for so long?"

"I was unwell before that," Madeleine reminded her. "I am sure I only needed some more rest. Perhaps, I had not fully recovered from the first episode."

Gaëlle nodded. "Of course." She stepped back to admire her work. "To the gardens, then?"

"Yes," Madeleine answered. "You are not the only one who has felt trapped within four walls."

Just then, there was a knock at the door. Gaëlle went to open it, then stepped aside to reveal Sarah in the doorway. "Your father requests your presence in his study, Lady Madeleine."

"Am I found out?" Madeleine said to herself, her heart beating double-time in her chest. "Did he say why?" she asked aloud.

Sarah shook her head. "No; he did not. Should I—should I have asked?"

"No. No matter. I will go, now."

Sarah looked relieved. She smiled and then ducked out of the room and disappeared down the hallway without another word.

"Not with a grain of sugar would I trust that girl," Gaëlle confided in a whisper, as Madeleine crossed the room. She shuddered. "Something about her isn't quite right."

"She is an odd girl," Madeleine agreed. "Wait here. I will return, shortly."

She found the door to the study half-open when she arrived. Basile was standing by the window, his back to her, though it was obvious he had heard her come in. On either side of him were shelves of books that looked new and untouched, despite being as old as his marriage.

It was Charlotte who had given him the study, as much to feed his growing self-importance as to give herself room to write her plays, undisturbed, in her own study. He seldom used it, but for when there were bills to be paid and money to be made. Though words confounded him, he was handy with numbers, perhaps suspiciously so.

"You called for me, Father?"

"Yes." He did not move from the window. Nor did he turn to face her.

"Is something amiss?"

"You have been absent from the dinner table for some days now."

"I have not been well."

"I see. And are you well, now?"

"I believe so."

"Good, as there is an important matter I believe you can shed light upon. Take a seat."

Did I leave some evidence of my meddling? Madeleine wondered again, her eyes roaming the room for any sign of why she had been summoned. The desk had been cleared of the letters she had seen before. In fact, Regina had brought the letter, expertly resealed, just the day before. Had they not seen it open on his desk with their own eyes, they would be none the wiser.

"You never met my mother," he began, "but she was a pious woman, however much good it did her. When I told her I meant to marry your mother, she said, 'the witch's daughter, you mean?!'" He laughed then and turned to face Madeleine. "She was not the only one who believed your family to be... eccentric with—some would say—remarkable capabilities. Your grandmother was especially renowned for her sorcery, and I have heard whispers that you take after her. Is this true?"

"I am a woman of science."

He gave a wry smile, and then returned his attention to the window. "Your pretence at modesty is unnecessary. I could use your talent in interpreting a dream I had a few nights ago. It has weighed heavily upon my mind. It runs thus.

"For some inconceivable reason, I was at your grandmother's *château* in Lamoreaux. It was a lovely day: warm, windy, birds chirping in the trees. I thought Charlotte might like to take a walk with me and sought after her to make my request. I searched her rooms at the castle, the study, the library, the kitchen; I could not find her.

"At long last, I thought it best to take the walk without her, or it seemed to me I would not be able to take it at all. As I walked, I ventured onto the farm, and into the holding area for the chickens. I am not certain what called my attention to the place, but as I walked, I noticed something in one of the coops.

"As I drew nearer, I noticed it was Charlotte. Her back was to me, but I knew it was my wife. It was a strange thing that she should be inside the coops. After all, even your grandmother has servants to fetch the eggs.

"I called for her, but she did not answer. As I drew nearer, I noticed she was bent over something. When she turned around, I was horrified to see she was holding a serpent in her arms, lovingly cradling it like a babe."

"'Charlotte!' cried I. 'What is it you hold? Set it down!'

"She looked up at me and smiled. 'This is my child,' said she. 'Is she not the most beautiful girl in all the world?'"

For a while, he said nothing more, and the silence stretched on between them. At long last, he asked, "Have you any idea what such a dream could mean?"

"None," Madeleine answered.

He turned to face her, his eyes bright with mischief. "I will tell you what it means. You are that snake, Madeleine. I warned Charlotte about you, the second you were born. I could see it in your eyes: a cold darkness I could not account for, like an ever-growing abyss. I see it in you even now.

"Since the dawn of your birth, a black shadow was cast upon my marriage. Charlotte petted and pampered you, discarding her duties as a wife to tend to you. You were a *demanding* baby. You would not be content with the nurse, or the servants—only Charlotte.

"You and Charlotte grew ever more attached, and she grew ever more *detached* from me. Your Mother may not, dear Madeleine, but I see your game. I see right through you."

"I know not of what you speak, Father. Why-ever would you think me a snake? Your daughter."

"You are your mother's daughter," he replied. "But more importantly, your grandmother's grandchild."

Madeleine narrowed her eyes at him but did not reply.

"Winter will be upon us in a month, I suspect. Your mother will begin her usual entreaties to see you. You will decline, if you are wise. I will go alone. Your company is neither necessary nor desired.

"It would not be proper for you to remain in Barfleur without a chaperone, so you will go to your grandmother. You will remain at the Château de Lamoreaux until I return from London. Do you understand me?"

"I hear you, Father."

"I do not wish for you to *hear* me," he said, the mischief fading into anger. "That is not what I asked. Do you *understand* me?"

"I understand the words you have said," Madeleine replied, standing. "Whether or not I agree is altogether a different matter."

"I did not ask for your agreement."

"Good, because I haven't the intent to give it." She shut the door behind her.

"A snake?" Gaëlle shivered. "What would *ever* induce a father to refer to his own daughter as a serpent? The very symbol of temptation, deception, EVIL, as though he is a saint, himself!"

"Hatred and jealousy," Regina answered from the window. She had not left it since Madeleine told her story of the visit to Basile's study. "He disliked you since the moment you were born. I saw it in his eyes. We all did.

"At first, I thought it was because you were the wrong sex, in his eyes. He pestered Charlotte for another child—another son—but by then she had already begun to see his true colours. Now, I think he hates you because you remind him of your grandmother. They have never seen eye-to-eye."

Madeleine considered that for a moment. She had heard stories from the servants of Mamie's frequent visits to the Barfleur Estate, but Madeleine could count on one hand how many times Mamie had visited in her lifetime: her birth, when she fell ill at four years old, and her sixteenth birthday.

All other times, it was she and her mother who had gone to visit, leaving Basile alone in Barfleur. She had always assumed it was old age that kept Mamie in the countryside, but even she had to admit Mamie was a spritely old lady, with complaints of neither aches nor pains.

"Was there a falling out?" Madeleine enquired.

"Several," Regina answered. "Before you were born, your father's mother—Miss Dubois—made accusations against Mamie, claiming she did the Devil's work and blaming her for the death of Charlotte's firstborn. Mamie was a frequent face in Barfleur, back then. The people loved her.

"But the accusations threatened to tear Charlotte and Basile apart, and she took her leave. Your mother begged her to stay, but Mamie is too proud a woman to endure unwarranted impertinence in her own home.

"Miss Dubois died a few weeks later, and Basile blamed Mamie. He took it as confirmation that his mother had been right. That she was doing the Devil's work.

"And yet... he was smiling the day they buried her. I remember clearly the look on his face, and even more so, when he turned to some old friend of his and said, 'Mamie indeed did me a kindness.'"

"Why would he not love his own mother?" Madeleine asked. "Why would he be glad of her death?"

"Why does he not love his own daughter?" Regina returned. "And after all, if you will permit my saying so, you aren't particularly fond of him, either."

She did not wait for a reply. "In spite of her baseless accusations, and her over-enthusiasm for religion, Miss Dubois was a good woman. She loved her son and did not think it beneath her to speak with us. She was often in the kitchens and would ask us to help her put together meals for the poor and sick. She had a good heart. I can't imagine what kind of son would want a mother like that dead."

CHAPTER V

The Winter Enquiries

For two weeks, Madeleine deliberated over how much to share with her mother of all she had discovered. Gaëlle and Regina were all for telling the tale in its entirety, but even they did not know the full story. They had not seen the pup feeding the earth with the blood from her throat. They had only heard her scream.

And what of her illness? Though no one could bring themselves to say the words, an attempt may have very well been made upon her life. It was too much of a coincidence that she should fall ill, both times after having an unfavourable encounter with her father. Was it not reasonable to cast suspicion in his direction?

She was certain about one thing, however. Though she was confident writing in Old Romani would keep her secrets safe, she had decided it was best to let her mother know their letters had been tampered with. Now, the letters came more frequently than ever, but not in the regular post. They were delivered directly to her by Gaëlle. Eli himself put them in her hands after sailing with them from London to the port at Barfleur.

But, not today.

Madeleine was bidding farewell to her professor when her father entered the anteroom. *Monsieur* Rámon was a tall and lanky old man who had given up the rich trappings of aristocracy to pursue an academic life. He had never married, never fathered a child as best he knew, but was himself fatherly and kind.

"Your mother will be pleased to hear how well you've been getting on when you see her for the winter holiday, I'm sure," he was saying. "I will see her myself, a few days hence, after I have tended to some matters of urgent business in Paris. Take care and enjoy the break from our studies."

"Take care, *Monsieur!*"

When the door shut behind him, Basile advanced and presented her with a letter. "From your mother," he said. "No doubt she is now asking for you to visit her in London. You know the answer you must give."

Madeleine took the letter and returned to her room. She had dreaded its coming, which Charlotte had no doubt posted to avoid suspicion. On the one hand, she feared leaving her mother alone with the monster she had married. On the other, she feared her presence would only further incite his anger. And wouldn't Eli be there to protect her if evil should befall her, as he had always done?

The letter ran thus, in Old Romani:

My Dearest Madeleine,

It is the time of year I look forward to only as much as the summer. It feels like eternity has passed since I last saw you. I cannot wait to hear all that you have learned from Monsieur Rámon this year. He writes to me of you often, always praising your keen mind, and quick wit. He admires you, immensely. Says you take after your dear old Mamie.

Did I ever tell you, he fancied her in his younger days? I have always wondered if the heartbreak of her marrying another man is why he has never married. I suppose that is all romantic speculation.

Speaking of romance, I had the pleasure of seeing your dear Sir Jacob a few days ago. He had come to see one of my plays and looked as handsome as ever. My, he dresses well! I invited him behind the stage after the performance, and we talked for a few minutes. He is such an intelligent fellow!

Eli took him drinking thereafter, where I hear he attracted many a wandering eye, but Eli swears he not so much as glanced in their direction. He will soon return to France, I am told. No doubt he cannot long be separated from a certain young maiden who commands his heart from Barfleur.

Much as you take pleasure in feigning disinterest and stringing the poor lad along (I fear you are your grandmother's child, in this!), I know your heart will be glad to know that, even with the English Channel between you, he is yours.

It may also interest you to know that I recently made the acquaintance of the naturalist, Charles Darwin, through our dear Ada. An eccentric man, with rather unorthodox ideas! I have told him of your interest in the pure sciences and the man under whom you study. He is very much impressed and will no doubt consent to seeing you in the near future.

Now, I will get to the point of my letter. When will it suit you to travel to your dear mother? I would very much like to secure you an excellent cabin, on board a new ship I have only just learned of. I cannot wait to see you again. I look forward to hearing from you, post-haste!

Your Darling Mother.

Madeleine set the letter down on her desk and sighed. "No, Father," she said to herself. "I do not know the answer I must give. One answer may kill her, and the other may break her heart."

The smell of liquor and urine was the first to assault him, when he neared the tavern. It jarred his senses and woke him from the quiet languor he often slipped into after journeying by sea. The second assault came from two women. He had barely made it through the door when he found himself unhappily set between them.

Why they bothered, he never knew. Though he could call either of them by name, not once had he ever so much as favoured them with a look. He would not claim he had never enjoyed the pleasures of a woman before, but tossing coins next to her naked body in payment had an uncanny way of taking all the romance out of it.

"Will soldier not come upstairs with we?" the one who called herself

Joceline asked him in heavily accented English.

"I am afraid I have no need of your services tonight, ladies," he replied in French, extricating himself from their embrace and advancing towards the bartender.

On either side of him, men were wasted in their cups. Some had taken to song, and others to soliciting other ladies like Joceline and her friend. A few lay snoring by their drinks, while pickpockets relieved them of their francs.

"Sir Jacob," the bartender greeted him, "I see the ladies have already got their paws on ya'!" An Englishman of four-and-fifty years, he wore a thick curly mane and a full beard, all snow white, though his every movement spoke of lingering youth.

"So, they have," he replied. "The usual please, Archie." He passed a few coins to his friend.

Archie pocketed them without counting and pulled out a bottle of his best wine. "Straight from Bordeaux, this one. My best stuff." He then whistled loudly; a whistle answered. He jerked his head towards the thick, black curtains hanging in an archway at the back. "Go on. I'll bring 'em in."

Esther was a beautiful woman. No one could deny her that.

Even now, Jacob's heart quickened at the sight of her. It could have been the way her cat-like eyes followed him wherever he went. Or perhaps, it was the tight curling of raven ringlets about her neck and ears, as yet unstreaked by grey, though she was hardly a year or two younger than her white-haired husband. Or was it the exotic sun-kissed brown of her skin? Her full, rosebud lips?

Men would have paid a fortune to bed her. Indeed, many had tried, but Esther was devoutly loyal to the man who had taken one look at her and given a year's wages as a sailor to free her from bondage in the West Indies. She had not left his side since.

"You look well, Jacob," she observed. "But tired. What weighs so heavily on your mind?" Her English was perfect, though her accent was unmistakably Jamaican.

"It was an unpleasant trip back to Barfleur, and I confess, I am no friend of sailing."

The curtain before the small booth parted. Archie set down two glasses of wine before them both and pressed a kiss to his wife's cheek. She watched him go and then raised the glass to her lips.

"I fear the news I have for you is not precisely what you would like to hear after your long journey," Esther warned. "Would you prefer to get some rest, and return in the morning?"

"Is it Madeleine?" he said with wide eyes. "Is she well? Has she been harmed? Has she been betrothed to someone else?"

Esther failed to stifle her laugh. "She is not *betrothed* to anyone," she assured him. "Do not allow sentiment to overcome you, Jacob. Business first."

She then proceeded to update him on the current affairs of Barfleur and the neighbouring towns, with a bit of news from Paris: an easy job when one owned a tavern and employed ladies of the night with sharp ears. And even easier when you were the local West Indian healer and priestess of choice, for there were many coloured servants populating the household staff of the nobility and the bourgeoisie.

"And now for the real reason you have come," she said, "your Lady Love has not been in the best of health, I fear. She has not been seen in town for some time, though her lecturer does continue to frequent the home. Twice now, her servant, Regina, has come seeking remedies."

"Remedies for what? What did she say?"

"Regina is a true confidant. She did not disclose any details, aside from asking me to put an end to Basile's life—a not uncommon request of servants, as it relates to their masters—but when she asked for remedies, it was for poison."

"Poison!"

"Regina did not confirm it was for her mistress, but in my heart, I feel it is so. A servant of Dr. Frederik, however, did confirm that he was called to the house at *least* twice and that Madeleine was in a terrible state. These times coincided with the days Regina came to see me. Both times, the doctor could not diagnose her. It could be, he did not think to look for poison for such a lady. She is well loved."

"By all but her father," Jacob pointed out. "She is not the heir he wanted."

"Then he should have thought twice before marrying into the Moreau Family. The eldest is always a girl, and they rarely have another." She paused, and then added, "Will you call upon her, and see that she is well? As you are courting her, your presence will be welcome, I am sure."

"Ha! Prescription without possession availeth nothing," he quoted, bitterly. "Madeleine has not exactly accepted my 'courting'. I do not doubt that she cares for me, but she would trust me with her life sooner than she would trust me with her freedom and independence."

Esther reached across the table and rested a hand on his. "She will soon come to see you are just the man for her."

"What makes you so sure?"

"I see it in my crystal ball," said she, laughing.

On several occasions, some drunken fool had stumbled into the tavern, demanding to see the witch his servant or wife had been consulting with. In truth, Esther was more a doctor than a witch, and a woman of strong Faith, even if that Faith did in some ways depart from the traditional teachings of the Church.

"Go home and get some rest, Jacob. If something truly is amiss, she will need you at your best in the morning." She rose from her chair and took a small vial from the shelves behind her.

"A love potion?" he said in jest.

The smile she offered was sad. "If only. Half the problems brought to me every day would be resolved." She handed the vial to him. "To ease your nausea, and help you sleep."

Jacob did not hesitate to accept. He could not remember a time when Esther prescribed him a remedy that did not work, making him all the more grateful Regina had consulted with her.

"There is one more development that may or may not be of interest to you," she ventured, with apparent uncertainty.

"Yes?"

"Father Costello fell ill quite suddenly and passed away in his sleep. The doctor believes he died of natural causes."

"But you believe otherwise?"

Esther seemed reluctant to respond, but finally said, "I respect the Catholic Faith. It is not so very different from my own, or yours, but to them, I am a pagan. The only business a priest would have with me is an attempt at conversion.

"Yet, the day he died, one of the sisters came to see me. She had concealed herself, so I could not tell who she was, but she said she came on behalf of the Father and sought a remedy for poison.

"He died before she could return in time to administer it. And indeed, if he was so far advanced, and considering his age, I am not sure it would have helped."

"I see."

"It is probably nothing," Esther continued. "Perhaps Dr. Frederik is right, but I thought you should know. Forgive me, if you believe I have wasted your time on a triviality. I know you must be tired."

"You have never wasted my time on a triviality, Esther," he replied, his expression serious and thoughtful. "Were the symptoms in any way similar to those experienced by Lady Madeleine?"

"Yes," Esther answered, clearly relieved he had broached the topic himself. "I prescribed the very same antidote I did for her. The symptoms were exactly the same."

Dear Mother,

I have looked forward to spending the winter holiday with you, since I last saw you in the summertime. There is ever so much to do in London, and your company is always a welcome break from the shadow Father seems to cast over my life in Barfleur.

We have not been on the best of terms lately, and I think it best he visits you on his own. There are other reasons, as well, but I would rather not disclose them. I will remain here in Barfleur until such time as I can see you again on my own. I know these are not the words you wished to see, and it hurts me to write them.

I am sorry, Mother. I am sure I will see you soon. Only not as soon as we originally planned.

Love,

Madeleine.

"What does it say?" Gaëlle asked, leaning over her shoulder as she folded the letter.

"It says, we shan't be joining Mother in London," Madeleine answered, almost choking on the words. Was there ever a winter she had not spent in London, even before Charlotte's final move? If there had been one, she could not recall it to memory.

"Not go to London?" Gaëlle seemed to stagger backwards. She moved to the front of the study that had once been Charlotte's and faced her mistress. "But—but why?"

"I have made my decision, Gaëlle," Madeleine replied. "You will take this to Eli at the port, tomorrow. Mother has already telegraphed to confirm he is coming."

"I don't understand. Why are we not going?"

"I have made my decision!" Madeleine snapped, her fists coming down on the desk in a heavy thud, while tears stung her eyes. "Leave me, Gaëlle."

She ran to her side. *"Mademoiselle*, I did not mean to question you. I know you must have your reasons. Madeleine-"

Madeleine buried her face in her hands. "Ellie, please. Leave me."

An hour before dinner, a caller appeared in the anteroom. As per Basile's orders, Sarah answered the door, but once a request was made for Madeleine's presence, Sarah called for one of the coloured servants to find her.

"I will go," Regina offered, removing her apron. She clicked her teeth at the servant, who had scampered down the hallway, and pointed back to the kitchen. "I will be just a moment, Sir. Please excuse my attire. It is almost time for dinner."

"Excuse *me* for intruding. I had intended to come earlier, but business in town detained me."

"Of course." She headed down the hallway, and then up to the second floor to begin her search for Madeleine. She was not in her bedchamber, but Gaëlle's position outside Charlotte's writing room was a good indication of where her mistress might be. She was wringing her hands in obvious distress and looked quite anxious.

"Oh, Regina. I finally done it," said she in *Kreyol*. "I gone too far and anger Madeleine. Basile was right. A servant no have no place befriending her mistress. I never seen her so upset. She'll never forgive me; I know she won't."

"What happened?"

"I don't know if is my place to say, Regina, but maybe she'll tell you. In any case, I made argument with *Mademoiselle*, and she order me out the room."

Regina looked at her with obvious incredulity. "Madeleine? *Ordered* you out?"

"Yes; but we should leave her alone for now, I think. She vex with me."

"I cannot. She has a visitor. Step aside."

Gaëlle stood her ground. "I can't, Regina. I truly upset her. We must leave her be."

"Step aside, or I'll move you myself."

Reluctantly, Gaëlle scooted from the door, though she ensured she was out of view when Regina slipped in and shut it behind her. Regina found her mistress still sitting at the desk, staring at nothing and no one in particular.

"Madeleine?"

She returned from her thoughts, with a start. "Regina! I—I did not see you come in."

"Evidently. You have a visitor."

Madeleine groaned. "I cannot see visitors, today. I will be dining in my room."

"I believe you want to see this one. 'Tis Sir Jacob. I daresay it been a month since we last saw him in Barfleur. I imagine he should be very disappointed if you did not receive him."

Madeleine hesitated for a moment. "Did he say why he had come?"

"Does a gentleman ever need cause to see the Lady he is courting?"

Madeleine sighed. "Will he ever give up?"

"I do not foresee it; no." When Madeleine did not reply, she decided to try her luck. "Madeleine, Gaëlle tell me you were very upset, earlier. Is something amiss?"

"I shan't be visiting with Mother this winter."

"I saw that coming," Regina confessed. "It is a wise choice. You must forgive Gaëlle for her impertinence. She young and in love. She was thinking of Eli."

"Of course. Tell Sir Jacob I will be down in a moment."

"Yes, *Mademoiselle.*"

Regina started towards the door.

"And will you ask him to stay for dinner, please?"

Regina smiled to herself. She knew despite Madeleine's best efforts to remain passive, she was deeply enamoured with the British soldier. "Yes, with pleasure!"

When she exited the room, Gaëlle was still waiting anxiously outside. Regina grabbed her by an elbow and dragged her down the hallway.

"She is indeed upset, you naughty girl! Come and make yourself useful in the kitchens. You laze about enough today."

CHAPTER VI

Broken Hearts

Jacob rose from his chair, but it was only the coloured servant who had returned. She was wearing that knowing smile she often had whenever she saw him.

"Lady Madeleine comes down soon, Sir," she said in her best English. "You would like something to drink or eat, while you wait; yes? Some coffee, or some tea?"

"No, no, thank you," he returned in French. "Regina, is it?"

"Yes, Sir," she answered in French. "The Lady has also invited you to stay for dinner, if it please you, Sir."

A light immediately kindled in his eyes. "Certainly, if I am not intruding."

Once she had left the room, he set his hat down on an end table and looked into the mirror above it. As he feared, the hat had left a flat circle at the very top of his head. He mussed his hair up a bit, and then instantly regretted it. It looked as though he had spent the evening in the violent embrace of a hurricane.

The rest of his person, however, showed impeccable though not over-bearing attention to his appearance. The high collar of his white shirt was crisp and clean, accented all the more by the low cut of his vest. His pants were tailored close to his lean and muscular legs, and his shoes were spotless.

"What a dandy you are, Sir Jacob! Ever the charmer of the fairer sex."

He turned to find Madeleine standing in the doorway. She was not the perfect image of health, but there was an unbroken strength in her that attracted him far more than mere beauty ever could. Her raven hair, usually braided or pinned up, was loose today. It shone a bluish black even in the fading evening light. Her large, dark eyes watched him with some amusement.

"A dandy?" he returned, affecting as though she had wounded him. "And it may or may not please you to know I can hardly remember the last time I so much as looked at another woman."

"Perhaps, 'tis time you did."

The suggestion cut him, but he would not dare let her see how much. "You will find I am not so easily thwarted, Madeleine. Once I have set myself upon a course, I am honour-bound to pursue it."

"So I very well see. Will you take a walk with me outside, while we wait for dinner to be prepared?"

He offered a hand. "I would love to."

Jacob could think of a hundred beautiful maidens who would have made for an easier pursuit; yet, he could never set Madeleine aside, and he needn't ask himself why. It was her fierce independence, her sharp mind, and equally sharp tongue. He was drawn to her wit and her defiance, and the intellectual challenge she presented, even in her most silent moments.

No; it did not surprise him she had no desire to marry, but he hoped to convince her it would not mean the end of her ambitions if she married *him*.

"You grow more beautiful by the day, Madeleine."

She glanced at him for a moment, and then returned her attention to the path ahead. "And you grow ever more charming."

"So you say, and yet you will not give me the honour of your hand."

"A man must be more than charming to be a husband, I think."

He smiled. "This is true. What other qualities do you believe he should possess?"

"He should be healthy, in possession of a good constitution, for our child will need them."

"I haven't so much as caught a cold since I was at my father's knees."

"He should be intelligent, so as not to bore me at dinner."

"Graduated top of my class in Cambridge."

"And he should be handsome, I think. Who wants ugly children?"

"Well... I confess, there you have me beat."

She laughed and turned to face him, pausing so suddenly that one of the servants carrying the lantern close behind almost walked into her. Jacob's breath stopped for a moment, as her eyes washed over him in obvious calculation.

"I think you would do," she decided, and resumed her walk, "*if* I wanted to submit to the shackles of marriage, that is."

"But you do not," he concluded.

"But I do not," she confirmed.

"You break my heart, Madeleine. I would not dare shackle a free spirit such as you! I want you at my side, not behind me: so you may share my light and grow, rather than dwindle away in my shadow. I would wait a thousand years for you!"

"Such a cheap promise to make, when you know good and well you will be dead in less than a hundred. Not even a tenth of the time served! Men and their shallow promises!"

He could not help but laugh at her exclamation and the sheer truth of it.

By then, they had reached the pond she had been guiding them towards. She took a seat in the grass and gestured for him to do the same. She then slipped her hand through the crook of his arm and rested a head upon his shoulder. He very cautiously put an arm about her waist.

"Can we not be friends, Sir Jacob? Is that not enough?" She looked up at him and found his face within a breath of her own.

"It is a start," he answered, placing a hand beneath her chin, and tilting her head up to his. For a second, he thought he had her, but just as quickly as the opportunity had presented itself, it was lost.

She turned away from him. "Then, I fear you break your own heart."

Her words tore through him, but he resolved not to let the bruise linger. "I heard you were unwell, and that you had not been seen in town for some time."

"I have been… indisposed for a while; yes. I am better now."

"Do you know what the trouble may have been?"

"The doctor could find nothing wrong," she answered. "But as always, Regina found a remedy."

"She is a true friend—of mine, as well, if she has done you so great a service. And I am sure London will restore some life to you when you go."

"I shan't be going to London," she replied. "It is a long story I cannot share, but I will be spending the winter here, in Barfleur."

"Lady Charlotte will be heartbroken."

"Indeed."

"You must have very good reason, I am sure."

"I do, though I wonder if I have made the right choice."

"I am sure you made the decision you thought best. Trust that decision; I do." He lifted her hand from her lap and pressed it to his lips.

There was the sound of rushed footsteps and then, "It is time for dinner, *Mademoiselle,* Sir." Gaëlle did a hurried curtsy, while she tried to catch her breath. She looked suspiciously from Madeleine to Jacob as they stood. "I did not mean to interrupt."

"Oh, how I wish you were interrupting something deliciously scandalous!" Jacob lamented.

Gaëlle giggled.

Jacob allowed himself the liberty of slipping an arm about Madeleine's waist again, as she had not stopped him the first time. "Come, my Lady. Dinner calls."

"When are you going back to London?" Madeleine enquired.

"I had planned on escorting you back myself, but as you are staying, so will I."

CHAPTER VII

Facts & Fibs

"Zir Jacob.... eh, zat pleasure brings your illustrious... er... presents to dining wit' us," Basile said, in what English he could muster.

"Thank you, *Monsieur* Dubois-Moreau," Jacob answered in French. "I am only too happy I was invited to dine with you. You do me a great honour."

"I am sure the *real* honour is being in the company of my daughter," he returned. "Beautiful, is she not? You would do *me* a great honour if you took her off my hands."

"Father!" Madeleine interjected.

"Whatever is the matter, dear? Let us not pretend we do not know he has come to bask in the glow of your sunlight. Him, and more others than I can count; however, he is the only one you seem to show any interest in, so I may as well peg my hopes on him."

Despite Basile's crude remarks, Jacob could not help but feel pleased at the colour in Madeleine's cheeks when her father mentioned her particular favour for him. Even so, he was too much a gentleman to prolong her suffering.

"Madeleine tells me she will not be visiting her mother in London, this winter," he said, changing the subject. "Will you be going, *Monsieur?*"

"Ah, she did, did she? Yes; she has classes with *Monsieur* Rámon and must stay behind to complete those. Such is the sacrifice of education!"

Jacob looked at Madeleine. She said not a word, but he did not fail to miss the clenching of her jaw and the way her hand tightened on her glass of wine.

"Indeed," Jacob agreed. "Education is always a worthy sacrifice."

Basile scoffed at that. "Education is lost on women. It is men who should sit in a classroom or study under noteworthy professors. A woman's place is in the home—a lesson my dear wife also seems to have missed."

"You will forgive my saying so, but I disagree. Lady Moreau is an excellent addition to London. Her plays are absolutely fascinating. I saw *The Hound* just last week, and it was the best I have seen in years.

"Many are calling her 'the female Alexandre Dumas', a title well-deserved, I think, though they might very well have just called her the 'English Dumas' and left her sex out of it.

"I am sure Madeleine will benefit from her education as well, no matter how she chooses to spend it."

Basile regarded the British soldier with burgeoning distaste. "I see clearly now why Madeleine is so taken with you."

"You flatter me, *Monsieur* Dubois-Moreau."

"I assure you, *Monsieur* Andrews," he returned, stabbing at his pork, "I do not."

"He is so very handsome!" Gaëlle gushed, their falling out some hours before now long forgotten. She fell into the featherbed with dreamy eyes. "Oh, that such a handsome man should but *look* in my direction! How are you not lost in those blue eyes when he fixes them upon you? Like the very depths of the ocean, they are! The clearest summer sky!"

"Easy; you look away," Madeleine quipped. "He is handsome and ever a delight to have in my company," she admitted after a while. "But to be married and owned. I could never live the life I wish."

"He sounds like an open-minded enough gentleman. Only observe how he stood up to Basile tonight, and how he spoke of Charlotte and her plays. 'The English Dumas', he called her!"

"Eavesdropping again, were you?"

"Why, always!"

"'Tis easy to say the words, and even easier to pretend they were never said when time comes to put them into action."

"I do not believe Sir Jacob is capable of such a thing. It is not unprecedented that a learned man should fall in love with, and encourage, a learned woman.

"Why, only look at our Ada: a wife and now a mother of three, but also a mathematician! The Earl has never, so far as I know, turned her away from her education. Indeed, I daresay he allows the Countess a good deal more freedom than she earns."

"I concede to your point, Ellie. The Countess of Lovelace is indeed a freer woman than most, but there is no guarantee that Sir Jacob is such a man as Lord Lovelace. I am sure Mother never believed *Monsieur* Dubois would be the self-centred, puffed up puss he is. Yet, here we are, and there he is."

Gaëlle had no response for that and was only too happy when Regina knocked and let herself into the room. "Did I miss the gossip?"

"Madeleine is in a mood," Gaëlle announced.

Regina glanced at her. "What's amiss?"

Madeleine sighed. "I wish I could go back to the happy days of childhood. Things were so much simpler then."

"Well, you can be a child right here with Ol' Regina." She sat in the chair and patted the bed. "Come, come. I tell you a story."

Madeleine tossed her brush aside, and scrambled into bed, next to Gaëlle.

"Now, what sort of tale should I tell? What special request will you make tonight?"

"Tell me about your home," Madeleine answered.

Regina looked at her with some surprise. "France is my home now, and surely you don't care to hear about Haiti."

"But I do, Regina. You've never told me how you came to be here. How did you meet Mother?"

She smiled. "It's not a day I am like to forget, and since you ask so very nicely, I must oblige!"

Regina shut her eyes, inhaled deeply, recalling to mind the bittersweet memories of life in the West Indies. "Now, keep in mind, I wasn't there for the start of the slave rebellion, but I heard stories," she began.

"When the rebellion was a-coming, my sister, Jeanne-Louise, the *mambo asogwe*—High Priestess of our community—and Master's consort, warned the Master. She begged him to leave, but when she refused to go with him, to leave her people to fight for freedom without her, the Master decided he too was a-staying. Master did his best to keep her safe, but not long after I was born, Jeanne tired of hiding behind our locked doors. She decided to take her rightful place as a *mambo asogwe,* that is, amongst the rebels.

"Master did not approve, especially after Toussaint declared any religion but that of Rome would not be tolerated in Saint-Domingue, as Haiti was called then. But Jeanne would not be deterred. Night after night she left us and came home unscathed. It made her brave and perhaps a little foolish, for one night in late 1803, just days before the war ended, she ventured out and was never seen again. Eli, born earlier that year, never knew his mother.

"Though we mourned our loss, we were not much surprised, for Haitian liberty was bought with blood and fire, and many perished. *Matant,* the head of the house slaves, told me that when the rebellion started, and the burnings with it, Master and her and the rest of his faithful lot remained on the top floor of the home. As the black night was lit with flames on all sides, Jeanne-Louise would pray and pray to *Bondye.* Several times the household saw the rebels put torches to the field, but the fields would not burn.

"Planter neighbours who had shunned Master for his kindness to us, now came rapping at his doors. The rebels cut them down where they stood. Men, women, children—all. No one was spared. More than once, they set fire to the house, but again, Jeanne prayed and prayed, and like the fields, it did not burn. After a time, the rebels troubled us no more. They saw we were protected by a greater power: the power of *Bondye*.

"I was born nine years into the Revolution. I was four years old when it ended, and at the end of the war, we found that we had bought our freedom at a heavy price. All 'round me, my people died of sickness and starvation. I will never forget the smell. That sad, sickening scent of death and smoke that lingered in the air wherever we went.

"In truth, we presided over ruin. The roads had been torn up, and the rotting cadavers of men and horses had been thrown into the rivers and wells to poison them, for when the French made their final stand, neither Toussaint nor Dessalines would suffer the earth, bathed with the sweat of slaves who had toiled to build *the Pearl of the Antilles,* to furnish our enemies with the refreshments they needed to put us once more into bondage.

"This ruin, and the loss we all suffered, led to quarrels among us— even more so after the French took Toussaint. Dessalines did his best to restore order, and succeeded for the most part, but some people— almost all *machotara*—claimed it was better we had remained under the rule of the planters.

"Most of us, however, believed freedom at any cost meant the freedom to die with dignity and respect, and without chains. We believed what Toussaint believed, that having confronted danger to obtain our liberty, we would not balk at confronting death to keep it! My mother was of the latter belief, but it was an easy belief to hold on Les Moreaux. *Seigneur* Bernard-Moreau had always been a kind master, a trait he learned from a wife he would mourn for from the day he landed on that cursed island, to the day he died amongst us.

"With independence now declared, and us all left to rule the rubble from which we should rebuild, Dessalines turned against the few

Whites allowed to remain, and they in turn rose up against Master. They threatened Master and accused him of siding with the Blacks against them, which I suppose was not altogether false, for he encouraged all who would take up arms on Les Moreaux to fight. For this and more, Toussaint, and later, Dessalines himself, had eventually considered Master an ally.

"Though I would not say Master could claim either man in any great familiarity as a friend, we were thought of favourably, or at least tolerably, by them, and it would be to Master's ruin in the end. With Toussaint taken, racial tensions rising, and much of Haiti burned to the ground, the Whites who remained grew desperate and sought revenge. The men had gone to fight, so it was mostly us women and children who tended the fields, and with neither Toussaint, nor eventually our *mambo*, to keep us safe, one by one people began to disappear.

"To keep the peace and to protect us, Master married the daughter of one of the ruined planters, just six months after the loss of his Jeanne. He fathered two children with the new woman before he grieved himself into sickness and died in the spring of 1806.

"When Master died, his will left all to Eli, and named him Master of the plantation, but allowed the wife to manage the affairs until such time as Eli came of age, or until his daughter from an undissolved marriage in France come to stake her claim. This made it apparent his Haitian marriage was a sham, but he asked the lawyer not to let this secret get out. Even so, the wife was bitter about all this—naturally, I suppose—and did not miss an opportunity to make her dissatisfaction known.

"One summer afternoon, she had Eli tied to the whipping pole and mercilessly whipped for stealing sugar from the pantry. I knew for a fact he had not done it, as I had done it myself, and had confessed to her from the start, but she would not, for anything, miss the opportunity to punish Eli for being the Master's beloved son and heir. When the Blacks refused to whip him, she tied them to the nearby post and hired one of the White overseers to whip them all.

"We were in the middle of this charade when a carriage stopped before the Great House and out stepped the most beautiful Lady I had ever seen: coal black hair, big brown eyes, and such kindness. I knew instantly, this young Miss must be the planter's female heir.

"She was horrified to see her brother treated thus. When the wife insisted Eli be punished further, Charlotte jumped before her brother and dared the overseer to raise the whip. Alas, the man was at first more terrified of the Planter Miss than Charlotte and, like a fool, raised the whip. Then, we heard a loud chi-chick from the carriage, as the barrel of a rifle poked out through the window. All of a sudden, he knew where his loyalties must lie, and wisely lowered the hand.

"Charlotte untied Eli, dirtying her beautiful dress that must have been of the finest silk from Lyons, just to carry the half-conscious, blood-ed little boy inside. She dressed him herself, and I marvelled that this *grand blanc* from France knew about as much of healing as my Jeanne-Louise. And when she heard her father had only just passed, how she wept!

"You could not pity Charlotte when she wept. You either wanted to weep too or make it right for her. It was impossible not to see strength in her tears, the defiance in her eyes, and the firm set of her mouth. When she cried, hers was not a face of helplessness. It was a face that said, 'I will get through this!'

"Naturally, I admired her from the start. We all did. Little Eli, only three then, worshipped the very ground she walked on. He was untouchable when he was at her heels, and so he could never be convinced to leave his big sister. We often called him *la ti lonbraj*, the little shadow.

"She stayed with us for some months, the best I ever spent on Haitian soil. When she announced she was denouncing her right to Les Moreaux and returning to France, I thought my very world would end. Eli especially, was heartbroken. So, imagine our surprise when she packed us all into her ship, and took us back to France with her: Eli, Betha, Gaëlle's mother, myself, and half a dozen others.

"Eli, she sent off to boarding school with some of the best boys in England. He could pass for White, you know, so he had a mostly easy time. And he was handsome, and charming, and won his teachers so easily; it was a wonder he ever had to study. Charlotte stole away to see him often, set him in England, gave him her playhouse to manage, and the rest you know of your Uncle Eli.

"The rest of us spent some time with her at Lamoreaux, where we met Mamie and became intimate friends with her. Oh, a lovelier woman we had not met, save for Charlotte. And when we thought of how Master had grieved for her, we did not wonder why.

"When Charlotte decided to strike out on her own, some months later, we came with her to Barfleur to form her household for the manor, and there she met your goat of a father. The rest of our humble history, I believe you know quite well. And so here I end my rambling, for there is nothing left to tell."

"Oh, poor Uncle Eli!" Madeleine exclaimed. "What a wicked stepmother he had! I am so happy Mother found him when she did. He would not have lasted. Not at all—her little shadow. You have never told me that story before, Regina."

"I have not," she admitted, "and now that I have, I am all in pieces. You shouldn't have asked." She lifted her apron to dab at her eyes.

Still, Madeleine pressed. "But how did Mamie not know about Eli, until some years ago? How come they have never met?"

"She knew all along," Regina answered, her voice raw with emotion. "But she chose not to interfere, as is her way. And anyway, Eli was a little terrified of her, maybe even now. His father often told us terrifying stories about the *Seigneuresse* Moreau in France. It was all in jest, of course, but Eli took it to heart, young as he was."

"Well, I am so glad Mother found you and Eli, and brought you all to be here with us," Madeleine said in earnest. She then relaxed in bed, staring dreamily at the ceiling. "But I wonder what, at one-and-twenty, sent her to Haiti by herself."

"I have oft' wondered that myself, Maddie," Regina confessed. "But, I think only Charlotte can answer that."

CHAPTER VIII

A Warning from a Witch

Madeleine woke with a start, the drip, drip, drip of blood from the pup's throat weighing heavily on her mind. For three consecutive nights the same dream had haunted her, each time growing with intensity. Even now, she could almost swear she still heard the gurgle of the pup's last breath.

Gaëlle was slow to wake, but soon summoned a maid to make the bed and another to fetch the water. She then helped Madeleine to attend to her toilet. Gaëlle tried to tempt her mistress with some of the bright colours Charlotte had gifted her with last summer, but as was not uncommon, Madeleine chose a dress that was a sombre black.

"You and Miss Charlotte seem almost predisposed to black cloth," Gaëlle teased. "Is it any wonder people whisper that you are witches?" She laughed. "How about a nice red ribbon to tie your braid today, at least?"

"As you wish, Ellie."

When her friend left the room to rummage through the box of ribbons, Madeleine released the sigh she had been holding in, and tried once more to clear the images from her mind. A woman of letters, she prided herself on being rational and logical, but this was an increasingly difficult position to hold, as the youngest member of a matriarchy of clairvoyant women.

Though Gaëlle meant no harm, her jest was not without substance, and much as Madeline hated to admit it, barring his serpentine allegations, Basile was not far from the truth, either. Her grandmother oft' filled the countryside with news, good and bad, she learned in her dreams. Likewise, Madeleine had, perhaps more often than could pass for mere coincidence, predicted an incident or two for family and friends.

Those who knew her family well claimed their foresight came from a great-great-grandmother who had once belonged to a roaming *Tzigane* tribe, before love and religion made a civilised Frenchwoman out of her. They claimed she had practiced her old rituals in secret—long after accepting the Catholic Faith as her own—and that she had passed her skills down the genetic line.

"This one's a witch," Madeleine's cousins would joke when she crossed paths with them, while visiting at the family estate in Lamoreaux, or the original family seat in Bourgogne.

But, she had always ignored them. She was of noble birth, after all, and educated, besides. Instead, she clung desperately to science and logic and the natural order of the world. A few coincidences would not change that.

Or would they?

"Are you sure you don't want to come?" She could almost hear the disappointment in her mother's voice, even as she read the letter.

"I know your father lied to me," Charlotte wrote. "I know you have no classes with *Monsieur* Rámon for Christmas. He cannot stop you from coming. He cannot stop me from seeing my child. You need only say you will come; I miss you, terribly."

Yet, a feeling of foreboding kept her in Barfleur. Her father's threatening gaze whenever she should chance to meet him in the hallways or the gardens did not help at all. She had taken to dining in her room with Regina and Gaëlle, neither of whom allowed her to partake of any food that had not been prepared and brought to her by them.

And the dreams, the cursed dreams would not leave her be. Day and night, they plagued her, stealing her sleep, and placing bags beneath her eyes. The dreams, even more than the threats, worried her horribly, so much so, she was willing to cast her scholarly pride aside to share it.

"Dear Mother," she wrote back. "Your guess runs not so very far from the truth; Father lied. I do not have classes, this winter. He has also threatened me, but it is not his threats that frighten me; it is his ease in delivering them. Something must have emboldened him recently, and I should like to stay and find out what it is, before it is too late."

There, she stopped. She was the intellectual, schooled in an era when education seemed all but lost on women, as Basile had so confidently declared. What favours did she offer her sex by then indulging in feminine fancies and fears? Yet, she felt she had to share the rest.

"There's something else," she added, the steel pen shaking as she scratched the words into the paper. She wrote of the horror she bore witness to night after night and the feeling of dread that lingered every morning.

There was still a slight tremor in her hand as she dipped the pen into the inkwell and paused to collect herself. Even now, the dream at once made her sick at heart and sick to the stomach. "I believe Father is up to something," she continued. "This is what the dream means. The lying about my classes, the threats for me to stay in France; it's all part of some sinister plan he's hatching.

"I told you about the counterfeit family seal in his study, but there is more. That same day, I also found letters with details of your movements and travels, as well as Eli's, mailed from a London address. Father must have hired someone to follow you."

The door to the study burst open. She was so startled, she spilled drops of ink all over the desk, peppering her papers with black.

"Women and their *bloody* letters," Basile bellowed, his eyes washing over the words without recognition. He then provided her with his verbal list of domestic duties.

Madeleine looked up at him with obvious curiosity and masked annoyance. She hadn't received such a list since a White servant had been added to the household a year prior. Basile had always considered himself too high a Frenchman to speak with the people of colour

Charlotte had hired, and Madeleine had tired of neglecting her studies to manage the house. "May I ask where Sarah is?"

"Her mother has taken to bed with a mysterious illness in London. I permitted her a week's leave to see her, so we have only the *nègres* here." When she said nothing in response, he asked, "Have you spoken with your grandmother about going to visit her in the country, while I'm gone? Is she who the letter is for?"

"The letter is for Sir Jacob," Madeleine replied, more sarcasm than lie.

He drew himself up with a pleased and proud look. "Very good," he commended her, and then he was almost pleasant. "It is good that you marry," he told her, though his own marriage provided no such evidence.

"If you were married, you would not need to go to your grandmother's house. You would not even be here. You would be with Sir Jacob: a soldier and knighted! You know the only reason he is still in Barfleur is for you."

"I do not for a second doubt it, Father." She set the letter aside. "But… I am not going to see Mamie. I am staying here."

A shadow passed over his face then, wiping clean the pleased smile that had been there only moments before. "You cannot stay here," he insisted. "It is improper for a young woman to be at home alone. People will talk."

Madeleine feigned confusion. "But you leave me here alone for days on end, while you visit with *Madame* Anglais up the street. It did not seem so improper for those four nights last week. Why now?"

At the mention of his affair, and with a married woman no less, his mood darkened. He clenched his fist, and worked his jaw, but the alleged letter to Sir Jacob before him brought back to memory her threat and gave him pause.

"In time, you will have no choice but to obey, you *insolent* and *ungrateful* excuse for a daughter!" he warned her. "You have brought me nothing but heartache and shame, since the day they placed you in my arms and called you mine." He then slammed the door shut and stalked off to his room to seethe and drink.

Madeleine pulled out the soiled letter, quickly rewrote it, and added the lines, "Be careful when he comes to London. He has grown unusually belligerent, and means you harm; I am sure of it."

After some thought, she closed the letter with, "I do miss you too, Mother. I will visit in the spring when work grounds him here. Affectionately Yours, Madeleine."

She then slipped down the stairs, into the kitchen, and handed the letter to Gaëlle. Eli was already waiting at the port, to spirit the letter off to London.

She watched through the kitchen window as Gaëlle crept across the yard under the cover of dusk, tiptoed through the gardens, and then stole over the fence. Even as the last of her confidant's shadow disappeared into the coming night to do her bidding, that feeling of foreboding took hold of her again. It was almost as though something—someone—deep, dark and sinister was watching and waiting and plotting.

"You okay, Maddie?" Regina asked in *Kreyol*. She took hold of her arm. "Some water? Maybe some coffee?"

"No; thank you."

Regina cocked an eyebrow at her. "Did the witch spy something in the future again?" she teased. "Maybe a nice, big, strong man, eh? Like *Monsieur* Andrews?" She winked. "Or maybe just Eli, ruffling Gaëlle's skirts, tonight."

Madeleine forced a smile: always grateful for her servant's offbeat and often inappropriate humour, but too preoccupied to give it the appreciation it was due.

"Upstairs you go, Maddie," Regina advised. "I'll bring up your dinner.

Wine and cheese too, yes?"

Madeleine nodded and started up the stairs to her room. The old floorboards creaked beneath her, as she climbed. She scoffed to herself, remembering Regina's long-standing joke, regarding the disrepair of the house.

"I could almost swear your mother married a carpenter," she had said, while she put the clean laundry away. "With the state of this house, I might think she married a sheep herder, instead."

Proud though he was, Basile's pride did not discourage him from accepting a monthly allowance from his wife. In thanks, virtually every shilling Charlotte sent home to pay for maintenance of himself and the house bought pretty bonnets and satin underclothes for other women, while Madeleine's floors, and women's beds, creaked on.

"I've done what I can," she reassured herself as she looked out from her window and into the garden, waiting for some sign of Gaëlle's safe return.

But, had her dreams provided better foresight of the dangers ahead, perhaps Madeleine would have sent more than mere words to protect her mother from harm.

CHAPTER IX

An Unwelcome Surprise

William Scott IV was an ageing attorney with a highly successful practice in the heart of London. He had inherited his profession from his father, and his father before him, and his father before that. With this inheritance had come a client list featuring some of the oldest, wealthiest, and most respectable names in London and abroad: from Dukes and Ladies and Earls, to merchants and tradesmen of considerable means.

Lord Pierre Moreau, the *1st Seigneur de Lamoreaux*, had first contracted the services of William Scott's great-grandfather when he sought to circumvent the ever-changing inheritance laws in pre-revolutionary France, to ensure his wife and only heir would not be disinherited, come what may with volatile French laws and his ailing health.

The landmark case not only birthed the Moreau Matriarchy, it launched the William Scott brand as the pioneers of law, geared towards the needs of the higher social classes and liberal women. Four generations later, and Charlotte found herself seated in the writing room with the second-youngest of the direct line.

"I've checked it a thousand times over; it still holds," he assured her. "Your marriage is governed under French law, but your property is still safely held by English trustees, as has ever been the case, since *Seigneur* Pierre Moreau—according to my father's notes." He set a copy of the marriage contract and will down before her.

For a time, he stared at the papers, shuffling them about anxiously. When he finally raised his bespectacled eyes to hers, he could mask his concern no longer. "Charlotte, forgive me if I presume myself to be too… too familiar, but you are in perfect health. Is there a reason you wish to make checks on your final affairs?"

"Please consider it a paranoid precaution at present, William. You have always been kind to me and my family. I trust we may rely upon your services, should we have further need of them."

"Without a doubt, *Madame.* You have the word of myself and my son, that 'tis so."

"Then, I am content."

Just then a knock sounded at the door, and the man she had so wanted to see rushed in with great urgency. "Lady Moreau, I came as soon as I received your message!"

"Thank you, George," said she to her new visitor.

She then politely dismissed her attorney. William donned his hat, bid *adieu* to his client and her guest, and left the room with a heavy heart and a troubled mind.

George's mind was no less troubled. It showed in the very depth of his hazel eyes, and the furrowed eyebrows of his unwrinkled face. Still, he waited patiently for Charlotte to explain the urgency of her message. "Come at once, George! I need you!" it had said, with no explanation. He had almost expected to arrive and find her dead.

She turned away from the intensity of his gaze, strolled across the room and stood before an oil painting, fading with age. It was framed in gold and showed a woman with Charlotte's coal-black hair and brown eyes, though the fashion of her dress was dated. In her lap laid a black cat, dozing lazily while she petted him.

"Do you know who this is?" she asked.

"I have always assumed it was you."

"And as a child, I assumed it was Mamie, and Madeleine, for a time, believed it was me. But, it is Maria Moreau: the first of our matriarchy, my mother's grandmother." For a time, she stood, staring, remembering what she fought for, remembering what was important. *The fight continues, Maria.*

Her mind was recalled to the present by the touch of George's hand to her elbow. His palm was damp, his hands shaking. She inhaled deeply, trying to quell the flutter of nerves his touch evoked.

"Charlotte, you know I care for you. If you are in trouble, if you are in danger, you need only ask. Ask anything of me. I would not deny you; I could not."

Emboldened by the fact she had not rejected him, had not cast him aside, he embraced her. Charlotte shut her eyes, half parts savouring the feel of his body against her own, and half parts reminding herself she could not have him. "You are young."

"I will age."

"You are... innocent."

"Not half as innocent as you would think."

"I am married."

"And I am an attorney by education, albeit not quite so well practiced as William."

She turned to face him, her hand resting on his cheek, smoothly shaved. He was not a handsome man: his nose was crooked and his jaw too square and firm, but there wasn't another face that delighted her more. His eyes were kind, his hands gentle if unsteady, and his voice put her at ease on her worst of days.

"I know what people say about me," Charlotte replied. "I cannot risk further scandal to Madeleine. She is not yet married. She is but one-and-twenty. I would rather not see her begin womanhood with her reputation already besmirched, and by her mother, no less."

"Sir Jacob does not strike me as a man who cares much for the gossip of bored housewives who lack your grace and ambition."

"Men strike different tunes, the closer they draw to the flames of marriage," she replied, bitterly. "Take it from me."

"We are not all so bad, Charlotte," he said, turning his head to place a kiss in the palm of her hand.

The wooden floor seemed to slip out from beneath her as he drew closer, but not for long. She was older, wiser, and still in possession of her good senses. She withdrew and returned her attention to the portrait of Maria Moreau.

His defeated sigh put an ache in her heart. "I am sorry, George; truly. But, we cannot be together."

"And yet, I will not be apart from you, either," was his good-natured reply. "I am not so easily thwarted. There is something amiss; I know there is. Confide in me. Whatever needs doing, I am your man." When she did not reply, he voiced his greatest fear, "Has a threat been made against your life?"

"Yes."

"By whom?"

Charlotte inhaled a sharp breath. "My husband."

Her confession did not surprise him. It was common knowledge that Basile had little love, if any, for his wife, and far less for her accomplishments.

"Tell me what you need, my love, and henceforth consider it done."

Long after her guests had gone, Charlotte sat in her sumptuous velvet sofa, sinking into a vortex of misery. She had always been a woman bent on completing things: her plays, her studies, her role as a mother in Madeleine's life. There was still so much to witness, and so many lessons to teach, so many unpredictable tales that had not yet played out.

Madeleine was as fierce and strong-willed as Mamie, and that gave her hope. After all, Mamie was the very woman who claimed to marry only to pass on her legacy in a child. She had then quickly dispatched of her husband with ten thousand pounds in thanks, and a free trip to Saint-Domingue on the family's last remaining ship.

Charlotte had hoped to rebuild the Moreau fleet, when she finally tired of her poetry and rhymes and songs and plays. It would have been her last gift to the matriarchy, before passing the torch to Madeleine.

Her dear Madeleine would be motherless and alone in the world, now. And would Basile be content enough to stop there? Would her daughter be next? Who would protect her? Recognising her own helplessness and dashed dreams, the tears finally came.

"Madame!" Eli entered the room with a tray of tea and pastries. He set them down on an end table by the archway and hurried towards her. "Are you not well, *Madame?* What did the lawyer say?"

"The marriage settlement holds," Charlotte assured him. It was not the first time she would be grateful for her mother's wisdom.

"He is only marrying you for wealth and title; I've seen it," Mamie had warned her, while she brewed one of her strange teas of honey and herbs. "You would do well not to marry this one."

But, Charlotte had loved Basile once. And much to her relief, the five thousand pounds Mamie offered as dowry had pleased him and his family easily; they had come from so much less. She had believed a man of little means might prove less haughty than her other suitors, but time had proven that notion wrong.

"Madeleine will inherit all—if not in name, then in practice, all the same," she told Eli. "And you will be provided for as well. You and Betha."

"You are kind, *Madame,* but you should think of yourself," Eli reminded her.

It had been some days since Charlotte had read him Madeleine's letter, and longer still since he had delivered it. There was no doubt in their minds that Basile had finally hatched some plan to dispose of her, which would not include ten thousand pounds and a trip to the West Indies.

"We could go back to Haiti," Eli suggested. "You renounced your claim, but I am next in line; by right, that plantation belongs to me, now. The sham-wife would not dare contest it." He added, "I would give it all back to you. You have given me far more than I could ever have hoped for, here. You could write Madeleine in secret and explain. I would bring the letter myself once you were settled."

"And give up my dreams? My work? My art?" Charlotte said, stubbornly.

"Would you rather give up your life?!" Eli was at the end of his patience. He had made this suggestion before, and her answer had been no different.

"I *have* no life without my work. Without it, I am just another babbling woman whose education has made her too far-reaching for her sex. Men will trample over me as they have always wanted to do. As *my husband* has always wanted to do!"

Eli studied her for a moment, and then calmly crossed the room to fetch her tea and biscuits. "I would kill him if you ask it," he said in a low whisper. "You need only say the word."

"I will *not* have my brother hang."

He met her eyes for a brief moment as he set the tray down, and then looked away. "What will you do, then?"

"I will send you back to France to protect Madeleine. I cannot have you anywhere near here. You and Betha must go. Should anything happen to me, or him, they will suspect you first.

"Make a show of your leaving. Tarry on the streets and say goodbye to your friends in the taverns, tonight. Let everyone know you are leaving for France in the morning. That gives two days for Basile to arrive."

"And what will you do?"

"What mothers do best in times of grief; I'll weep," she answered. "And I'll sing and work and finish the last play I am like to write." After a moment's pause, she added thoughtfully, "I will give you a letter to bring to Madeleine. She will blame herself for this."

"We both shall," Eli replied.

"Go out and drink, Eli. You will only drive me to fretful distraction with all this talk of my mortality. Tell Betha to meet me in the study."

She sipped a bit of her tea, had a bite of biscuit, and then swept from the parlour and into the study she used for writing. The marriage settlement and will had already been locked away. Her desk was now littered with pages from her most recent play, about a pompous knight whose pride and jealousy drove him to murder his betrothed. *How fitting!*

Betha came in quickly to adjust the gas lamps in the room, bringing with her the unfinished tea and biscuits. She then helped to clear a writing space on the desk.

"Are you truly sending us back to Barfleur, Miss?" she asked. "I'd sooner be here."

Charlotte sighed, deeply. "Betha, I am flattered by your loyalty, and Eli's; truly. Still, I would not die peacefully, if I accepted it. You are... not the right colour for justice. You would hang, just like Eli. No trial. No truth."

Betha's eyes watered with three decades of history between them. "You will hire someone else then to protect you when Eli and I are gone?"

"I will think on it."

Betha did not look satisfied with the answer and seemed to drag her feet as she left the room.

Finally, alone with her thoughts, Charlotte let the tears come. There was misery at the sudden end to what felt like the very prime of her life, and regret for having not married one of the many wealthy suitors her mother had suggested.

For a moment, she even let herself think of the life she might have had if she had never borne Basile a child. But no, Madeleine was perhaps the only good thing to come from her mistake, and she would have wanted no other child but the feisty feline she had birthed.

Finding her resolve, she dried her eyes and penned her parting words to her only child. As she wrote, she felt herself grow stronger, calmer. She would defy Basile as she had always done, and she would win, as she had always done.

She would make plans, perhaps set traps. Though these plans continued to take root in her mind, she mentioned none of these to her daughter: nothing that would alarm her or beg her help. Nothing that would put her in harm's way.

Suddenly, the sound of silver trays and spoons colliding with china and hardwood floors reverberated throughout the house, swiftly followed by the raised voices of an angry man and a frightened woman.

Charlotte grabbed a letter opener and ran to the door to see what mischief was afoot. It was not like Eli to make such a violent entrance, not even after a night of drinking. He had barely been gone an hour.

"Get off me, *négresse!*" the man barked in French. He threw Betha aside and strolled into the parlour. Behind him, he left a mess of cheeses, vegetable broth, wine, and broken glass strewn across the floor.

He was richly dressed in a bronze-coloured swallowtail frock coat with golden buttons and the matching top hat upon his head. A coarse, black beard now peppered with white fought valiantly to reclaim ownership of his cheeks and chin, and his moustache was expertly curled. Though he did make a fine picture, no man of high birth would have dressed so ostentatiously without occasion or worn such colours in the streets of London.

Betha curtsied. "Miss," she began nervously, "I tried to warn him you were busy, and should not be disturbed."

"Basile," Charlotte said, with wide eyes. "I had not expected you for another two days. You said you would arrive on Thursday."

He closed the distance between them, and smiled with that singular charm that had once melted her heart so many eons ago. "So I did, my darling, but I thought you might enjoy a surprise. Did you miss me, love? Come. Give your dear husband a kiss."

His words and the brilliant white smile that accompanied them had long ceased to fool her. When his eyes met hers, she saw the same jealous greed where love should have lived, and where hatred had sat for so many years.

With a casual flick of the wrist, she stuck the letter opener into her hair. *I could stab him with it,* she thought to herself. *Once in the neck or the heart, and I could be done with him forever.*

CHAPTER X

Ladies & Letters

Long before his hand had ever left red marks across her face, before he grew to envy the very qualities for which he had married her, it was his snoring that had driven them to separate sleeping quarters. His nasal trumpeting was singularly terrible tonight. The very house seemed to shake when he drew breath. She could hear it even through the thick walls that separated them.

It was, however, a useful signal that he was indisposed for the rest of the night. She lit the lantern next to her bed, crept from her room, and then into the study. For hours, she wrote, not the play that so mirrored her life, but the letters that might save it.

She then crept from the study into Betha's room, just across the hall from her own. She found her friend awake in bed, with a candle lit and a book balanced upon her knees. "Impossible to sleep when he begins to blow his trumpet," she jested. "Would you like me to fetch you anything?"

Charlotte set the lantern down and handed the letters to Betha. "Eli is still at the tavern," she said, "so I am entrusting these to you. Some are for London and some for France. You must have them all delivered at your earliest convenience and make arrangements to be absent in the morning."

"Then, you have hired protection?" she guessed, her voice hopeful.

"In my own way, yes," Charlotte parried. She picked up her lantern and started for the door. "Do try to get some rest, Betha. You will need it. Dark roads lie ahead, but whatever happens, please never doubt that there are few I count as dear to me as yourself and Eli. God be with you."

❖

Despite its ominous name, the Hangman's Pub catered to the tastes of the wealthiest in London. It attracted the patronage of noble faces as high in rank as royalty, and it was not uncommonly frequented by nobles from as far south as Greece and Italy and as far north as Russia and Germany.

Though most of those patrons were men, women also frequented the tavern: mostly socialite widows and beautiful commoners who were willing to risk scandal if it increased their chances of attracting a wealthy husband. Some men had also brought their mistresses along, and others, their wives.

As Eli searched the room for an empty table, someone slipped an arm around his shoulder, and leaned unsteadily against him. "Well, hullo there, Elijah! The most handsome, generous man in all of England! Care to buy your dearest friend a drink?"

"You are drunk, John."

His friend patted him on the back and laughed. "That I am, my man. That I am! Now, how about that drink? I am one step ahead, you see, for already I have a seat for us!" He released his friend and led the way through a bevy of beautiful women. There was none among them who did not look up to cast a favourable eye in Eli's direction.

He had dressed smartly for the occasion, intent on drawing attention to himself, as Charlotte had instructed. But truth be told, Eli needed no embellishments. More than once, his heritage had come into question as a youth, but now that he was older and wiser, he found that hiding in plain sight served him best.

He looked and sounded every bit a Frenchman, if only a shade darker. He had dark, curling hair, which a ribbon held back from his freckled face, and watchful hazel-green eyes. The only tell-tale signs of the mulatto that had been his mother was his high cheekbones and the fullness of his lips. Yet, they only served to make him more handsome, and devilishly so.

Already, a few women were sizing him up from a distance, no doubt calculating his age, social rank, and means. Some recognised him as the manager of The Lady's Playhouse, while others sought any excuse to make his acquaintance.

"You certainly have a way of making every man in any room hate you, when you step inside," John jested. He had the face of a bulldog, the hair of a wet rat, and teeth like a drunken checkerboard. Still, he dressed well and spent often, and that got him all the attention he desired.

"A blessing and a curse," Eli replied, seating himself on the long, empty sofa his friend had chosen for the night. "These women don't want husbands, not truly. They want a handsome bank and a pretty title."

John laughed, heartily. "I do confess, I fail to see how this is a disadvantage!"

Eli summoned the barmaid, while John loudly invited all the ladies in the room to make themselves comfortable at his side. In seconds, the sofa bore every shape, size, and disposition of the fairer sex. Their eyes were fixed eagerly upon Eli, but a few were not above sharing their affections with John.

"I do enjoy basking in the glory of your presence," said he, smiling. When Eli did not reply, John turned to face him, taking note of the brooding look that had settled on his friend's face. "What ails you, Elijah? I would not call you a laughing man, and yet there is an air about you that is more sombre than usual."

"I leave for Barfleur in the morning," Eli answered, a little louder than was necessary.

"This is routine; is it not?" John replied. "Why the sour mood?"

"I shall be there a while, this time. I have some unpleasant business to attend to."

"Planted a little seedling in a Barfleur garden, did you?" John winked at him.

Eli managed a chuckle and began to fill his pipe, while a busty brunette drew closer to him. "What's your name, lass?" he asked.

"Janice," she answered.

"Janice," he repeated. "That's a beautiful name." He puffed on his pipe as he lit it, then inhaled deeply, threw his head back, and exhaled blue rings of smoke.

"How long have you been in London?"

"Since I was four years old, if memory serves," he answered.

Janice giggled. "You still sound very French."

"I do," he agreed.

"Have you never heard about doing what the Romans do in Rome?"

"Indeed, I have," he answered, passing his pipe to John. "That is why I came to London, where I may do as I damn well please."

She giggled, again. "You are a man of good humour; I can tell!"

"When it moves me to be."

"Strange you should be here alone," she ventured, resting a hand upon his chest. "A handsome man like you must have some beautiful lady waiting for you."

"I do." He removed his gold pocket watch and flicked it open in one fluid motion, revealing the time on one half, and a daguerreotype of Gaëlle on the other.

Every summer she came to London, he would pay to have a new one taken. She loved the fuss, the dresses, the powder, and the pictures, while the photographer frowned at the subject he was forced to capture.

"Surely, you jest!" Janice said, laughing. "She's a negro."

"So am I," he replied.

She laughed even harder. "You really are quite funny!"

Eli chuckled to himself, as though enjoying a private joke. Without another word, he puffed on his pipe, shut his eyes, and blew more smoke into the ceiling.

The crow of a cock in the distance woke Eli, as did the sudden stop of the hansom he had hired. To his left, John looked about in a daze, as though he did not recognise his own quarters.

Though Eli cherished their friendship, John had always been troubled. The two had met in college, but only one had graduated. John had wavered between wealth and poverty ever since, with a penchant for falling into questionable company.

"I—I can manage from here," John said, as he stumbled from the hansom. Halfway to the door of his apartment, he almost fell flat on his face, but managed to reclaim his balance.

"Wasted the night in his cups, that one," the driver noted. He wrinkled his nose at the putrid smells that lingered in the air of the East End slum John now called home.

Old Nichol Street was flanked by grimy tenements: people stacked one upon the other in damp, dirty, poorly ventilated rooms. And now, with winter upon them, the broken windows looking out into the streets were stuffed with everything from old clothes to last week's newspapers, to keep the cold out and the warmth in.

"Better 'e should drink less an' live better than suffocate in this 'ere stink o' Ol' Nick!"

"I pay you to drive me, not judge my companions," Eli snapped.

"I apologise, m'lord! No 'arm intended."

Eli did not reply. He dozed again, waking when the hansom stopped before the small, but elegant home Charlotte owned on the outskirts of West End. Betha was waiting in the anteroom when he entered. The more she told him of all that had happened in his absence, the more apprehension and anger waged war within him.

"We must deliver the letters," she told him.

"Yes; we must."

"I think we should start with this one, for George," Betha suggested. "He is closest, and the least likely to be put off by us waking him at this hour."

Eli nodded, and then led the way back out the door he had only just stumbled through. He was pleased to see the driver had not yet left the property, as he had stopped to give his horse a good brush before the morning traffic.

"It seems I still have further need of your services, sir."

The driver cast a suspicious look at Betha. "Is the coloured one coming, too?"

"She goes where I go, but if you object, I am sure there is a driver who would far more appreciate a day's wages for a morning's work."

"Oh no, not me, m'lord! Would never object, I wouldn't. Just wanted to make sure she was coming with you, is all!" He set his brush down and opened the door for Betha to enter. Eli helped her in, and then followed after.

"I tire of their prejudice," Eli said in *Kreyol*.

"We don't all have the privilege of passing for White, cousin," Betha answered, though she very nearly did herself. She was a few shades too dark, to be sure, but all other features she bore were strikingly Caucasian: from her grey eyes to her freckled nose and strawberry-blonde hair.

"One should have no need to pass for White to be treated with common decency."

"Decency is not so common, Eli. Not in Haiti, nor France, nor here. But let us not dwell on this. We must put our heads together to help the Miss, and that is a far more pressing matter than curing ignorance and stupidity."

CHAPTER XI

Fists Fly

All morning long, they did indeed put their heads together, but could find no solution that would ensure Charlotte's safety. Their deliberating was made all the more difficult by the cocked ears of the nosey driver, and their frequent stops.

Breakfast was well underway when they returned to the London house. Basile was nursing a headache and was in one of his sour moods. It only intensified when Eli sauntered through the door, leaning in the doorway, while he lit up his pipe.

"You!" Basile said, pointing. "You dare come here, while I am visiting. You dare!"

"I live here," Eli returned. "When last I checked, you do not, *Monsieur*. As you say, you are 'visiting'."

Basile sprung up from his seat. "Charlotte has assured me you will be on your way to France within the hour. If I catch a whiff of you thereafter, the next time your scent reaches noses, it will not be the perfume you wear now to dazzle women!"

"Dazzle women..." Eli repeated, with a chuckle. "Is that why you think I am here? To dazzle your wife?"

Basile turned purple with rage. "You are a fool if you think some upstart half-breed like yourself could win the affections of Charlotte Moreau."

I have seen her dazzled by less, if we are to include the likes of you, Eli wanted to say, but he held his tongue and turned to his sister. Charlotte looked as though she had not slept a wink all night. There were bags beneath her eyes, and, for the first time, he could see her years upon her. The streaks of grey dulling the once raven hair. The wrinkles now carving lines into her olive skin.

"I received your request and the tickets. Betha and I will be leaving for Barfleur within the hour, as you instructed. All other business has been tended to."

"Thank you, Eli," she returned. "I trust you understand. Basile and I are grateful for the privacy."

Basile was even more puffed up than usual, at the thought of Eli cast out of the house. "You need not explain to the little half-breed *why* he is being sent away. I am sure even he understands when he is unwanted, however much he hangs around you like a lost puppy in London."

His headache now forgotten, he sipped at his coffee with a supercilious smile. "Go back to your *négresse* in Barfleur, half-breed. I have no doubt that at this very moment, she is corrupting my daughter with some pagan or deceitful idea. Low-cunning little traitors, the whole lot of you! Not an ounce of loyalty, faithfulness, or gratefulness to be had! No knowledge of your place!"

Eli could feel his face grow warm with the beginnings of rage. It was one thing to insult him, and another to insult his family and the lady who commanded his affections. "I am sure you would know all about the qualities of faithfulness and loyalty, after the sensational stories that come to us from the very heart of Barfleur, *Monsieur* Dubois."

Basile sprung up from his chair again, and closed the distance between them with angry strides. "Do you accuse me? Do you *dare* bring such accusations to a gentleman?"

"You are no gentleman. You are an over-proud peasant with a Lady for a wife. She deserves better in a man than you!"

Basile's fist came up at his face within seconds, but Eli was no stranger to confrontation. He ducked, grabbed the offending hand, twisted it, and prepared to plant his own fist in Basile's face.

"Élian! Enough!"

Eli turned to look at his sister, his fist inches from Basile's now frightened face. It took every ounce of self-control to quell the bloodlust that had taken hold of him. Finally mastering his anger, he straightened Basile's shirt and picked up his pipe from where it had fallen.

"I apologise, Charlotte. It is never my wish to embarrass you. I lost my head. It will not happen again." He then turned and left the room.

The echoes of the argument that then ensued between husband and wife followed him to his bedchamber as he checked to ensure he had packed all he needed.

"You will not patronise my workers!"

"Your *servants*," Basile corrected her. "The sooner you and your daughter recognise the difference, the better off we all shall be. Did you see him try to lay his hand on me? I should have it removed. One word in the right ears and he would be undone!"

"If you speak an ill word against Eli, I will strike your name from the Moreau line as sure as English rain, Basile. Do *not* test me. I have had enough of this!" He heard her footsteps down the hall, followed by the angry slamming of a door.

A heavy silence settled over the house thereafter, interrupted only by Basile, alone at breakfast, loudly stabbing at his meal and clinking the china.

Eli had always been fascinated by ships and life at sea. From as early as boyhood, he had climbed to the tallest hills in Haiti with Regina, and looked down at the ships docking miles away. He had wondered what it was like to ride the wooden beasts out to sea, to be part and parcel of the bobbing movements they made as they rode the waves and wind that drove them to their destinations.

He had dreamed of being a sailor then, had held on to that dream even while he studied at Cambridge, but Charlotte had not wished to see him enter into any service with such a high risk of peril. Indeed, it would have broken his heart to be separated from his sister for long—and Gaëlle.

And so, he had confined his love to the journeys he took around Europe. Every so often, Charlotte presented him with an errand that showed him more and more of the world beyond the borders of London. He had seen the Parthenon in Greece, stood in the shadow of the Colosseum in Italy, debated with the monks of Jerónimos in Portugal, walked through the best Bordeaux vineyards in France, and stood where the giants had once roamed in Ireland.

By train, carriage, horseback, and on foot, he had seen all these places had to offer: savoured their foods, enjoyed the company of their people, learned their languages. Even then, there was nothing he looked forward to so much as standing on the deck of a ship, with nothing but blue skies and seas in all direction. No land in sight.

Unfortunately, Betha did not share his enthusiasm. She spent most of the journey bent at the waist, either heaving into a bucket, or over the side of the ship. She drank little, ate less, and spoke none at all. Eli wished he could comfort her, but had learned long ago that Betha preferred to endure her misery alone.

"Negroes," the Irish captain began, not unkindly. "They never do take well to the sea. Me always wondered why that was."

"Have you ever been aboard a slave ship?" Eli returned, accepting the brandy the sailor offered.

"No, and glad I am of it. Dreadful things, they are. Dreadful, too, the plight of the negroes still lost in the West Indies."

"Indeed," Eli agreed. "I have been aboard a slave ship. It is worse than dreadful. Humans stacked one upon the other, cramped, without space to move. The air reeks of human filth and death. And the moaning, the cries for help. You needn't speak their language to understand the desperation, the cries for mercy, the confusion, the sadness, the fear, and grief.

"If for generations, that was your memory of the sea—or ocean— passed down from African to West Indian, I don't imagine you would learn to find favour with the sea, either. You would learn to fear it, to hate it, even."

"And yet, you love the ocean," the sailor noted, accepting the brandy Eli now handed back to him, and taking a long swig of it.

"I do," Eli confessed. "I have never been a man who allowed himself to be mastered by his fears."

The sailor laughed at this. "And that's what makes you a better man than a good half of the crew I got here! I don't know what burdens your heart, Eli. I hope it's not women troubles, but whatever it is, me thinks you're a grand man for putting it right." Without waiting for a reply, the sailor hobbled off to tend the ship.

Eli inhaled deeply, wanting to believe the sailor's estimation of him were true. And what of his own assertion that he was not a man to be mastered by his own fears? His own emotions? Had he not allowed Basile to get under his skin that very morning? He regretted the way he had reacted now, though he did not regret defending his lady.

Gaëlle had held a special place in his heart since childhood. After her mother passed, he had watched over her, protected her. And as they had grown older, that protection grew to fondness, and then to affection. It was only their mutual love for Madeleine that delayed their union. They could not leave the only heiress of the direct Moreau line unprotected, much as she believed she needed no one's protection but her own.

And yet, I have left the Head of the Moreau line to fend for herself.

Though Mamie was by title, *Marquise de Lamoreaux,* and the head of the family, she had long since passed responsibility to her daughter, to enjoy the quiet peace of pursuing her passions. It was Charlotte who now presided over the Moreau Family, and who wrote letters to settle disputes in the village of Lamoreaux, where the family had once held their feudal rights.

A gust of wind washed over his face, bringing with it the salty spray of the ocean. He could feel his curls coming undone from the ribbon which held them back, the tendrils brushing against the collar of his coat, caressing his face. When he opened his eyes, he saw Betha to his right, emptying herself into the sea.

He drew up beside her. On any other day, she would have turned away from him in embarrassment, but on any other day Charlotte would have been safely with them. Today, though she was not particularly friendly, she was at the very least willing to listen.

"I can think of only one solution to our predicament," he said, drawing near to her ear to fight the much louder wind. "I cannot be in two places at once. I cannot protect both Charlotte and Madeleine. I must choose."

"Then surely, you choose Madeleine. Charlotte would not have it any other way."

"Indeed, she would not," Eli agreed. "And yet, I must choose my sister. My mind is decided upon the matter. You need not waste any time dissuading me. Basile, after all, is not in Barfleur. He is on English shores, and upon England, I must focus my solutions."

Betha was quiet for a time. Her disapproval echoed in the silence. "What will you do?"

"Rid her of Basile myself, if I must," he answered. "But I believe I know a man, who knows a man, who can be relied upon to do us all a kindly favour."

"Should I ask?"

"You should not. The less you know, the better. If anyone must hang, let it be only me. I owe Charlotte my life. If I must give mine so she may keep her own, I do it gladly. All I have, I have because of the kindness she showed a poor little negro orphan boy, who any other sister might have seen as her rival and disposed of without a second thought."

CHAPTER XII

The Beginning of Scandal

Madame Anglais was an infamous woman of five-and-thirty. Seventeen years prior, she had appeared in town, well-dressed, well-loved, and well-sought after. With ease, she had wooed the wealthiest baron in Barfleur, a soon-to-be unfortunate, *Monsieur* Pierre Anglais.

After wedding, each learned the other had grossly misrepresented their wealth. The young bride had escaped a ruined family in Italy, and the young groom had gambled away half his recent inheritance in London, only months before.

Thus, a promising love turned sour, while each complained about the other's past deception, but said not a word of each other's present indiscretions. And so, it was at some risk to her reputation that young Madeleine found herself at the residence of *Madame* Anglais.

The large Gothic Rayonnant-style manor sat on a small hill in the centre of a well-manicured lawn. The oldest manor in Barfleur, the walls stood proud and strong, though weather and age had turned the whitewashed walls to various shades of brown and mildew.

Inside the stately manor, furnishings were sparse and the provisions poor. The anteroom, however, kept the secret well. It featured golden fixtures, animal-skin rugs, and expensive Italian paintings.

"*Signora* Anglais will appear shortly," a maid announced from the archway to the left of the room. She was plump and pleasant, if a little shy, with a heavy Italian accent. "May I offer you something? Wine? Cheese? Coffee?"

"No, but I thank you for asking."

"Then you do not mind waiting here, while *Signora* dresses?" She gestured to a white, upholstered chair with lion heads carved into the armrests.

"I don't mind at all. Thank you."

The maid then left Madeleine to her thoughts.

It was not mere happenstance that had sent the young heiress to the home of *Madame* Anglais. It was common knowledge that Basile spent an inordinate amount of time in her company, often neglecting to return home altogether, and always while *Monsieur* Anglais was abroad. Surely, if he had hatched some sinister plan, she had a hand in it.

At length, *Madame* Anglais appeared. She floated into the room wearing a dress of the most expensive fabrics from Milan. The bright red of the dress complemented her dark hair, now streaked with white, and her dark eyes. About her neck, she wore a pearl necklace, and large rings adorned her fingers. She had never been known for modesty or subtle charm.

"Oh, you must forgive me, *Mademoiselle*," said she. Nearly two decades of residing in France had done much to temper her Italian accent, but its combination with French now created a lilt that was almost Wallachian. "I was not expecting company, you see, and was not at all dressed to receive a visitor as distinguished as yourself."

Madeleine kissed both cheeks and settled into the chair once more. *Madame* Anglais chose the larger one adjacent to her and extended the maid's prior offer for refreshments. Again, Madeleine politely declined.

Madame Anglais fidgeted with her hands for a bit, and then asked, "To what do I owe this pleasure, *Mademoiselle*? It is not often you come to visit at the Château d'Anglais. The manor has not seen a Moreau for many moons, now."

"Indeed. Pray, forgive the intrusion," Madeleine conceded. "It is only that I hoped you could help me resolve some personal matters at home, involving my father."

Madame Anglais's eyes widened. For a moment, she struggled to find the words to string together a coherent response. Finally, she regained her composure, lifted her chin and said, "I have no idea what you mean to imply, child. Your father and I are only acquaintances in passing. There is nothing else between us. Indeed, I might even venture to say I barely know the man."

Madeleine feigned confusion and pulled a piece of paper from the pockets of her dress. "I mean to surprise Father, while he's away visiting with Mother at the London house. I'm afraid I spend more time in books than learning how to beautify a home and know your skills would far surpass my own. That was my reason for coming. I did not mean to cause offence."

Madame Anglais's entire demeanour changed after this admission. She was filled at once with an odd mix of guilt, regret, and pride. Nevertheless, she then launched into expert advice on how the Barfleur Estate might be better improved.

As she listened, Madeleine felt strongly that *Madame* Anglais had thought long and hard on this before. After an hour or so of pretending to take notes, and nodding from time to time, she put an end to the farce and thanked her for her expertise.

"Do come again if you have need of my assistance, and I hope I haven't bored you," the baroness told her guest. "Father always put me in charge of these things in Italy, especially after Mother passed away. He said I had an eye for making a beautiful home."

"That you do," Madeleine replied. "I'll call again, should I need further assistance. And do let me know, if ever you should have need of mine."

Though only an hour or so had passed in the company of the baroness, a marked change had taken place outside. Already, the first tinge of orange had stretched itself across the sky, heralding the twilight. A steady wind had picked up, pushing Madeleine's dark tresses back from her face, while the skirts of her dress swept at her feet.

"Did you not come by carriage? Should I send for one?" *Madame* Anglais enquired. "It seems awfully cold and the darkness will be upon us, soon.

Surely, it is not safe for a young girl like yourself to be travelling alone."

"I appreciate your thoughtfulness, *Madame* Anglais, but I rather look forward to the walk. I am sure you may have heard I have not been well. The fresh air can only serve to improve my health."

"Indeed, I have not heard those rumours," *Madame* Anglais professed. "You appear to be in excellent health!"

"You are kind to say so. I am mostly recovered, now. Have a wonderful evening and thank you again for your advice."

CHAPTER XIII

Prejudice & Honour

With the towering manor and the silhouette of *Madame* Anglais behind her, Madeleine made her way through the winding streets of Barfleur to the local merchant. A man of eight-and-fifty, old age had not been kind to him. Already he was white-haired, with gaunt eyes, sagging skin, and a stooping posture.

Madeleine did not fail to notice the look of surprise in his eyes when he saw her, for she was unaccompanied, and more often than not her coloured servants were trusted with the shopping. Nor did she fail to notice the look that betrayed the fact he had sniffed an opportunity. He immediately summoned his twin boys from the back of the store. They were home from college to help their father with the shop.

The boys were a year or two shy of twenty with barely a stubble upon their chins and the naivety of youth still shining in their brown eyes. They had the bearing of the well-learned and the charm of boys who were not unaccustomed to the company of young women. On any other day, she would have been tempted to pick their brains on everything from physics to philosophy, but today her mind wandered elsewhere.

The sky was now burning bright with orange flames. Surely, Gaëlle had not been caught. Should she have stayed a while longer? Maybe distracted the maids by requesting refreshments, after all? Had she finally put her companion's neck at too great a risk?

"Have you seen my friend, Gaëlle?" she enquired, her eyes still fixed on the streets as half a dozen traps raced by, the clippity-clops of horseshoes echoing against the cobblestones.

"The *négresse* from your household, *Mademoiselle?*" one of the twins asked. It was hard to say which one. They were identical in every way, save that one was a half inch taller than the other.

She turned to face them. "I believe I said my *friend.*" If their father expected his sons to be invited into high society through her, they could begin by showing respect for her valued companions.

"I don't believe we have," the shorter twin answered.

"I am expecting her," she explained. "Would you mind if I waited here a while? I am sure she is just a little late."

"Of course!" the merchant piped up, though the exhaustion of the day's work had already begun to weigh upon him. "I'm sure Olivier and Thibaut will not mind keeping your company, while I tend to the last of business for the evening." He gestured to a few waiting customers. Madeleine had not even noticed when they entered the shop, so set was her mind upon Gaëlle and how she fared.

In spite of their father's less than altruistic intentions, the boys did make fine company. They shared stories of life at *Université de Paris*, and of trips to Asia and Africa with their father for trade.

"Father was a soldier in his youth," Thibaut, the shorter one, explained. "When he was injured, he thought it was the end of his career, but all those years serving abroad taught him much about ships and trade and the ways of the different people of the world. We have enjoyed travelling with him, though it is sometimes dangerous."

"We once had our carriage overtaken by some *nègres*," Olivier volunteered next. He had noticed the keen interest in Madeleine's eyes at the mention of danger and sought to play it up to his advantage. "Luckily, father knew the uncle of one of the savages, and we were able to escape with our lives and all our possessions. We-"

"Brother," Thibaut interrupted. Unlike his younger twin, he had not failed to notice the sudden change that overcame the heiress.

"No, Thibaut. Do let him finish," she said, her expression darkening.

Olivier, still oblivious as to how he had erred, looked from his brother to Madeleine with a puzzled expression.

"Pardon me, *monsieur*. Is *Mademoiselle* Moreau here? She was to wait for me, and I am afraid I am a little late."

"Well," Madeleine stood, her chin lifted, "my little savage has summoned me. You will excuse me, I am sure."

Behind her, she could hear Thibaut chastising his brother for his loose tongue, but it was not his words that bothered her; it was the contents of his heart. Better a loose tongue than a lying one, after all. And Thibaut— did he share his brother's feelings? Had they on prior occasions laughed together about the *nègres* and savages? Was it a stronger sense of morality or propriety which moved him now to silence his brother?

The merchant was reading the shopping list presented to him by Gaëlle when Madeleine appeared. "I am so sorry to come so late, *monsieur*," Gaëlle was saying. "Other errands for the *Mademoiselle* detained me for longer than expected."

The merchant was clearly annoyed, but perked up when he saw Madeleine approaching. "I will have these for you in just a moment."

"Thank you, *monsieur*," Madeleine cut in. "I fear I sent Gaëlle on one errand too many before her stop here, today."

When he was out of earshot, Gaëlle turned again to her mistress. "It is done," she said. "I believe I have found just the thing. You will be proud, I think. You will thank me with a new dress!"

"Is that all it takes to reward you for so dangerous a mission?"

Gaëlle smiled. "Your friendship is all the reward I can ask for, Madeleine. The dress is just a wonderful bonus. How oft' you forget, I am here to serve you."

"Friends do not serve friends," Madeleine replied, regretting for perhaps the hundredth time their differences in station.

"There you are wrong, Madeleine. Good friends serve each other. I count myself lucky to have been in your favour for as long as memory tells me."

Madeleine squeezed her hand and was about to reply when Gaëlle's distraction caught her attention. Thibaut had just appeared and was waiting politely for a moment to interrupt.

"I must apologise, Madeleine, for the behaviour of my brother," he said in earnest.

"It is not his behaviour that concerns me, but his prejudice," she returned, perhaps more haughtily than she originally intended. In any case, she was not sorry.

It was Olivier who brought the goods out, looking sheepish. His face burned red when Gaëlle turned to look at him, her own face the picture of innocence and genuine curiosity.

"It is growing late," the merchant noted as Gaëlle stepped forward to settle the bill. "An attractive young heiress should not walk home alone. I know my boys will be happy to accompany you."

"You are too kind, but I believe *Mademoiselle* Moreau's safety might be better entrusted to a soldier than two green boys," came a voice from behind.

The *green boys* did not take the slight well. Olivier narrowed his eyes at the newcomer, and Thibaut watched him thoughtfully with a dark expression. Nevertheless, neither spoke a word in response. They knew better than to challenge a knighted soldier. After all, they carried naught but knowledge, whilst he carried a pistol and the vengeance of the British crown.

Outside the merchant's shop, a steady wind blew. It rustled the last of autumn's fiery foliage in the trees and sent dead leaves scurrying along the cobblestone streets ahead of them. Only their feet echoed on the cobblestones now, for though the occasional gas lamp lit their way, the shadowy streets were long since deserted. There was neither hansom nor hackney to be seen, and already, Madeleine regretted not taking the carriage. Still, it could not have been avoided. It had been safer not to take her driver into her confidence.

"Isn't the breeze lovely!" Gaëlle exclaimed in English, for the benefit of the soldier.

"Quite so!" Jacob agreed, reaching towards her. "Let me help you with your load, Gaëlle. And if you would be so kind as to walk ahead, so your mistress and I can speak in private, it would not go unappreciated." He pitched her a coin.

She caught it easily, but did not move ahead until Madeleine nodded in consent.

"Nice of you to carry the goods for Gaëlle," Madeleine commended him.

"She is a lady, if not by title then by sex, and by the distinguished company she keeps," he replied.

"Olivier and Thibaut would say otherwise," Madeleine replied, her tone bitter. *"Nègres*, they called her and all people of colour—savages. And then their father, seeing a window into the noble circles through me, of course: the daughter of the noblewoman who marries beneath her, and whose entire family has taken to befriending coloureds.

"And me to sit there a-smiling all the while, as if I do not feel myself used and my companions abused! Oh, that I were a man and could put a fist to their proud faces!"

Sir Jacob listened to her fiery soliloquy, half incensed and half amused, for she was never as attractive to him as when she was in a fresh temper. "They meant no harm, I am sure," said he, his voice low and soothing. "Even educated men are oft' fools, perhaps more so than most, since we naturally believe college has taught us everything."

"Well, I am indeed thankful that you are not a fool in these matters, though I am sure you are thrice the fool in others," she teased, her spirits already lifting, for she was as quick to recover as she was to fly into a temper.

"Quite so! For here I am, pursuing a woman who has turned her very heart against marriage, in hopes that she will marry me. Has ever a more impossible thing been attempted?"

She laughed, then. "You know, Sir Jacob, at one-and-twenty I am much older than many a man prefers his woman."

"Truly? I should not have noticed, had you not mentioned it, for you are exactly as I love mine." He turned to look at her, but Madeleine looked straight ahead. She knew his game too well. He had been three years at playing it now.

"I am also more stubborn than most men have use for," she pointed out.

She could feel the mischief in his grin beside her. "A strong man seeks an equal; a weak man seeks a slave."

"A strong man oft' seeks a strong woman he believes he can conquer," she bantered. "You must excuse my cynicism, Sir Jacob, for I am the birth-child of a country which had the good sense to declare the Rights of Man, but then the audacity to turn and say, 'Oh, but not you, women; and not you, Blacks!'"

"A worthy observation," Jacob commended her, "but I am of a country where a girl, the very age as yourself, sits upon our throne. Ask any man from her court and they will tell you she is a force to be reckoned with.

"And even before her time, let me see, we had Elizabeth I, who reigned for four-and-forty years; and before her, Bloody Mary—though some may argue she showed more tyranny than true strength.

"Thus, we Englishmen are no strangers to the rule of women, though I confess, we do not often make wives of them. For my part, I am not too proud to say it is *you* who has conquered me, with your wit, and charm, and beauty. There is no other like you in all the world."

"For your sake, that may be a good thing."

It was his turn to laugh. "Are you suggesting you would be so terrible a companion?"

"Is that not what they say of the Moreaux? That we are a family of women who have forgotten our place?"

"As long as you agree your place is beside me, I have no quarrel with the other places you may or may not remember."

She tried not to smile, but already the unbidden curving of her lips betrayed her. Thankfully, the wind did much to conceal her face from his, by way of her hair. "I will keep that in mind, Sir Jacob—for future reference, of course."

"Of course," he replied, enjoying his own private smile.

It was not much longer before they arrived at the entrance to her estate. Gaëlle approached to take the goods, and then darted through the open gate.

"You are such good company, Sir Jacob," Madeleine said, only then meeting his gaze. "Perhaps, too much so." She looked about them, observing the shadows creeping in at every corner and every turn. "I should leave you now, as the town does love to talk."

"Yes, and of your father especially," he returned in a tone that was as gentle as it was serious. He looked deeply disturbed by what he meant to share, yet also resolute. *"Monsieur* Dubois soils your mother's good name with his licentiousness, but I daresay one can expect little more from a Frenchman, if I may be so frank."

Madeleine soothed his apparent fear that he may have offended her with a smile. "And do you propose an Englishman might be better?"

The spark of playful mischief returned to his cerulean eyes, then. "Well, *Mademoiselle!* I am afraid I can only swear for this one, so choose wisely." His hands twitched behind him. He had not forgotten how close he had come to kissing her in the garden, beneath the dying sun. How he longed now to reach up and curl a lock of those pitch-black coils about his fingers.

He was on the verge of finding the nerve when Gaëlle bolted from the house, coming to an abrupt halt a few feet away. She was out of breath but determined to deliver her message. "I am so sorry to interrupt," she said, evidently shaken. "Madeleine, you are needed inside, *immediately*, if you can forgive my directness."

Jacob's hand rested on his holster. "Is there trouble?"

"No, no, Sir. Just family matters to attend to," Gaëlle replied, but her eyes belied the calm she now tried to exude.

"Wait inside please, Gaëlle. I will follow within the minute." Madeleine returned her attention to Jacob. "It was a pleasure speaking with you as always. Thank you for walking us home, and for helping Gaëlle. It is not often that people bother to be kind to her."

"I only wish I could do it more often." Finally plucking up some courage, he took her hand and pressed it to his lips. "Good night, Madeleine." He then turned on his heels and went off into the night, with his heart thundering pleasantly in his chest.

CHAPTER XIV

Discovering Deceit

She was surprised to find Eli pacing the anteroom when she entered. Betha was also with him, sobbing softly in a chaise lounge at the other end of the room. Panic rose like bile in Madeleine's throat.

"Where is Mother?" she demanded. "Why are you not with her? Why are you *here?*"

"Charlotte is in London with your father," Eli answered. He took a swig from the glass of brandy Regina had brought him earlier, trying to steady his nerves. "She asked me to give you this." He took an envelope from the breast-pocket of his travel coat and offered it to her.

"And I took this from *Madame* Anglais's study," Gaëlle piped up, holding the leather-bound journal she had found, while snooping around the Château d'Anglais.

"Father said he was delivering gifts in the countryside to his family. That he would be gone until the day before his trip," Madeleine pointed out.

"He lied," Regina joined in.

In her distraction, Madeleine had not noticed her in the room. Somewhere in the far reaches of her mind, she now remembered duty: that dinner was to be prepared, and that rooms should be readied for the guests. But at the forefront of her mind were words yet unread.

She sank into one of the chairs by Betha and opened her mother's letter.

My Dearest Madeleine,

You have always been gifted in ways neither I, nor even your grand-mother, ever enjoyed. We could but hope for your skill, though perhaps the burden of knowledge would be greater than we ladies could bear.

Even so, I must suggest that perhaps just this once, this vision is but a fancy of yours, born from hatred of your father. I wish you would not hate him so. Our soured marriage has no doubt tainted your idea of the man I married, and who fathered you, but he is a good and honest man, who means us well in his own way.

Please, do not share these dreams of yours with anyone else, least of all Mamie. It would only cause needless worry and concern, and perhaps, great scandal.

I have never felt safer in London, and at your father's unexpected arrival, I have sent Eli and Betha back to Barfleur to give us some privacy, long overdue.

I do apologise for the short notice, but I thought you could use Betha and Eli's company to pass the holidays, as you will not have mine in London. I have sent gifts that I am sure you will all enjoy, and I do hope you will be so kind as to deliver your grandmother's before the holidays are over.

With all my Love,

Charlotte

Madeleine read the letter again, and again, and again, before finally addressing Eli. "Was she deep in her cups when she wrote this?" she said, angrily. "Mad, perhaps? Has she taken leave of her senses?"

Eli was so engrossed in the journal Gaëlle had found that he barely looked up. "You need to see this, Madeleine," he said. "It is written in Italian; I will translate.

"Basile has gone to London to do the deed. I trust the imbecile will be successful, and that by the end of the winter holiday, he shall be a rich widower, and I, his bride."

Had a stranger stumbled upon the study, they might have believed a hurricane from the West Indies had settled on French shores overnight and torn through the room. There was not a thing left in its rightful place.

Severina had emptied all the drawers and strewn their contents all about the desk and the floor. Bills and letters and newspapers and novels lay mingled together with the occasional sighting of a ruby or pearl.

The books that had once lined the shelves in alphabetical order by author now lay at the foot of the cases. Some had been shaken open and dropped, then stomped on. A few showed unfortunate signs of not surviving Hurricane Severina.

"Signora!" a familiar cry came from the door.

Severina turned towards the maid. "Have you or *any* of the servants entered this room?"

"Of course not, *Signora!*" she answered. "I have not set foot inside without your leave, and always in your presence; nor have I ever observed anyone but your husband entering the room."

Fear pierced Severina's heart. "Did you say my husband?"

"Yes, *Signora.* I saw him enter just last night."

"Did you see what he did, while he was inside?"

"The door was closed, *Signora.* I did not observe him. Is something missing? Should I alert the servants to keep an eye for anything in particular?"

Severina did not immediately furnish her with a response. Why had Pierre come into the study? Though she had never outright banned him from it, it was she who managed their affairs, since he had proven himself more adept at spending than making money.

Had he discovered her private journal? And what would he make of it, if he had? He could not read a word of Italian, and he would not dare risk scandal to his own name by bringing into his confidence someone who could. She then had no reason to despair over the missing journal she had torn the room apart to find.

"No," she finally answered. She then stepped over a pile of books and out through the door. "I expect this to be cleaned up by the end of the day and trust you alone to do it."

The maid nodded. *"Yes, Signora.* I will tend to it, now."

She was no less suspicious of her husband when he sauntered into the dining hall later that evening. As they had neither elderly parents still alive, nor children, nor guests, they dined alone. A dozen chairs on either side separated Severina from her husband, but not a movement he made escaped her notice.

When the servant set his food down before him, Pierre made a face. "Is this a sign of the depths we have sunk to?"

Severina looked down at her own plate. It was not a meal fit for a baron and his wife, living in a manor upon a hill, but it was all they could afford. The wine was cheap, the cheese had already begun to show a bit of mould, and the meat was not as fresh as it could be.

"Our finances have been especially strained this month."

"Indeed," Pierre replied, scraping the mould from his cheese. He winced when he tasted the wine, but then sighed and emptied his glass in one gulp. The servant rushed forward to refill it. "If I recall, I warned you about buying that property on the outskirts of Paris. It looked about ready to cave in from the start."

"They assured me it was sound," Severina said, tensing for a fight.

"And I assured you, it was not—advice you should have honoured from a husband who is no stranger to managing properties. I suppose you women see the independence of the Moreau Matriarchs and naturally assume you can do the same. After five generations, they make it look easy; it is not."

He sipped his wine again. "We will need to reduce our household. We cannot afford to keep them all, and it is only you and me who need looking after. Personally, I am not opposed to looking after myself, if this is the quality of meals I must accept to have the house I am hardly in kept tidy."

"You are an inconsiderate, ill-bred fool!" Severina returned. "People would talk if we let our household go!"

"And what is it to us, if they do?" Pierre challenged her, unruffled by her anger. "The lion does not concern himself with the bleating of sheep."

"If memory serves, while our sheep were relatively well-behaved in Italy, yours almost brought all of France to its knees for need of bread."

Pierre seemed about to respond but thought better of it and held his tongue. Thereafter, dinner was a clatter of dishes and cups and forks, complemented by the awkward silence of a loveless marriage.

Some minutes of this carried on before Severina interrupted with, "The servants tell me you were in the study."

"I was."

"On what account?"

He looked up with some surprise at her sharpness: an eyebrow arched, a bitter smirk upon his lips. "There was a book I had an interest in and I thought I might find it there."

"Did you?"

"Yes."

Severina narrowed her eyes at her husband, trying to decide whether or not it was worth pressing him further. His pale grey eyes rose from his plate to meet her brown ones across the table. For a while, neither blinked nor swallowed.

Finally, Pierre chuckled to himself and lifted his glass of wine. "Careful, wife. Or I may begin to think you love me, yet."

"Unlikely."

"As is your God, and yet you believe," he said in that teasing voice that made her want to bash him over the head with the pitcher of wine. "Why should I not also have Faith?"

She scowled at him, her hand automatically going up to clutch the silver cross she wore around her neck. Try as he might to engage her in conversation thereafter, she would not say a word. And as his efforts went ignored, he at long last finished his poor repast and retired to bed, alone.

The following morning, she woke to a knock at her bedroom door. A quick glance towards her window showed that the sun had long since risen, and it was fast approaching noon. She had tossed and turned all night, only slipping into the arms of sleep just before the first rays of sunrise had begun to steal across the sky.

The knock sounded again, and this time the door opened. She was just about to give the servant a strong talking to when her husband entered. He was evidently dressed for riding and looked about her room with some amusement. It had been a long time since he last set foot inside it.

"Severina," he began, his eyes finally settling upon her. "I waited for you at breakfast, but you did not come down. Are you not well?"

"Why-ever should you care if I am well or not?"

The accusation wounded him. "You may have opted to ignore that I am your husband, but I have always treated you as my wife."

The truth of his words filled her with guilt, but only for a second. "What do you want, husband?"

"It's a lovely day. I don't believe it will be this warm again for some time, with winter almost upon us. I thought you might like to come riding with me."

She did enjoy an afternoon ride in the woods and often went alone when she could not find a trusted partner, but there was no company she detested in all the world as much as her husband's. She rose from the bed, walked to the window, and looked out at the woods bordering the Château d'Anglais.

"I thought a small picnic might earn me some forgiveness for my thoughtless comment at dinner," Pierre said, startling her as he closed his hands about her waist. "I did not mean to mock your beliefs, however foreign they are to me."

She went stock still, and when he touched his lips to her neck, it roused her anger. She turned around and shoved him away. "I am not your plaything!"

He looked back at her, with more injury to his heart than his pride. Though he had never forgiven her for her deception, he cared for her no less than he had on their wedding night. Unfortunately, the feeling had never been mutual between them.

"Please leave, Pierre. I have no desire to go riding with you."

He did not need to be told twice. In a moment, he was gone.

She waited until she saw his horse galloping from the yard, with the stable boy following close behind, before rushing to his room. For an hour she searched the sparse belongings he kept in his bedchamber, but she could not find the cursed journal!

She returned to her room in greater distress than she had left it. Surely, he would not have wanted her if he had found a way to read the journal. He would have been angry about Basile. Or would it have somehow made her a more attractive conquest, in the twisted mind of a gambler who enjoyed high stakes?

And if not him? Then who had taken it? And what did they know? For there were worse things she feared would be discovered if the journal fell into the wrong hands. After all, what was an extramarital affair compared to the act of taking a life?

CHAPTER XV

The Blackened Château

"Do you think it mere happenstance that Charlotte sent gifts for you to bring to Mamie?" Eli pointed out. "She wants you to go to Lamoreaux."

"How do we know we are not playing into his hands?" Madeleine returned. "We're doing exactly what he told me to do from the very beginning: the very direction he *threatened* me to take."

"I don't understand it myself, Madeleine, but I do know you are not safe here. Let me escort you to Lamoreaux, and then I will return to London to do what I can for your mother. The longer you take to be persuaded, the longer you delay the assistance I could provide."

"I should be in London!" Madeleine exclaimed. "I warned her! Why did she not listen?"

"Not for ten thousand pounds would I allow you to board a ship to England."

"Oh? And how do you propose to stop me?" she challenged him, chin lifted.

"With your own common sense. Basile and Severina intend to wipe out the entire Moreau Matriarchy. Neither Charlotte nor Mamie can produce another heir. You are the last of the line, Madeleine. All hope rests with you. You cannot put yourself in danger."

And so it was that Madeleine found herself in her carriage, headed for the countryside. Though she was glad for Eli's protection, and the company of Gaëlle and Regina, for a long time she fumed in silence as the horses picked their way along the rocky and perilous path.

The closer they drew to the family estate, however, the more she looked forward to seeing Mamie again. Surely, Mamie would have the answers she sought. In fact, now that she thought about it, how could Mamie not have known that her only child was in danger?

"Believing in magic now, are you?" she asked herself, but there was no easy answer.

Looking for a distraction, she turned to Eli. He sat across from her in the carriage with an arm around Gaëlle, who was dosing quietly on his shoulder. "Uncle, why are you frightened of Mamie?"

Eli's eyes widened at the blunt accusation. "Whatever planted such a notion in your head?!" he asked, though already he glanced with unmasked suspicion in his aunt's direction.

Regina laughed. "Do you deny it?"

"I am not *frightened* of your grandmother," Eli said in answer to Madeleine's question. "I admit, I was as a child. *Papa* told me a lot of stories about her. Indeed, Charlotte and I have often joked that she must have inherited her storytelling skills from *Papa.*

"He said the *Seigneuresse* was a powerful woman, intimidating, beautiful, kind: a force to be reckoned with. A woman likely to suck the very air out of your lungs, but who brought life to those around her. He called her his dark paradox."

"That sounds accurate!" Regina said, laughing. Unlike Eli, she was well-acquainted with Mamie, and always looked forward to spending time with the now *Marquise.*

"I know he loved my mother, but I'm sure he loved your grandmother twice as much, until the day he died," Eli said. Thereafter, a faraway look had crept into his eyes, and Madeleine knew he was back in Haiti, seeing his homeland through the scared, innocent eyes of a child.

Scarcely half a day had passed before they came upon that last great hill. The carriage slowed considerably, and Madeleine could hear the horses struggle to make it up and over as soon as possible. They, too, knew the end of their journey was near, and were only too eager to get it over and done with.

The young heiress drew the curtains aside and opened the window, just as Lamoreaux rose up to meet her. Set on fertile land in a valley through which a river had run for centuries, the townspeople flourished under the care of the eldest Moreau. It was one of the few rural towns through which a train ran, connecting them to Paris with all its culture and commerce.

For this reason, Lamoreaux was not so backward as the rest of rural France, where the wealthy seemed an evergreen presence, while the poor wilted away. Mamie was to thank for all this, the shepherdess who was never too far from her flock.

She watched over them from a *château* set upon a small hill to the west, where the river curved before disappearing into the untamed woods. Though the *château* brought back fond memories of adventure and exploration for Madeleine, it was nonetheless like a dark spectre against the first dust of winter snow.

"Exactly as *Papa* described," Eli said, looking out at the high stone walls. He then quoted the late *Monsieur* Bernard-Moreau, "And her eyes were e'er upon the villagers beneath her: every chick, every child, every blade of grass, every kind deed, and every injustice. Naught escaped her prying eyes."

Madeleine turned to look at him, savouring the sheer wonder upon his face. "Welcome to my home, Uncle Eli. Isn't it beautiful?"

"It is, but is there a reason the walls are blackened?" he asked. "Is that from fire?"

"Yes," Madeleine answered. "After the storming of the Bastille, villagers from a neighbouring town came to Lamoreaux and set the *château* on fire. I suppose they believed they were doing the villagers here a kindness, but they were mistaken.

"When everyone else had been starving on mere bread and vegetables, Mamie had seen to the needs of her people. Long before the bread riots started, French production was already lagging behind the British. Mamie herself went to Britain to learn their secret and brought it back to her people, giving loans where necessary to help them improve, and working with *gros fermiers*.

"Within a decade, our little town was transformed and flourishing, turning mere peasant farmers into merchants. It is perhaps the only countryside in all of France where more than half the homes have piped water, and a good third are lit by gas and burn a light outside their gates for passers-by.

"The villagers did not forget her kindness, nor her wisdom. And so, they drove the outsiders from the town, put the fire out, and rescued Mamie from the blaze. When Mamie repaired the damage done by the fire, she decided to keep the blackened stone walls facing the village as a reminder."

"A reminder of what?" Eli prompted.

"Loyalty."

When at last they neared the blackened Château de Lamoreaux, they were greeted at the lowered drawbridge by an old woman, smoking a pipe. Her white hair was worn long and loose, dishevelled as much by the wind as by neglect. Her feet were bare, and she was clad in a simple black dress with no adornments. There were no rings on her fingers, no jewels about her neck.

For a moment, they wondered if a servant had been sent ahead to greet them, and if so, how? They had not sent a message ahead of their coming.

Yet, as they drew nearer, there was no mistaking the old woman's effortless pride and grace as anything else but the result of noble birth. And in her face, there was a beauty that knew no age. It was the face of Charlotte, the face of Madeleine.

"Mamie!" Her granddaughter had never been happier to see her. She flew from the carriage and into her arms. "I meant to surprise you!" she said in Old Romani.

"Surprise a seer? Ha!" Mamie hugged her granddaughter tightly, and then stepped aside for the carriage to enter.

"You saw us coming over the hill!" Madeleine guessed.

Mamie laughed at that. "You mistake me for a purveyor of cheap tricks; I am insulted!"

As it passed, Eli jumped down and made his way to the old woman, almost sheepishly. He removed his hat and bowed. Whatever respect he owed to Charlotte, he knew the *Marquise de Lamoreaux* commanded twice as much.

"Madame, I am-"

"Elijah Bernard, when it suits you to pass for a proper Englishman," she finished for him, "or Élian Bernard, as your father named you: my late husband's eldest son, and rightful heir to his Haitian estate."

Eli looked at first surprised, and then embarrassed. "I am a bastard," he said matter-of-factly, "and not of pure blood."

Mamie scoffed at that and puffed on her pipe. "I trust that Charlotte and Madeleine must have shown you by now how very little we care for 'pure blood' in this family. You are nearly a Moreau yourself, and welcome under my roof at any time."

She then fixed him with that gaze of hers that seemed to see through the skin and into the heart. It made the strongest of men feel naked; vulnerable. "But you will not be staying, will you? You plan to leave tonight and will politely request to borrow one of my horses to return to Barfleur, where you will then go on to London to watch over my daughter."

Eli seemed to stumble over his words for a moment, as he struggled to simultaneously come to grips with her knowledge and find the proper response. "Yes, if it's not too much to ask; I hoped to hurry back to Charlotte."

"I already asked the servants to ready my fastest horse for you. He's waiting in the stable," she said, turning, and starting the trek up the hill towards the *château*. "But first, you will sup with us. I've already set a table for eight and will not be refused."

There was a feast waiting inside when they entered: roasted meats, steamed vegetables, baked pies, fresh fruits, and the best wine and cheese from Paris.

Conversation flowed easily as Mamie's Wallachian paramour shared stories of his travels across Eastern Europe, and Mamie delighted the ladies by reading the future from the palm of their hands. But, at long last, the festivities came to an end, and it was time for Eli to leave.

"Should you not rest first?" Gaëlle suggested, when she found him getting acquainted with the black beauty Mamie had readied for him.

Eli turned to face her, steeling his heart against the sadness in her eyes and the quiver of her lips. He took her hands in his. "I rested on my way here, my love. I cannot delay. I must return to Charlotte before harm comes to her: before it is too late."

The tears came, then. "Promise me you will be careful, Eli. This is an awful mess that is upon us—murder, no less. If I should lose you..."

"Do not say such things," said he, releasing her hands to cup her face in his. "You must be strong. We cannot allow our love for each other to compromise our loyalty to those who furnished us with all we have."

"You speak only truth," she conceded, "but it breaks my heart no less."

"Be patient just a while longer, Gaëlle, for when I return to France, I mean to make you my wife."

"A poor choice you have made," she said through her tears, while her caramel cheeks turned purple with pleasure. "Your English friends will not think highly of it."

"Then they are not true friends," he said, offering her the brown leather-bound pages that held the damning thoughts of *Madame* Severina Anglais. "I wish I had the time to go over this, but I do not.

"Her entries are infrequent. Mostly, she complains about her husband, frets over money, and gloats about the men she seduces. She is none-theless of uncommon intelligence; I give her that."

"If she was, that journal would never exist."

Eli smiled, but it did not reach his tired eyes. "Right you are, *ma chérie*. And if there is a clue, I know Madeleine will find it. Will you see that she gets it?"

"Of course," Gaëlle answered, trying hard to swallow the stubborn lump in her throat.

Eli pressed his lips to hers, and then in an instant, was upon his horse and galloping over the drawbridge.

As the hour drew late, Mamie's lover respectfully retired to the guest quarters two acres south of the main house, leaving the Moreau ladies to speak in private. Or so Madeleine had hoped.

"Your mother sent me gifts," Mamie said to her when they were alone in the study, "but you wish to speak with me first."

"Yes."

"I will have Charlotte's gifts, now," Mamie replied. "We will talk on the morrow. Your usual suite has been prepared for you."

Mamie was not a woman the wise argued with, so Madeleine complied in silence, and then made her way up to the attic suite with Gaëlle trailing behind her. The attic had been scrubbed clean with fresh linen and clean clothes set out for her: a project which would have taken Mamie's servants at least a few days to accomplish.

Gaëlle's and Regina's rooms were also prepared. The two rooms were the first set, facing each other, at the bottom of the staircase leading down from Madeleine's attic suite. The driver had long retired to a separate wing, feeling over-tired from the long journey into the countryside.

"How did she know you were coming?" Gaëlle asked, in obvious wonderment.

"Indeed, how does Mamie know half the things she does?" Madeleine returned, taking her seat before the mirror and undoing the ribbon she had used to tie her hair.

Gaëlle quickly grabbed a brush and began to run it through her mistress's curls. "Your grandmother terrifies me," she confessed. "I would bet my life she does not hear 'no' very often, not even from you. Not even from men.

"She has this confidence. You know she is in charge when she enters a room, and that she's good at it. Some people fumble with authority, you know? It is as if she knows exactly what to do with it."

"Perhaps, that is what it takes to be a matriarch," Madeleine replied.

"And will you be like that when your time comes?"

"Perhaps. And perhaps not. A true leader must find their own way of inspiring loyalty and trust in the people around them. This is Mamie's way. When the time comes, I must find my own. I only pray that the time comes later, rather than sooner."

CHAPTER XVI

Secrets Told

Whether from travel or worry, exhaustion kept Madeleine in bed until almost noon. When she finally descended from the attic, she found Mamie waiting patiently at the foot of the main staircase.

"I thought you should be awake by now," she greeted her.

"Good morning, Mamie. I didn't mean to oversleep."

"You had a long day and a long trip. I would be surprised if you had not." She gestured to the large back room where she did her readings. "Wait inside. I will let the servants know to prepare your breakfast."

Like most rooms in Mamie's home, the reading room was not short of books. The only window in the room opened to the east, making it cool in the summertime and warm in the winter. It was large and fitted with a seat strewn with cushions and blankets. On either side of the window were shelves and shelves of books on astronomy, botany, medicine, and theology. Most of these had creases in the leather, cracks in the spines, and strips of paper used as bookmarks.

Yet, the reading that took place in this room was often not the literary kind, but divination. The fireplace in the corner of the room held a large metal cauldron, which almost always seemed to be boiling some brew or another, sometimes for weeks at a time. Today, the smell was earthy and herbal, with a touch of mint and lavender. On either side of the fireplace were large wooden cabinets containing various herbs, spices, liquids, bones, teeth, samples of earth, and other various odd bits and ends.

In a cosy corner, adjacent to the fireplace and across from the window seat, was the reading table with two chairs: one for Mamie and one for those who sought her services. In the opposite corner of the room, some twenty feet from the door it faced, was her writing desk.

Mamie spent many an afternoon leaning against it, facing the red velvet chaise which stood between herself and the door. There, many of her clients often spilled their greatest fears and sources of despair, while she listened with keen ears. Mamie had learned long ago that some of the greatest ills of the heart and mind were almost instantly cured by naught but a listening ear.

As the scent of tobacco filled the room, Madeleine turned away from the window to find Mamie sitting at the reading table, puffing on her pipe in quiet contemplation. Her hair was up today, tied into a haphazard knot atop her head. She must have been gardening earlier, as the maid who came in with food quickly removed her dirt-stained gloves after setting down the food.

The meal smelled delicious, but when Madeleine sat down to eat, she found that a belly full of thoughts soon robbed her of her appetite. The freshly baked *brioche,* steaming hot cup of *café au lait,* the sweet scent of rich honey, and the small block of delectably pungent cheese were no match for where her mind wandered. Had Eli returned to Barfleur safely? Was he now on his way to London? Would he make it there in time? And what would it mean, if he did not?

"I thought you had much and more to say, child," Mamie began in Old Romani. When Madeleine did not reply, she reached across the table and took her hands. "Something weighs heavy upon your heart, and all those who came with you. Much as I know you love your Mamie, you did not come just to see me. Tell me all."

Madeleine needed no further encouragement. She shared the mysterious illness that had come over her, the recurring nightmare that had kept her up night after night, what she believed it meant, and then, finally, her tears.

She hated the tears most of all, and, worse, how small they made her feel. "I wish I was as strong as you, Mamie," she lamented. "Or better, I wish I were a man, unburdened by female weakness."

Mamie stroked the back of her hands. "Even strong men weep. Love and empathy are not weaknesses."

She released Madeleine's hands and leaned back in her chair with eyes shut, as though to keep a painful memory at bay. "My husband wept when I left him—when I sent him away." After a long, thoughtful pause, she added, "Seeing Eli is like watching a ghost parade as flesh before my eyes."

She stood then and crossed the room to retrieve one of Charlotte's gifts from a locked drawer in her writing desk. "Do you know what this is?"

"I do not, Mamie."

"It is the original copy of Charlotte's marriage settlement, and a new will reaffirming that, should death befall her, you stand to inherit all through our trustees in London. On paper, almost all our property belongs to these trustees, but it is ours in the sense that matters most—its use and wealth. I pray I live to see the day when our own names may be writ upon the line."

She took her seat before Madeleine again. "Now, your mother asked me not to share this with you, just as she asked you not to share your suspicions. As is her way, she wants us to believe she has it all under control. I am wont to interfere, and she long ago told me when I first made an attempt to interfere in her marriage, she will not be rescued by her *maman* every time things go awry.

"And you, she means to keep safe, as you are impulsive by nature and would naturally fly to London." Madeleine could not keep her cheeks from flushing with the truth of her grandmother's guesswork. "She knows us better than we give her credit for, and so should also know better than to think we would listen. She never doubted you, Madeleine. You deserve to know that."

Mamie paused to shake the ashes from her pipe. "Indeed, who would doubt you? You are especially gifted. Some of us are blessed with the gift of seeing, like me; and others with the gift of intuition, like your mother. You are blessed with both, but also the gift of interpretation.

"You see more than I ever did at your age, without trying; imagine what you might accomplish with training. I have skill, but you—you have talent, for it is one thing to see and another to feel, but it is the interpretation that matters most. Man sees many things in his life-time, but makes little sense of it all."

Madeleine had heard similar words before. "I don't want to be a seer, Mamie. I want to finish my schooling."

"As did your mother, and so she did. We are Moreaux and we choose our own paths, whatever they may be. Still, before you choose your mother's path in place of my own, there is something about our family you must know."

Madeleine eyed her curiously but did not interrupt.

Mamie lit her pipe again and savoured the warmth moving through her lungs. For a time, Madeleine thought she might not say another word, after all, but then she asked, "Do you believe yourself superior to people like Eli, or Regina?"

"Superior in station and prestige," Madeleine answered honestly, "but never in intellect or skill, or worthiness of fair treatment."

"That is a good answer," Mamie decided. She looked pleased. "It is good that you understand this, because you see, we are very much like them."

"They are human, same as us."

Mamie nodded. "Yes, and they are mulatto; same as us."

Madeleine wrinkled her brow in confusion. "The Roma?"

Mamie shook her head. "We are not Roma, Madeleine, not *true* Roma. My grandmother, your great-great-grandmother did live with the Roma, and learned their language, their rituals, and their secrets.

"But before that, she was a *quadroon* in Haiti. She was the daughter of a planter, and a mulatto slave. Maria, they called her, and Olga, the mother."

Mamie paused to puff on her pipe, blue smoke clouding her face. "Maria was like Eli: the African in her, barely obvious. And so she was accepted into high society, learned her letters, learned their language and customs, and wooed their men. But, at the end of every night, she returned to her mother to learn something far more powerful than Latin and arithmetic.

"Olga was a healer and a good one. Even the *grand blancs* often preferred her services to a French doctor, but this would be to her detriment, in the end. One day, a planter's son fell ill, and Olga realised she could not heal him. She explained this to the father, but he insisted on her caring for him. When the lad died, he had Olga flogged and hanged. Angry and desperate, Maria turned to the darker arts and called on the Devil to do her bidding."

"She sold her soul?" Madeleine looked horrified.

A final curl of smoke passed through Mamie's lips, and then she set the pipe down. "She offered it to him, desperate as she was. Whether he took it or not, or how much of it he claimed, she never knew. But, however much it was, it proved to be enough. A terrible storm blew through Saint-Domingue that night, such as they had never seen before. And when the sun came up that morning, the planter was dead, and Maria was long gone.

"She arrived in France a beautiful and mysterious woman, but with a dark past and empty pockets, so she joined a group of local *Tziganes* as a seer. She was more powerful than them, you see? And so, they respected her and feared her, while she grew rich from peddling her wisdom for gold.

"Despite her success within their circles and her love for travel, Maria had always preferred the finer things in life—the balls, the wine, the gentlemen—and so when the time was right, she wooed a wealthy Frenchman and left the gipsy life behind.

"Her husband died without ever knowing her secret, and thereafter it is only the eldest women in the line who carry the burden of that knowledge. It has since been passed from mother to child at one-and-twenty years old. I pray Charlotte will forgive my presumption, but it is time you knew the truth.

"We may not look like them, act like them, or even talk like them. A few generations have watered down our origins and made us passable, like all the rest. But, we are *not* like the rest.

"Our matriarchy did not come about because we see ourselves as better, or even equal to the men. It was because *Seigneuresse* Maria Moreau knew what it was to be a slave: to be owned and own nothing. She had only one child, and she was determined to see my mother have it all.

"But perhaps, more important than this, was the fact that she married a good man, and good father, who did not want to see his widow and only child disinherited, because of their sex." She fell silent, then, watching Madeleine's expression change from shock, to confusion, and then finally to acceptance.

A distant look now crept into Mamie's dark eyes. "If it comes to it, Madeleine, the Moreaux will once again call on Old Friends to do our bidding, though preferably not my grandmother's Friend," were her ominous words. "The wrongs against your mother—against my only child—will not go unpunished, while I still draw breath."

CHAPTER XVII

Blood & Fire

A thick fog had settled over London, bringing with it cold wind and rain. The chill seemed to bite through his coat, while the wind howled through the rooftops overhead. It gnawed at his flesh and unsettled his nerves, already worn raw by lack of sleep and the risks which lay behind and before him.

He flicked open his pocket watch and checked the time. It was half past midnight. "Late," he observed to himself, barely a whisper.

"On the contrary. I imagine I've been here for upwards of ten minutes," came a voice from his left, joined by a brief flash of fire and the smell of a pipe.

"First rate, this," the shadow against the wall decided. "Say, how much does tobacco like this cost?"

The gentleman's hand flew to his pocket. Sure enough, both his pipe and tobacco were gone. "How did you...?"

"I'm not paid for hows: only whats and my discretion." There was the click of a cocked barrel, and the press of cold metal to the back of his head, while the stranger in the shadows continued to smoke. "Who is your man?"

"My man is John and the hills are green and golden beyond."

"Blood red is the sunset o'er yonder," recited the shadow.

"And dark is the night that follows," answered the gentleman.

"Very well," the shadow decided, pocketing his gun once more. "So, do tell, what would a respectable gentleman like yourself ask of a crook like me?"

The purple bruises were visible for only a brief moment as the lightning lashed the night sky. It was quickly followed by a lingering darkness.

Then, the guttural roar of thunder would ricochet through the pitch-black night like the cries of an angry beast.

Still, it was not the thunder that woke her; it was the wind. Its eerie wail echoed throughout the house, like the ghost of a distraught and motherless child. It sent a chill through her and peppered her skin with beads of fear.

On any other night, Charlotte would have closed her eyes and slept in sweet bliss, while Mother Nature raged outside her window. But not today—not tonight.

That morning, she had woken with a sickening feeling in the pit of her stomach that today was the day she would draw her last breath. She could never tell how these morbid intuitions found her, but when they did, it was impossible to shake them.

With the fear set in her heart, everything that day seemed to confirm it. Basile had been unusually quiet, his eyes ever seeking her out as she went about her usual routine. And when he drank more than his fill at dinner, was she mistaken, or had she noticed a tremor in his hands?

Now, she lay awake, awaiting the inevitable. How would it happen? Had she been poisoned at dinner, like Madeleine? Or was he brute enough to dirty his own hands, like she suspected?

While she waited, not a sound in the house escaped her. Yet, what put her most on guard was the silence coming from Basile's bedchamber. All night, not a snore had come through the walls.

But, as hour after hour passed without further incident, her frayed nerves brought her to exhaustion. She had only just slipped into the tempting arms of sleep when the wind slammed a tree branch into the window.

Her eyes flew open, just as Basile raised his hands above her head. A brutal flash of lightning showed the thin blade as he brought it down full force and planted it in her breast.

Monsieur Popescu was not an imposing man. He was of middle height and slim build with a face that could have been as much forty as sixty. His honey-coloured eyes were bright and clear with the sharpness of intelligence, and his wavy black hair was worn long and neatly tied back from his face.

Most days, he smoked much and spoke little, his brows furrowed with deep thought and a book open upon his lap. To a stranger, he might have appeared to be brooding, but those who were well-acquainted with him knew that even the briefest address could break this grave expression and give way to pleasant and animated chatter.

And so it was with some surprise that Madeleine found him sitting in the back parlour, a dark expression etched into his face, an English newspaper spread upon his lap, and his pipe held but long forgotten. He did not speak to her when she entered the room and did not reply when she asked him what so troubled his thoughts.

"Monsieur, has Mamie yet returned from the village?" she tried again, taking a few steps in his direction.

He jumped with a start in his chair as though he had seen a ghost. "My dear, Madeleine! How you trouble a poor man's heart with this cat-like stealth!"

"Monsieur!" she cried, herself startled by his reaction. "You grow quite pale, sir. What is it that ails you? Surely, I was not so very quiet, as I did bid you hello you when I came in."

He removed his reading spectacles and rubbed his eyes as though massaging away a headache. "Have a seat here, child," he said, gesturing to the velvet sofa adjacent to himself. "I imagine no news has come to you from—from London?"

"News of what, sir?" Madeleine asked, now anxiously glancing at the paper in his lap. She could smell ill news in the air, like a grand *château* slowly burning to the ground.

He studied her for a moment and then took a deep draw of his pipe as though to steady his nerves. "Your grandmother is not a woman the wise take issue with, and yet I could not sleep easy if I did not speak of what I saw today. Understand, I do not question her conviction that your mother is well—though she must also confess that *seeing* is an art, not a science. It calls for Faith instead of indisputable facts, however often the facts later come to life.

"And—and even a seer may oft' be blind to that which they need most see. Where were her visions when you lay in a sickbed with poison upon your lips? Or when Basile set his hand against your mother, years ago? True, she is much occupied by the peasantry who look to her always for guidance, but it shows a hole in her formidable strength and reminds us that she is wise but not omniscient—does it not?

"And so, would it not be better if you were yourself presented with the facts presented to us, and drew your own inferences?"

Madeleine had felt her heart skip a beat or two at the mention of her mother's health. And his roundabout way of speaking did not much soothe her apprehension, either. "Please, *monsieur!* Speak plainly."

He lifted the papers from his lap. "I have circled it with ink—the article which may be of interest to you."

The Daily Courant: *December* 21, 1839

HUSBAND CHARGED ON SUSPICION OF MURDER. LADY WIFE STILL MISSING.

by George Walker

Scotland Yard confirmed on Wednesday, December 18, a most terrible turn of events involving the well-loved English playwright, come to us from French shores, the Lady Charlotte Moreau. The Lady has disappeared from her London home, and her estranged husband, Lord Basile Dubois-Moreau, was taken into police custody on December 19 to answer for her disappearance, alongside other charges.

Workers at The Lady's Playhouse first raised the alarm when Lady Moreau did not appear on time for work, and summoned the police. Inspector Garland, who was in the station when the summons came, selected four brave officers, and escorted the workers to the residence of Lady Moreau.

Upon arrival, the officers found the courageous household had cornered Lord Dubois-Moreau in the Lady's bedchamber, as he tried to flee a bloody scene. He was immediately arrested and charged by the good Inspector Garland on suspicion of murder. Scotland Yard officers then conducted a thorough search of the property, but found not a trace of Lady Moreau or the weapon used against her in what appears to be a brutal attack.

However, a letter was found, penned and signed by the Lady, herself. Police say, in the letter, the unfortunate Lady expressed fear for her life at the hands of her foul-tempered husband, who she claims has been violent with her before.

With no body found, the police have not confirmed Lady Moreau's death. However, the local physician, John Arthur, has told *The Daily Courant* that it would not be possible for the Lady to survive such heavy loss of blood.

Lord Basile Dubois-Moreau remains in custody, while the search for his Lady wife continues. It has been reported that Chief Inspector Brown, also of Scotland Yard, will be joining the investigation.

Madeleine was so engrossed in the newspaper that she hardly noticed when her grandmother came in, or when she gestured for *Monsieur* Popescu to leave them.

"You may remember George," Mamie said. "The only journalist who bothers to write honest reviews about Charlotte's plays in London."

Madeleine glared at her grandmother as hot, angry tears filled her eyes. "You speak to me now of plays, with this horror spread upon my lap? Your daughter—*my mother*—is..." A tremor of anger and despair took hold of her.

"I have not dreamed your mother's death," Mamie said, unmoved. "I do not believe her dead, but Basile will likely rot in prison, all the same."

On any other day, with any other risk before her, Madeleine might have believed her. But as she looked upon her grandmother's face, she could not shake *Monsieur* Popescu's scepticism: *even a seer may oft' be blind to that which they need most see.* And did not every hero—or heroine—who had suffered too long a string of successes eventually fall prey to their own hubris? Would this be Mamie's?

CHAPTER XVIII

Obsession

The Daily Courant: *December 22, 1839*

LADY CHARLOTTE MOREAU'S DAMNING LETTER ACCUSES HUSBAND OF HER OWN MURDER

by George Walker

On December 13, 1839, I, George Walker, received a letter delivered in person by one of the Lady Charlotte Moreau's most trusted companions. Upon its delivery, I was warned not to open the letter until the time was right. When asked how I would know when such a time had come, I was told only that I would not be in doubt when indeed that time was upon me.

Naturally, I brooded over the contents of the letter for days but refused to betray her ladyship's trust. A mere week later, when *The Daily Courant* learned of the alleged murder of Lady Moreau, I knew without a doubt that it was time to open the letter.

What I read will forever leave a bruise upon mine heart. Here are the words as they were given to me, unedited, by the Lady Charlotte Moreau, herself:

If this letter has fallen into the hands of the public or the police, then the worst has finally come to pass. I am finished. I am dead. And I must congratulate my husband, the self-styled Marquis de Lamoreaux, Basile Dubois-Moreau.

Here is my story.

He was a carpenter when I first laid eyes upon him: a young and handsome man with swarthy skin; dark hair; and a fierce tangle of a beard. He had responded to my ad in the papers to fix the roof of my then newly purchased manor in Barfleur.

My mother, who had come from Lamoreaux to see me established, met him at the very instant I did. And where I saw longing and the promise of happiness with Basile, she saw danger ahead.

"You would be wise not to marry this one," were the first words she uttered the moment he had gone.

But I did marry him, and perhaps even worse, begged my mother not to interfere, come what may. Strong women are not made by coddling, I reminded her.

If you know anything of my mother, the Marquise of Lamoreaux, you know I was a very foolish girl indeed not to listen. I suppose, when one waits to be five-and-twenty to be struck with love for the first time, one is entitled to a certain amount of naivety, and, of this, I had plenty.

For months, long after my roof was fixed, Basile lingered. He brought me flowers and played his violin in the gardens beneath the sunset. His voice was melodic and sweet. I fell in love as any woman paid such seemingly earnest attentions would have.

More fool I, for they were not earnest! Not long after we married, the flowers stopped coming and the singing went quiet. The violin was put away in the attic, where only spiders play those lovely strings, now.

A year later, I gave birth to our first child; a month later, he was gone. The doctors said his little heart had just not been strong enough. His birth defect was deemed a rarity, no reason why I should fear trying again.

But I did fear it. In my seven-and-twenty years of life, I had never felt loss and grief such as this. Never truly felt pain. And that day, I did. When I buried my child, I buried a bit of my heart with him, I never thought I could reclaim.

I did my duties as a wife but was ever-careful not to fall pregnant again. I could not bear a second loss. It was

not enough for Basile, and so began his infamous legacy of straying from his marriage bed.

I did not fault him, or the children who sprang up among the peasants in Barfleur, with his dark hair and swarthy face. I did what I could for the mothers, though they always suspected me of some treachery. I did not fault them for falling prey to the same charms that had won my heart.

As the children grew, my heart longed for one of my own, and so fear gave way to motherly desire. When I fell pregnant with Madeleine, the old Basile returned. He cared for me as though I were a delicate flower, fawned over me, let the other women alone.

But after Madeleine was born, when he found himself no longer the centre of my universe, a jealousy set in such as I had never seen in a man. He ordered her nursery be moved further down the hallway, and once locked Madeleine from the room when a burglar had come in to do us mischief. She had been awake, had heard the noise, and came to tell us, and Basile shut the door while I slept. It was Betha—her Nanny, at this time—who found her, and Regina—our head of staff at the Barfleur Estate—who cornered the thief with a machete.

When Madeleine continued to distinguish herself as being of singular intelligence, his hatred of her grew. When I insisted Madeleine be allowed to con-

tinue her education, an argument ensued, and he struck me across the face. Madeleine had heard the commotion and came to the room in my defence. She witnessed the scene, entire.

That was the day I knew I could no longer pretend to be a wife, for sake of being a mother. Unwilling to soil my daughter's prospects in love and marriage and to lose my favour with Rome and God, I did not attempt to divorce Basile. Instead, I moved to London to start my life anew.

I all but begged Madeleine to give up her education and come with me, but never was a more determined child born. She chose to brave the dragon for her letters, and thus my own words thrown at my mother when I was five-and-twenty were thrown at me by a young lady of just eighteen: strong women are not coddled by their mothers.

This dragon, my beloved husband, made a show of coming to the London house every so often to ward off talk about being deserted by his wife. To spare Madeleine's honour, I allowed it.

His love for our daughter did not grow in my absence. Instead, his resentment and jealousy increased tenfold. He sent private investigators to watch me and intercepted letters between Madeleine and me.

I could not just sit by and do nothing, so I sent a spy to infiltrate the house in my stead, though it did little good when my daughter, my only living child, found herself poisoned by the one man in the world she should trust to protect her.

When I later learned I would be next, I was not surprised. I made preparations for my daughter's safety, for there was no guarantee, with me disposed of, she would not be turned upon. I then gathered my closest allies and did what I could to ensure my own survival. Anything but running away like the scared little sheep women are always expected to be.

Yet, even lions die.

For how long he has hated me, I cannot tell. I find myself wondering if he had always loathed me. If our marriage and my heart were just stepping stones on the ladder of his ambition. Indeed, how foolish I must have been all these years to believe he ever truly cared for me!

I have no doubt that if I am gone, my daughter will be set upon, next. I beg of the authorities to see to her safety, and to punish Basile Dubois to the fullest extent of the law.

Mark my words. He is a guilty man, and I have no doubt that if he is set free, he will strike again.

The Daily Courant sold like hot bread that day. There wasn't a soul in all of England or France who had not read the letter or heard tell of it from a friend. In truth, people could speak of little else.

There was pity for Charlotte, mixed with some feeling that she had deserved her fate. A woman such as her, who did not know her place, would have angered and disgraced any husband. Even so, there wasn't a single soul unconvinced of Basile's guilt and greed.

"My daughter is not dead," Mamie said, when Madeleine had finished reading yet another newspaper clipping heralding the news.

Madeleine did not reply. She set it down, and returned to bed, while Gaëlle fretted outside her locked door, unable to go in but unwilling to leave her.

"I fear she's gone mad," Gaëlle confessed to Mamie, when hunger finally brought her down to the dinner table. "Should we not open the door? Surely, there is another key."

"If I know my granddaughter as well as I believe I do, it is bolted from the inside, making a key little more than a decorative item at present."

"What if she does herself harm?" Gaëlle pointed out.

"Madeleine is not about to miss the opportunity to see her father swing for his crimes."

"But she hasn't eaten."

"She has not," Mamie confirmed. After a lengthy pause, she added, "We live our lives as best we can, we Moreaux. We pride ourselves on being kind, and fair, and a pillar of support for anyone who needs it. But there is one vice we cannot seem to rid ourselves of."

"Pray tell, what vice is that?"

"Vengeance," Mamie answered, her eyes aflame. "In times like these, it sustains us; it is all we eat, breathe, and sleep; it is all we think about. And when a Moreau sips from the cup of vengeance, we have appetite for little else."

Gaëlle could neither find the words nor the courage to respond to Mamie. Gone was the benevolent old woman of charity and love. In her stead was the cunning and determination of something feral, albeit tempered by experience and wisdom.

"Not while I still draw breath," Mamie muttered in a voice so low, Gaëlle was not at first sure she had spoken. Then, the old woman turned and disappeared into her reading room.

"Me should never have given her that book!" Gaëlle confided to Regina in *Kreyol*. "She obsessed!"

"She looking for clues," Regina pointed out, her eyes never leaving her needlework. "She the only one, aside from Eli, who speak Italian. We can't help, Gaëlle. Patience. Let her work."

"And pray tell, when she gone mad, what then? We just let her work then, too?"

Regina did not take the bait. Instead, she returned her full attention to the dark blue fabric in her hands, while Gaëlle paced the room with obvious impatience.

In the neighbouring rooms, there was the sound of chatter, and the crude accent of the peasantry. They had come to pay their respects to Mamie, to wish her well, and offer their assistance in any way possible.

"Why does she not tell them Charlotte lives, if that is truly her belief?" Gaëlle said in a whisper. "Why play along with this madness?"

It was *Monsieur* Popescu who spoke up, his bespectacled gaze still fixed upon the very article that had created such an uproar, and a frown upon his face. "Because if Charlotte wanted people to know she was alive, they would."

Four storeys overhead, in the belly of the attic, Madeleine worked tirelessly to translate the Anglais diary. It kept her occupied, preventing her mind from straying into dangerous territory. Why wallow in misery, when she could potentially solve the mystery of her mother's disappearance?

She laboured night and day, eating little, and sleeping less. Soon, her appearance began to tell the tale of her exertion. Her dark tresses became a matted tangle of curls, and there were bags beneath her eyes from lack of sleep.

The desk she worked at also told of her hard labour. Alongside a notebook, an Italian dictionary, a map of Italy, and a steel nib pen, with an inkwell stained with black, there were pages upon pages of writing scattered all about, numbered for later reorganising.

A week of this passed before Madeleine finally flew down the stairs one evening to share her findings: the stolen journal in one hand and a bundle of papers under the other. She found Mamie in the reading room alone, an old book with yellowing pages spread before her and a scowl on her face.

"I have done it!" Madeleine announced. "I translated it all. There was not much to go on. She is a terribly petty and self-important woman, with very little substance to her rambling, and often goes an entire year without writing a word, only to start up again. Still, what I did find was worth putting up with her trifles."

CHAPTER XIX

The Diary of Severina

Madeleine set the papers down upon the old leather-bound book that had so captured Mamie's attention. On the left page was Baphomet with red-rimmed eyes, while the right was now covered by translations from Severina's diary.

When Mamie did not move to read them, Madeleine lifted one from the top of the pile and began to read aloud.

January 23, 1833

When she enters a room, there is neither man nor woman who does not take notice. There is an effortless grace in her gait that commands the attention of everyone within sight of her. Something regal and yet not over-proud in her bearing. While other women scramble to buy the latest styles from Paris, she is always simply but beautifully dressed, and ever in black. Rather than take away from her beauty, it seems to accentuate it.

Her only adornment is a near century old silver ring, adorned with South African diamonds encircling a garnet diamond, rumoured to have been taken from the hilt of the sword of the first Seigneur of Lamoreaux, who earned his title in service to the King. On any other woman's finger, it would look old-fashioned; dated. On hers, it tells of an unbroken legacy.

What a fool her peasant husband oft' looks in her presence, stumbling where her feet are sure, fumbling through manners when she sets new heights in propriety.

There is not a woman I hate in all the world as much as she.

September 18, 1835

She is rarely seen without the company of her coloured servant, a girl her age or older, with uncommon beauty for a negro. That her mother would choose someone of unequal birth to keep her daughter's company is hardly surprising, considering her choice in a husband.

How simple and helpless he must feel under the spell of these women, to whom every door is opened and nothing is denied. What a fool a man must be to marry a Moreau!

March 21, 1836

When I shared my plans with Pierre, he immediately warned me that the sunshine would not last, and he was certain it would rain today. Naturally, I contradicted him, but by the time we had breakfasted, the sky had become dark and a wicked wind had picked up.

Unwilling to admit he was right, I insisted on going through with my walk, and declined his invitation to take me in the carriage. I had not been gone for ten minutes when the first shower of rain descended upon me, to the ruin of my newly bought dress.

Just as the worst of it came down, a carriage stopped at my feet. Inside was Monsieur Dubois-Moreau. He offered me a ride home, and knowing I would be silly to decline, in I stepped.

He gave me his coat, as I was shaking and cold, and offered me some of the most exquisite wine. He was kind and gentle and lifted my spirits with easy conversation, in spite of my obvious embarrassment.

It is not difficult to see how he persuaded his wife to overlook his low birth. He is a handsome man, with a perpetual and contagious smile, and a splendidly curled moustache, as is now the fashion.

There was none of the self-consciousness I usually see in him when Lady Charlotte is about. What a better man he is without her, and it took naught but an hour in my bedchamber to persuade him he is a better man with me. A man so easily swayed surely cannot be much satisfied with his wife.

What else of hers could I reach out and take with ease if it pleased me, I wonder?

November 14, 1836

When we meet, Basile says little and less of his wife. But today, there was a darkness in his eyes upon which I fully intended to shed some light. It was a burden he was glad to share, when I presented the opportunity to him.

His daughter, no doubt under encouragement from her mother, has got the idea in her head that she should further her education. Basile has warned that this will make it difficult for her to find a suitor, a reasonable fear any good father with his daughter's best interest at heart should have.

After all, why should she remain a burden at home? I have advised Basile to put his foot down, come what may.

November 26, 1836

Basile is furious with me. He claims my meddling has cost him dearly. And perhaps it has, but I confess to a certain pride in the matter, for he took my advice. Charlotte apparently did not take the affront well and has left for London. Madeleine will remain in Barfleur and will be tutored by a retired professor.

I have suggested divorce to Basile, since his wife is naturalised English herself, and divorce is the very basis of English religion! It would not be so frowned upon, I think, with that in mind. After all, he and I should make a much happier couple.

But, he will not let her go. He suspects that his rival is a young Creole Frenchman she has been particularly close with, since years before he first made her acquaintance.

The very thought of them together fills him with jealousy and rage. I have never seen a man in such a passion as when he thinks of Charlotte in the arms of another man. He will not think of divorcing her, and, I do believe, would rather see her dead than happy with another.

This suits me perfectly, for a world without Charlotte Moreau is by all means a better one. I have convinced Basile that we can surely manage the thing. Whenever he is in doubt, I need only remind him of the handsome Frenchman from the West Indies.

April 5, 1837

Basile and I have stumbled upon a complication in our plans. Due to an agreement signed, and witnessed by the Church of England no less, upon the death of Charlotte, it is Madeleine who inherits, through trustees set upon English soil.

Basile confesses he until now had forgotten about the agreement, set in place the day his wife gave birth to a son, so many years ago. But with the son no longer living, "The Oldest Living Child" as the document states, would be Madeleine.

While ownership of the property rests with the trustees, use of the property is what seems to be "inherited" by these women. It is a terribly complicated process, no doubt set in place to circumvent changing inheritance laws in France and the likelihood of a husband seizing ownership of their property.

If Charlotte dies, then use of the property passes to Madeleine. And, upon the death of these women, only the Barfleur property will go to Basile, while the rest of the Moreau legacy will go to whomever Mamie has appointed in her last will and testament (likely some relative of the longer established Moreau line in Bourgogne). It is madness!

Still, the way is clear, of course. We must get rid of Madeleine, whose company with peasants and coloured servants should leave no shortage of suspects from which the Gendarmerie Nationale may choose. And Mamie, being older than the very Earth itself, is long overdue to return to it.

Basile, though he despises the poor girl, seems to have some conscience where she is concerned. I cannot imagine why. He has never a kind word to say about her and blames her for the distance between himself and his wife, far more than he blames me. He refers to her as "a snake in the grass", quite an odd way for a man to think of his child.

I have asked him if he suspects his daughter belongs to another man, as I cannot imagine why else he should hate her so. He assures me she does not, and that she carries a mark on her skin that is present in his entire family; it was the first thing his mother looked for at her birth. He also expresses fear of crossing the Marquise and confesses he does believe the old hag possesses a dangerous power that could do us harm. He blames her for the death of his mother, the one person who had courage enough to stand up to the old woman's tyranny.

I confess, I believe it all to be utter rubbish, but he holds strongly to the belief. I have no reservations. Charlotte must die to free him, Madeleine to end the Moreau Matriarchy, and the old lady to pass use of the Barfleur Estate to us.

July 21, 1839

Basile is back from his summer visit to London to see that woman. Why he insists upon these formalities, I cannot imagine. Does he not look more the fool, when all must know she is in love with the West Indian?

It appears the man is also getting bolder, as Basile says he seems to have set his residence there some six months, now. He also escorted Madeleine into high society on a few occasions, accompanied by the coloured girl that is ever at her side, despite her father's insistence to the contrary. Charlotte evidently trusts the man and Basile is as jealous as I have ever seen him.

He is in one of his dark, hot-headed moods, and no longer wants to make a clean business of this. I have convinced him to hire a man, if he must insist upon something bloody. He cannot afford to soil his hands; I cannot afford to lose him. Not now.

November 8, 1839

I have found a man in London, for Basile continues to speak of doing the deed himself. The price was dear, but I will blame it on a bad investment in Paris. I am sure I will be repaid tenfold when the deed is done, and the Moreau Matriarchy is no more.

November 22, 1839

It has been a fortnight since the man was set upon her trail, yet naught have we heard from him.

Has he met some grave misfortune along the way? Or was Basile's apprehension not so very far from the truth? Is the old Marquise really as formidable as he claims?

But, why even entertain those thoughts? An old woman—decades beyond the strength of her prime—is no match for a renowned assassin.

November 24, 1839

What kind of sorcery is this? These Moreau women continue to plague me like the very leprosy of Egypt! For a second time, Madeleine has eluded the very jaws of death just as it means to clamp down upon her.

I cannot imagine how! I made sure it was Doctor Frederik who was summoned to see to her. And though he feels for the girl, even begged for her life, in the end he chose his reputation. He would not risk news of his affair with my servant, while he is betrothed to the heiress of the Lombard Estates, for she is as pious as she is wealthy.

In any case, the little witch must suspect, for I am told a certain servant now sees to every detail of her meals herself. And nothing goes to her mistress's lips that was not entirely handled by her.

And if she truly suspects, will she be able to trace the attempts back to her father? To me?

November 29, 1839

Is there a cure for woman's weakness? Do the Moreaux suffer from it too, or has years of independence rid it from their system?

Though I consider myself a woman of stout heart and strong constitution, I confess to a tremble in my hands and a pain in my heart as it begins to dawn on me the weight of my decisions and actions this past year.

And the uncertainty! What indeed has become of the man sent to Lamoreaux?!

It has become too much to bear, and I knew Basile would only mock it as woman's weakness, or otherwise remind me that he warned me about the old witch.

So, I turned to the only other man in whom I have always confided my greatest fears. It was a stupid thing to bare my intentions to a priest, but I was overcome with fear and perhaps had not put enough thought into it.

Naturally, he found me out. After all, how many women are there in this French town who confess in his native language? Rather than grant me absolution, he has condemned me, and has threatened to stand in the way of my plans to the best of his ability, though his tongue remains bound by the seal of the confessional.

If Basile learns what I have done, I should not wonder that he might be done with me. I must make it right before I am found out.

Father Castello must die.

December 3, 1839

My heart is heavy. Surely mere repentance will not earn my forgiveness in the eyes of God. Have I lost my way? Am I beyond redemption? And is it love that blinds me? Or the sinful call of ambition?

A good man will take his last breath today, and his death shall be upon my hands. It is no easy task to take an innocent life. It is harder still to kill a priest.

I am damned.

December 10, 1839

Basile has taken notice of my dark mood, which no doubt now weighs heavily upon him, as well. Like me, he is filled with doubt.

We no longer pass our time together planning for happiness, but for failure. Whatever shall we do, if things do not go according to plan? So far, nothing has, and I dare not tell him the crime I have committed against God and man.

Thankfully, all is not lost. There is an old villa in Rocchetta Alta that belonged to my mother's family. I have received a modest income from its inhabitants since her passing and have filed it away without Pierre's knowledge. I believe it is the perfect place to flee to if crisis should indeed come upon us, and the money I have saved should sustain us for a time.

This is not the ending I imagined. Indeed, if I could go back to the beginning, I might never have started upon this cursed journey. Not for a hundred-thousand francs a year. Not for Basile.

December 11, 1839

All three Moreau women continue to draw breath, in spite of all we have done. I am beginning to see some truth in what I had originally thought of as mere peasant's superstition in Basile.

We had even attempted to intercept the correspondence that so frequently flows between mother and daughter, but they write in a language neither of us understand. We believe we have since been suspected, for the letters have slowed of late.

We must strike before they have time to plot against us, and cannot involve anyone else that might betray us, for it is certain now that our attempts have not gone unnoticed.

Basile has gone to London to do the deed. I trust the imbecile will be successful, and that by the end of the winter holiday, he shall be a rich widower, and I, his bride.

CHAPTER XX

Gone

Mamie set the papers down in the order Madeleine had so carefully arranged them, before her wild dash down the stairs.

"You have been busy," she noted. Though her expression was thoughtful, she did not seem to share her granddaughter's enthusiasm or pride in her discoveries.

"We have the evidence to get them both convicted of murder!" Madeleine pointed out. "Is this not the very thing we needed?"

"I am not sure I trust justice for my daughter to the hands of the incompetent fools who call themselves officers of the law in London. That is a matter, I believe, best left in my own hands. *Itemba alibulali*—hope is not dead!"

"What hope?" Madeleine said, bitterly. "Magic? I don't believe in magic, Mamie."

"Yes; you believe in science. And I suppose it was science that warned you of your mother's danger, and which warned me of my own."

Only then did Madeleine remember the threat made against her grandmother's life. Embarrassment coloured her cheeks. "What—what became of the man they sent after you?"

"He is no more," was her vague reply.

"Did he come here?" Madeleine pressed, a chill running up her spine at the thought of an assassin visiting her elderly grandmother in the dead of night, bearing ill will.

"He tried." She lifted the leather-bound book that had so preoccupied her thoughts, revealing the newspaper clippings *Monsieur* Popescu had supplied her with earlier that day. She then slid them across the table to Madeleine.

"Here is the result of the law and science you put so much faith in.

For my part, I trust no further in Scotland Yard, but in the power of *Bondye*."

Madeleine glanced at the headlines and felt her heart sink.

The Daily Courant: *December* 28, 1839

RUTHLESS KILLER LORD DUBOIS SET FREE.
SCOTLAND YARD SAYS HANDS ARE TIED.

by George Walker

Despite overwhelming evidence against Lord Basile Dubois, the disgraced Frenchman has been released from police custody this morning, and into civilised society.

An anonymous source from Scotland Yard shared with *The Daily Courant* that an attorney from Rome, well-versed in English law, saw to his discharge on the grounds that the police has no clear evidence that a murder had even been committed, there being no body, no weapon, and no witnesses of the allegations.

"We cannot but admit that this is indeed a setback to our case," Chief Inspector Brown told *The Daily Courant.*

"Nevertheless, we continue to make energetic enquiries about the whereabouts of Lady Charlotte Moreau, for a sound conviction hangs upon her discovery—dead, or alive."

The *Gendarmerie Nationale* in Paris has also lent their resources to Scotland Yard, as the conspiracy to murder Lady Moreau, the daughter of the *Marquise de Lamoreaux*, is said to have begun in France.

Scotland Yard and the *Gendarmerie Nationale* are appealing to the humanity of the public, to come forward with any information they may have regarding the disappearance of the beloved Lady Moreau.

The Daily Courant: *December* 29, 1839

MURDERER OF BELOVED WEST END PLAYWRIGHT FLEES LONDON

by George Walker

Scotland Yard has worked tirelessly to discover the whereabouts of the unfortunate Lady Charlotte Moreau, who has now been missing for nigh a fortnight. Now, they are faced with news that the man believed to be destined for the rope, Basile Dubois, has absconded from London, breaking the terms of his release.

"Made it worse for himself, he has. Now, when we find him, we needn't press for only murder charges, for he has supplied us with new cause to hold him," Chief Inspector Brown told *The Daily Courant*. "Unfortunately, we must first find him!!"

Chief Inspector Brown believes that the best hope for catching this ruthless killer now rests in the capable hands of the French police.

"The *Gendarmerie Nationale* was promptly alerted of *Monsieur* Dubois's absconding. The Commissioner assures me that men and hounds are stationed at all ports and main roads in France," Chief Inspector Brown told *The Daily Courant*.

The Chief Inspector has requested that I, George Walker, accompany him to France to act as translator for Scotland Yard. I will henceforth follow the story from the place where it first birthed its roots of treachery, in the coastal town of Barfleur.

The Daily Courant: *December 31, 1839*

GENDARMERIE NATIONALE NAMES WIFE OF FRENCH NOBLE AS PERSON OF INTEREST IN DISAPPEARANCE OF RENOWNED PLAYWRIGHT, LADY CHARLOTTE MOREAU

by George Walker

The *Gendarmerie Nationale* is now making energetic enquiries after the whereabouts of Lady Severina Anglais. The Italian-French baroness and resident of Barfleur for some seventeen years, has been named a potential suspect in the case of the missing Lady Charlotte Moreau. Lady Anglais aroused the suspicion of the French police when her husband dutifully reported her missing following an unannounced extended absence.

The disappearance of Lord Pierre Anglais's wife coincides with Basile's flight from the rope in London. And, according to the local residents of Barfleur, there were rumours for some time of a romantic relationship between Basile Dubois and Lady Anglais.

Despite these incriminating details, the *Gendarmerie Nationale* urges the public to take care in drawing conclusions. "We have yet to ascertain what role *Madame* Severina Anglais may have played in the alleged murder of *Madame* Charlotte Moreau, or if she is herself a victim," Inspector Laurent cautions. "We are investigating the case from both angles."

The *Gendarmerie Nationale* continues

to hold firm to this objective stance, despite strong pressure from the King and the French nobility to find answers, and fast.

"We haven't a clue whether or not this is an isolated incident, or a matter that may be henceforth repeated against another nobleman or noblewoman," Count DeFonte confessed to *The Daily Courant,* as he waits eagerly for news of a woman he describes as a pillar of the Barfleur community. "What if Basile strikes again? And what of Lady Anglais—if she is in danger?!"

The Lord Anglais, however, professes no innocence on his wife's behalf, and has washed his hands clean of her. "She has harboured a strong hatred against Lady Charlotte for many years, though I thought it only petty jealousy, until now. Basile has also been less than kind to his wife on many an occasion, even attempting to upbraid her in public a few times in the year before she left for London. No doubt he and Severina found a common point to bond over in this."

The baron is rumoured to have been one of the many suitors Lady Charlotte Moreau turned away in her youth, to marry Lord Dubois, making him at first a suspect in the case. He has since been cleared of any suspicion by the *Gendarmerie Nationale* and continues to cooperate with the police.

Lord Anglais is not the only Barfleur resident convinced of the guilt of his wife and her alleged paramour. Reports of Lord Dubois-Moreau's drunken debauchery, serial infidelity, and unwarranted violence, continue to pour in at the station. However, the *Gendarmerie Nationale* are still unable to confirm any information as to the whereabouts of the murderer, or Lady Anglais.

Lady Charlotte Moreau disappeared from her London home on December 18, 1839. Her husband was cornered by her brave and loyal servants until Inspector Garland, and four brave officers of Scotland Yard, arrived to make the arrest.

The Lady Charlotte Moreau—a playwright, philanthropist, and dual citizen of France and England—would be succeeded by her only living child, Lady Madeleine Moreau, the great-great-granddaughter of the former *Seigneur* of Lamoreaux, the Most Honourable Pierre Moreau, who was the family's first naturalised citizen of Britain.

Madeleine set the newspapers down with trembling hands. "Will you do nothing?" It was more an accusation, than a question.

"In time, you will see I have worked hardest of all."

"How?" Madeleine shot at her. "Smoking idly in your garden and taking long walks with *Monsieur* Popescu?" She did not wait for a response. The loud slam of a door marked the end of the conversation.

Moments later, Mamie heard the creak of the door reopening. She walked to the window and looked out onto the garden, as her roses braved the cold in their glass enclosure, and soaked up the very last of the day's sunlight. They had never been brighter in the winter than they were now. How ironic that they would be provided with life by the man who had not too long ago come to take her own.

"She has seen the news?" Gaëlle guessed.

"Yes."

"Mayhap—mayhap it would have been better if I had brought it to her. Found some way to break it, gently."

"I believe the time for that is long gone," Mamie returned. "Madeleine is a girl no longer. She has seen the world for the cruel place it can be. There is no turning back from such a truth."

"That may be so," Gaëlle ventured, "but should we not take care with her? I fear she has suffered more than she can bear. She is not herself. Sometimes—if you can forgive my saying so—"

"Speak freely, Gaëlle."

"Sometimes I truly think she has gone mad. There is a look in her eye, of late. Like something wild. I saw it even just now when she left."

"I see," Mamie replied. "Keep a watch on her. A mad Moreau she may very well be, but a Moreau nonetheless."

After some hesitation, Gaëlle added, "I am worried about Eli, as well, Mamie. Not a word has he sent us since his disappearance."

"Me too, child," Mamie admitted, "but I have not seen his death, either. I believe he is safe."

Gaëlle breathed a sigh of relief. "I cannot tell you how much those words mean to me, Mamie, for he is my very heart! I will see to Madeleine. She will not leave my sight, if I can help it."

But as it so happened, Gaëlle was not the only one adept at giving the slip. For when the household woke the following morning, Madeleine Moreau had long gone.

CHAPTER XXI

Escape

The first layer of snow had already settled along the rocky precipice, and more was falling still. The wind whistled and howled and blew at the carriage with all its might, while the horses struggled to pick their way along the narrow road, uphill.

"Can we truly go no faster?" Basile growled. "Snails could overtake us at this pace!"

"And risk the horses taking a bad step?" Severina pointed out. "No; we cannot. Better a longer journey, than a journey not completed. We would freeze to death."

"I am *already* freezing to death!" Basile pulled his fur coats closer about himself. "I can already begin to see this place will not suit me."

His companion shot him a deadly look. "Oh? Would you rather be in a London cell? Or better, hanging from a noose? Just say the word, husband! You will find me ready to oblige!"

At the reminder of his close brush with death, the fierceness in his manner dissipated. He would have indeed been swinging from an English noose had she not interfered on his behalf, with a clever plan for escape at the ready.

He took her hand and pressed it to his lips. "I am sorry, Severina. I owe you my life and will not soon forget it."

The sudden change in him soothed her own fiery temper. And so, as quickly as discord had risen between them, it was settled. "This is my mother's homeland," she said. "Years have passed since the last time I set my eyes upon it."

Just then, the carriage came to an abrupt stop and there was the crunch of boots in the snow. Severina pulled the curtains back and watched as the driver threw the large, rusted metal gates open. The horses trotted ahead, and then waited patiently as he shut it behind them.

The worst of their journey had now passed. Indeed, it was almost over. Just up ahead was the Villa Martelli, which had belonged to her mother, and her mother's brother before her. It was not half the size of the majestic Château d'Anglais, but it compensated for this with homeliness.

The driver and his father before him, and even his father before, had been with her mother's family for as long as anyone could recall. As was his way, he did not speak as he helped her down from the carriage, and he stepped aside when his wife and daughter came to the door. The three made up the entire household that would now tend to her affairs, but she would make do.

"I shall comfort myself with the thought that we could do much worse," Basile remarked, as he looked around the anteroom, not nearly a quarter of the one that graced the Barfleur Estate.

Severina was in such excellent spirits at this point that Basile's mood could not darken her own. Even so, she did not fail to deliver a sound lashing of sharp wit. "Of course, I am sure you inherited far more magnificent quarters from your family, Basile. You should take me there one day, when this mess you have put us in is behind us."

He grunted at the slight, and turned to the driver to demand his luggage, but saw that it had already been brought in. The daughter, who still wore the rosy blush of prepubescent youth, had also come to help him out of his coat.

"The fire is tended to, *Signora*," the old lady told her in Italian. "I thought you and your new husband would be hungry, so me and the child prepared a meal for you. It is waiting in the dining hall."

"Thank you, Wilma. I truly am grateful for your assistance." Severina handed her a silver coin. "I will thank you properly when this misunderstanding is all behind us. You, Ines, and Giu may retire to bed. Basile and I can tend to matters on our own."

Basile, who spoke enough Italian to understand the exchange, did not look pleased with that arrangement. He waited until the woman and child left the room, and the husband had proceeded to take their bags up to the main suite they would occupy, to voice his thoughts on the matter. "Pour my own wine? Are they not servants?"

"You would be wise to treat them well, if you wish to remain a free man," Severina advised. "Might I remind you, we are fugitives of the law, with special thanks due to your incompetence?"

Basile bristled at the reminder. He had not slept a single night since his last encounter with Charlotte; nor had he spoken a word to Severina about what had passed, and he was glad she did not ask. The events of that night, and the morning that followed, weighed heavily upon his mind, if not his conscience. There was no logical explanation for what had happened, and yet, it had.

"I am tired, wife," he said to his new bride. "I am sure some sleep will better improve my mood, for I have certainly been less than courteous to you." He kissed her hand. "Come to bed, soon."

Severina met his changed mood with a smile. "Our suite is up the stairs, at the very end of the hall."

"Thank you."

"Should I bring you up a glass of wine?" she called after him.

"I would be a fool to decline such kindness. Thank you."

Yet, when she went up a few minutes later with the best from the cellar, he pretended to be asleep, and pretended longer still when she came to bed with hopes of intimacy between them.

It was not from any bitterness towards her, but a preoccupation with his blackened conscience and piqued curiosity. Try as he might, he could not scrub his last day with Charlotte from his mind. She had known what he meant to do, had suspected it all from the very beginning.

He had seen it in her eyes that day. Oh, how he wanted to hate her for the humiliation of being a lesser man to a greater woman! For the whispers in the streets of the Moreau who married beneath her—him, who could have had any woman he wanted in the small village he had once called home.

Yet, he could not help but admire her courage. She had stayed her ground, sent her most trusted servants away, and had not kept a man about to watch over her.

What else had she done?

And where did her body rest now?

As his mind swept through a thousand possibilities, sleep drifted further and further away from him. In the hour before the first cock heralded the coming of morning, exhaustion finally won, and he drifted off into a fitful sleep.

CHAPTER XXII

The Unexpected Visitor

Jacob had called at the Barfleur Estate thrice, in hopes of speaking with the Lady of the house. And just as many times, the household had turned him away with apologies and red-rimmed eyes.

The fate of all other visitors was the same. If Esther was right, even the *Gendarmerie Nationale* had yet to score an interview with Lady Madeleine, and the newly appointed Father Ricci had also been politely turned away. There was murder in the family and the murderer had gone free. The proud Moreaux, and their equally proud household, would not suffer Barfleur's pity. Not even from the *curé*. Not even from him.

Yet, he could not help feeling slighted. It was eating away at him that the woman he hoped to marry should be locked in her room with naught but tears and sorrow, and he could not comfort her. Had he not earned greater trust from her than that, even now?

A knock at the door roused him from his dark ruminations. With a sigh, he set aside the book he held, as yet unread, and went to see who could be calling at such a late hour. Outside, the fury of hell pounded on his window with heavy drops of rain, flashes of lightning, and roaring thunder. Everyone should be home and safe in their beds.

When he opened the door, he found his landlady standing in the corridor. The light from the candle only barely illuminated her wrinkled face, but he had lived so long beneath her roof that he fancied he could spot her shadow from a thousand miles away.

"There is someone here to see you, Sir," she said in English. "A young man— he did not give his name, but he looks a foreigner to me. I know you long since retired to bed, and told him as much, but he seems to have travelled so far to speak with you; I could not turn him away. And I thought, perhaps, you might trouble to see him, if only for a moment. I would not be surprised if he marched up here himself, so determined is he to see you."

Jacob could not conceal his confusion. "A gentleman?" he repeated. "At this hour?" Could one of the Moreau servants have come to ease his pain with news of Madeleine?

"Yes, and noble," the elderly woman cut into his thoughts. He had almost forgotten her for the moment, so deeply engrossed was he in his speculations.

"I could not see his face," she continued, "but it was his manner of speaking, Sir. He seems a very young, good-natured lad, and has the bearing of one who is used to being obeyed."

"Send him in," Jacob conceded, and then he returned to his apartments to tend to his toilet. He splashed some water on his face and slipped into a robe that provided enough modesty to receive a man of good standing at so inconvenient an hour.

All the while, he wondered at the identity of his visitor. Many of the coloured Moreau servants and employees had an air of high birth about them, like Eli, no doubt owing to the close and honoured society they kept with their mistresses, who offered them every advantage at their disposal.

But when his unexpected visitor entered the room, it was not Eli Bernard he saw. Indeed, he did not recognise the dark-haired man at all. Still, he was compelled to agree with the landlady that his dress and mannerism spoke of high society. Even so, he was in a pitiable state, visibly trembling from the wet and cold. The landlady gave him a sympathetic look, and then bowed out through the door, locking it behind her.

"Come by the fire, *Monsieur*," Jacob offered. "You must be freezing." He crossed the room to toss a few bits of wood onto the dying flames.

When he turned to face his guest again, he found the man had not moved an inch. He noticed also that he had not spoken a word since he entered. Jacob's interest was piqued, but he felt it would be indelicate to accost and interrogate the man too quickly.

Whoever he was, he truly had seen better days. His hair was uncommonly long and spilled from beneath a black sheepskin hat of Eastern European make. His black, double-breasted frock coat, embroidered in brightly coloured, elaborate designs, was soaked all the way through. Where the coat ended, mud-splattered trousers began. They were tucked into heavy leather boots that had been worn through and seemed a trifle too large for his feet.

"Would you like some tea?" Jacob tried again. "There is also coffee or some brandy, if you prefer."

The young man gave no answer, but his eyes now roamed the Englishman's humble abode. The knighted second son of a baron, and nephew of a Marchioness, Jacob was nonetheless a man of simple tastes. His apartment was scarcely furnished, and his only indulgence was evident in the shelves along the walls, stuffed to bursting with his favourite books.

While the man observed his choices in literature, Jacob observed him, and felt his heart quicken in his chest. He knew the proud dark eyes and those black ringlets. He knew that posture, that lithe physique, only barely concealed beneath the heavy cloak.

"Madeleine?" He approached her then, ripped the hat from her head, and cleared the black tendrils from her face. Her eyes were swollen and red, and where there had once been pride and determination, only grief and desperation remained. It broke his heart to see her thus.

"You promised me his head once," she said, her voice breaking. "You promised me that if I asked—were you only in jest? Did you mean it?"

"I did," he assured her. "I meant it. It was no jest."

Her body sighed in relief, and for a moment he thought she might faint. "I know I ask a difficult thing of you," she said, as tears mixed with drying rain on her cheeks. "I know I ask a selfish, devilish thing."

"And yet, I will do it without complaint, because you ask it of me."

Her eyes met his, the grief now replaced by cold calculation. He met her gaze with his own, and, after a moment, her expression softened, as though she had found the tacit reassurance she needed.

She unbuttoned her coat then, and let the barriers between her skin and his slide to the floor about her feet as she stepped out of the trousers and boots. She wore no shirt, and her hair, pushed back beyond her shoulders, hid little and less of her skin. His eyes washed over her with obvious admiration and desire, but hers did not leave his.

"I am willing to risk dishonour," she told him, "to be at your mercy. To marry you, if you should still want me when the deed is done."

Jacob inhaled deeply, struggling to remember every lesson he had ever learned about being a gentleman. Yet, he could not deny the effect she had upon him.

How simple—how easy it would be to reach out and take all she offered. After all, he would keep his word. He would never betray her, never take back his promise. Never resist the offer of her hand in marriage, given so freely. Yet, he bent to the floor, retrieved the coat she had let fall, and clothed her in it.

She stared at him, confused. "Do you not want me, then?" she asked, her eyes brimming with tears. "Will you not avenge me?"

"I will do precisely as you ask," he assured her, his eyes shut, his forehead now pressing against her own, "but not at any risk to your honour, and not like this. You grieve for your mother, and for your father's betrayal. I despise him more than I ever have, because it is his actions that have broken you, and that is a power no man should have over you—not even me. I will take you whole and mended, for only then will I know you come to me with full heart and no reservations."

He seemed to hesitate for a moment, as if regretting his decision, his thumb lingering on her skin. "I will escort you home. I know Gaëlle and the others must be filled with anxiety at your absence, and at so late an hour." He turned away from her then, but a touch to his cheek stayed him.

"I did not come from the Barfleur Estate," she confessed, her estimation of him growing tenfold. "I have not set foot there for quite some time. I came from Lamoreaux, dressed as you see me, in the clothes of my grandmother's friend. I can stay the night, if you like. No one would be the wiser."

The thought of her beneath him by the fire was almost more than he could bear. "Madeleine, I do love and respect you," he professed, "but I am only a man. Take care with the things you say. If you spend the night, I neither promise you your honour, nor mine."

There was a look of mischief in her eyes that stirred the very devil in him. Surely, just a taste, after all she had said and done, and all he meant to do on her behalf, could not be such an unchivalrous thing. He pressed his lips to hers, more intimacy than had ever before passed between them. Then, as the hands of lust took hold of him, planting carnal thoughts inside his head, he withdrew.

The smile had not left her eyes, nor had her hand left his cheek. "I have not always been open with you about my feelings, Sir Jacob, but I do hope you know I care for you. I come to you not from mere desperation, but because in my darkest hours and amidst the worst of maledictions I heaped at the feet of men, you alone remained unscathed."

She added, playfully, "I daresay not even my Uncle Eli can claim such an honour, for I know my Gaëlle is the very air he breathes, and though I approve of the match, I confess I disapprove of the separation it will cause me."

Her words set his heart beating even faster than the kiss had done. "I have but one favour to ask of you."

"Then consider it done, Sir Jacob," she replied. "What is it that you wish?"

"If you are to be my betrothed, and my wife, may we not now dispense with the formalities? I would much prefer if you called me Jacob, or Jack, or Jake—anything but *Sir.*"

"Jake," she tried out the name, "I have something to show you."

He tensed.

She laughed. "I know not what you think I mean by that, but I assure you, you have seen as much of my skin as you will for the night remaining. I will have to depend upon your honour though, I'm afraid. There is much you need to know, and it may take some time. Can you manage it?"

"I suspect you are enjoying this; aren't you?"

"I daresay, I am," she replied, "but you must pardon me for the change of mood." She took a leather pouch from an inside pocket of her coat and removed the translations she had made of *Madame* Anglais's diary. "I know where they are. Here is all the information you will need to find them."

Jacob's eyes widened as he skimmed through the words before him. "Where did you find this?"

"I have my methods," she parried. "As to the cost-"

"You needn't trouble your head about that." Jacob slowly sank into the old, threadbare sofa he had been attempting to read in, just minutes before, his eyes never leaving the papers before him. A dark horror seemed to creep over his face, the more he read. "Father Castello..." he murmured once, but said little else.

When he had finished, Madeleine was sitting on the floor by the fire, with her legs folded beneath her. He wondered what she thought of his humble quarters: the small bed in the corner, the reading area by the fire, his rows and rows and rows of books, the now tilting stack of penny dreadfuls, and the small table where he took his meals in private.

"Disappointed?" he asked her, setting the papers beneath the book he had tried to read earlier.

Startled, she turned to look at him, perhaps anxious that her wandering eye may have hurt his pride.

He only smiled. "Not so very luxurious, I grant," he said, looking around the apartment that had been his home for some two years now. "I developed very simple tastes as a soldier and find it best to maintain as a bachelor. Why squander my wealth on idle things now, when I can save it all to invest in my wife and our family, later?"

Madeleine blushed and turned away from him. "You are wiser than I would have once credited you for, Jake."

He chuckled. "I confess, I worry there is an insult hidden in there. Speak plainly. Enlighten me."

"I most certainly shall not," she teased. "A bit of mystery is always good for the mind, and even better for the heart."

It seemed eons had passed before she was standing in front of the Barfleur Estate, her secret safe, her honour spared, and his promise given. Yet, that old familiar feeling of foreboding was creeping in, again.

"You will be careful, Jacob?"

"Honourable gentlemen oft' keep their honour through friendships with dishonourable men," he returned. "Nothing will come back to you."

"Me?" She looked at him, eyes wide with incredulity. "I was thinking of *you*."

Jacob's heart did a somersault in his chest, but he was spared from finding the right words by the appearance of Betha. He had ridden ahead in the dead of night to alert the household and had brought a carriage back to his apartments to retrieve the young heiress, whom he learned had been missing for some time.

"Madeleine, oh you dreadful child! How you worried us! And what is this clothes you wear?" Betha greeted her with obvious relief. "We are forever in your debt, Sir Jacob!"

He was about to respond, when Madeleine pressed a kiss to his cheek and then disappeared up the garden path. Betha looked at him with a mix of surprise and approval, and then hurried after her mistress.

As the door shut, one of the servants brought the horse Jacob had left when he fetched the carriage. The horse had evidently been watered, brushed, and fed. Jacob pitched the servant a coin in thanks, and rode off into the coming sunrise, just as the first shot of red bled across the sky.

CHAPTER XXIII

A Frightening Tale

After fleeing Lamoreaux on foot, under the cover of nightfall, dressed in *Monsieur* Popescu's Sunday best, Madeleine had more than once questioned her sanity. She had walked for leagues, taken carriage rides with strangers, and often did without food and water. Her sustenance was vengeance and little else.

When she entered the sitting room Betha had led her into, she found herself questioning her sanity yet again. "Do my eyes deceive me?" she asked. "Mother, is that you?"

Charlotte struggled to sit upright on the sofa, where she reclined by the fire. She had withered down to skin and bones and had clearly lost her strength. There was a bruise on the left side of her face and neck, and the puff of a bandage beneath her purple nightgown.

"I survived," she replied, her voice barely a whisper.

"But Basile does not know it, and he cannot," said the anxious voice of a man in the armchair adjacent to her own. "Not yet."

Madeleine had never formally met the man, but needed no introduction. She had more than once caught a glimpse of him leaving her mother's company with flushed cheeks and hurried footsteps. *"Monsieur* Walker," she guessed. "Ever my mother's staunch supporter."

He reddened at the acknowledgement. "Yes, always." He looked about at the others who stood on the fringes of the room, unwilling to interrupt the reconciliation between mother and child.

Among them was Sarah, the timid servant Madeleine had hired the year before. Sarah did not look to be a servant, now. Her flaxen hair was pinned up beneath a white cap and she wore the dark uniform and white apron of a matron. In her hands, she held the blooded bandages she had only just changed.

"I do believe you could use a bit of privacy," George said, noting Madeleine's apparent confusion. "I will hurry back, now, before I am missed by the French detectives." He tipped his hat. "Lady Moreau and Lady Madeleine, may the hands of Fate be henceforth kinder to you both."

"Whatever your hand in this, Mister Walker, I cannot thank you enough," Madeleine replied.

He nodded, and left the room, taking the others with him.

Only then did Madeleine rush to Charlotte's side. "Oh Mother, whate'er has he done to you? We believed you dead!"

"So did I," she confessed, her eyes watering at the sight of her only living child. "Madeleine, how it pained my very heart when Mamie wrote to tell me you were gone! I was so sure an assassin had taken you, as you had taken nothing with you: no money, no food, or water, no horse. She was so sure you were on your way to Barfleur, but I feared I would never see you again."

Madeleine's brow furrowed at first with confusion, and then with realisation. "She knew you were here, all along?"

"She did not know for sure, at first. I had warned her of my plans, and the means I meant to take to ensure my escape. I could not burden you with that knowledge, with that false hope. I pray you can forgive me for that secrecy; I did it only to spare you."

Madeleine left her side to take one of the cushions from the armchairs. She threw it down on the floor before her mother. "I will forgive you, if you tell me all that has happened."

Charlotte nodded. She had expected the request. "I am very tired, Madeleine. My strength is not with me, but Miss Harper says I will recover if I only have the patience. Still, it is not a very long story, and I believe I can tell it all before sleep claims me."

She reached for a cup of water with trembling hands. Madeleine sprang up from the floor and placed the cup to her lips. Charlotte drank deeply, and then motioned for Madeleine to reclaim her seat.

"In the summer, I fell victim to the very same nightmare you did," she began. "Like you, it came for nights at a time. I could not sleep, for fear that I would dream of it again. Even so, I am not blessed with the gift of interpretation, as you and Mamie are. I do not automatically know the meaning of these things.

"The murderous dog could have been a rival playwright, or a jealous admirer. And the dead dog, could have... it could have been you. That it was you, was my first thought, and so when you insisted on hiring a White maid for the prejudiced fool, I saw my chance. I recommended Miss Harper—Sarah, to you—and sent her to Barfleur to be my spy. Even then, I did not dream Basile would have done you any true harm! I believed at most he would be a nuisance to your education, a fly in your ear, not a murderer!—but I digress."

She took a moment to recover her line of thought, then finding the thread, she resumed her tale. "The first time you were poisoned, Sarah noticed the signs and administered an antidote. By the second time, Regina had caught on and now began to watch all the servants in the house, keeping an especially keen eye on Sarah. In doing so, she found her out, but was sworn to secrecy for I could not risk Sarah throwing any suspicion upon her person by making herself familiar with you.

"When I then received your letter, interpreting our shared dream, I knew you must be right. Sarah taught Regina as best she could how to ascertain the signs of poison or any other likely threat against your health, and assuring me that you were in very capable hands, she took the first opportunity to return to London. There, we began to plot. At every available chance, she drew some of my blood, and put it away for future use.

"I did not tell Eli or Betha of my plans, for I believed the less they knew the better. I could not risk a noose for either of them, justice being what it is for those of Black heritage, however little. It has been but a few years since Britain freed the Blacks in the Indies. They would be hanged without trial! I would not—could not risk their lives to spare my own."

Madeleine touched her hand to her mother's in tacit reassurance that she understood.

Charlotte took a deep breath to calm her nerves, and then recommenced her story. "When Basile appeared unannounced, I knew I had to act swiftly, or all my planning would be for naught. I had warned George of the threat, and it took only a few letters delivered by Betha and Eli to spring things into action. I could not involve them further, so with the letters delivered, I sent Eli and Betha home to escort you to the safety of Lamoreaux.

"Day after day, I waited for Basile to strike, and when the day finally came, I knew it. I felt it as surely as I feel the suffering it has caused me, now. When the day passed without incident, I knew then that he meant to carry out his evil act under the cover of darkness, like the coward he is.

"It was storming that night and knowing what lay before me, I was determined to stay awake. Unfortunately, my body would not cooperate. I was weary with worry and had only just shut my eyes when I saw Basile above me. He was drunk and missed the mark, but I was stabbed all the same—two inches of vengeance buried in my chest.

"I had but a little strength left to prick him with the syringe Miss Harper had prepared for me. He fell almost instantly asleep, though a brief struggle between us served me the bruises you see here.

"I was in too much pain to move thereafter, and was growing weaker by the second. I prayed to *Bondye* for a miracle, and then fainted away with the words of prayer still upon my lips. Soon after, the window opened and who should come hopping onto my bedroom floor, with muddy shoes and soaked all the way through, but your Uncle Eli?

"He had brought an assassin with him, a dangerous man, for we never saw his face. He wore a hooded cloak and mask, and I could not help but think his rough accent was put on. So intent was he on keeping his identity from us! To think, I could pass him on the street tomorrow, and wouldn't have the slightest clue he was the man who helped save my life!

"I begged them to leave Basile to the noose, even after the assassin confessed Basile had tried to hire him to murder me first, for I knew another murder would only cause suspicion. And who would they suspect but Eli, who came running back to London after I had sent him away?!

"They fetched Miss Harper from the room I had hidden her in earlier that day. I fell unconscious before she arrived. When I woke, I was at William's home, hidden from the authorities until such time as they could move me. While I slept, Eli and Miss Harper had used the blood I stored to create the crime scene with the assassin's help. He was sure Basile had not been working alone and advised them to keep me hidden until an accomplice was found. I did not dream for a second that it would have been Severina. More fool I, for all the trust I misplaced and the treachery I did not perceive!

"I was weak from the loss of blood, and heavily sedated, so the rest is all a blur. Still, I know that in the days that followed, Eli made plans to bring me here. When I arrived, I was met with a letter from Mamie that you had only just gone missing. For a week we searched, but no sign!"

She looked the very picture of distress, mingled with desperate relief. "Oh, Madeleine! I thought for sure you were dead! They had already sent a man to Lamoreaux to take Mamie's life, and there you were, wandering along the road by yourself, without food or shelter, at the mercy of strangers! My beautiful girl! My only child!"

"I managed, and never once felt as though I was in any true danger," Madeleine replied. "I am not half so fragile as you would think, and there is safety in the dress of a man. Nevertheless, I do regret causing you grief, especially in this state."

"I daresay Gaëlle is more distressed than even I," Charlotte teased. "She will be here with Mamie and the others by the morrow. When Sir Jacob came tonight to borrow the carriage, I immediately dispatched Eli with news of your safe return. I had hoped for justice, but the law failed me as it has failed so many women before us."

"It was a woman who caused that," Madeleine pointed out. "Not a man. It was Severina who sent that lawyer." After a pause, she added, "Mother I have done a terrible thing, you may never forgive me for."

"What could you ever do that I would not forgive with a willing heart, Madeleine?" she said kindly, through her eyes betrayed the fear and concern now taking root.

"I asked Sir Jacob to dispose of him," she confessed. "I know it is a ghastly thing I ask, and yet even with you here, I feel no remorse."

"Madeleine..." Charlotte could find no other words.

"I offered my hand in marriage to Sir Jacob—to Jake—in exchange," she continued. "I will marry him as soon as he carries out my request."

For a time, Charlotte was silent. She wanted to tell Madeleine that it was indeed a terrible thing to wish her father dead. And yet, she too had thought of taking Basile's life when she woke to find him still sleeping soundly in her blood, and even more tempted when the assassin had offered so casually to do away with him.

"Like he ne'er existed, it would be, ma'am!" he had insisted, as though he were merely chatting about removing hungry caterpillars from a vegetable garden.

"I wish you had not taken such a decision into your own hands," Charlotte finally said. "It will weigh heavily on your conscience; you are too young for such burdens."

"I have carried greater in the past few weeks, when I believed I had lost my mother."

Charlotte could not prevent the tears from escaping her, then. "Do you love him at least, Madeleine. Truly, love him?"

"Yes," she admitted, "always, though, until recently, I would have preferred to die a spinster, even so."

Charlotte could not help but laugh, even as the tears streamed down her cheeks. "You are your grandmother's child. She loved my father, you know? Perhaps even more than he loved her. But, he made the mistake of trying to tame her, and Mamie could not stand it.

"I was three years old when she sent him away on that ship to Saint-Domingue, but I remember how much she cried. It was not an easy decision, but it was one she felt she had to make. Mamie always does things her own way."

She took Madeleine's hands. "I hope you will find a marriage neither like Mamie's nor my own. Sir Jacob is a liberal man, I think, and may understand that ours is a bid for equality and not superiority, however much it might look otherwise from the outside."

CHAPTER XXIV

The Burden of Guilt

Like a statue he sat, eyes fixed on nothing at all, while his mind roamed in deep contemplation. Had it not been for the occasional twitch of an eye or finger, she might have suspected someone had murdered him and propped him up in his seat.

"Is the meal not to your liking, *Signore?*" Wilma enquired, but he was too far away to hear her.

"He is probably exhausted from his trip, and the terrible ordeal he has suffered," Severina chimed in.

Wilma nodded, and hurried her daughter from the room. Only then did Severina move to touch his hand. Basile withdrew it in a flash and set almost accusatory eyes upon her.

"You startled me," he said by way of apology, when Severina fixed him with one of her calculating gazes.

"Are you well? You have not touched your food, and I am not sure you slept at all last night."

He met her eyes across the table, attempting to gauge what her response would be to the confession he intended to make. "Rina, what would you say, if I told you I am not at all sure what happened on the night of... on the night?"

Severina arched an eyebrow at what was clearly the beginning of an admission she did not want to hear. "Go on."

"I met with the ruffian you suggested, and he refused the job: promising that he would ensure no another assassin took the work either. I was furious and returned to the manor with every intention of doing the deed myself.

"I was careful. I did nothing as far as I can see that let on to my plan. Yet, there was a knowing in her eyes that day as she watched me, and a proud resignation, as if she had accepted her fate, come what may. 'Do your worst, Basile!' her very eyes seemed to tell me! When she went to bed that night, she did not even lock her door. It was as though she was waiting for me.

"Even at dinner, I am loathe to admit, I found my nerves failing me. As you have seen, it would mean the noose if I was found out, and there were many arrows that could point to me. Frenchmen are not especially welcome in London, so I knew if one of their beloved nobles should die—even one born on French soil—suspicion should fall upon me and I would be ruined.

"Nevertheless, the thing had to be done, so when she went to bed, I waited and waited until I was sure she had fallen asleep. I went to the room, climbed onto the bed while she slept, and plunged the dagger deep in her chest.

"Never in my life have I fainted away. Yet, the next thing I remember is waking up in her blood, and the servants screaming. I felt weak; disoriented. It was some time before I could even try to make my way out of the room, and these servants set themselves upon me and made impossible my escape. The police arrived soon after and they grabbed me, roughing me up as though I was some common man!

"When they interrogated me about Charlotte, and I said I did not know where she was, it was no fib. It is the truth. I know not where her body lies, but surely, she could not live after what I had done. So much... so much blood." He raised his hands before him, and looked at them with disgust and horror, as though he could see the very stain of murder upon them. "Never in my life have I ever seen so much blood, not even on a birthing bed."

"A regular Macbeth, aren't we?" Severina mocked him, though she felt the very chill of death course through her spine. "Basile, do not be foolish."

"Ridicule me, if you must, but I tell you Severina: her soul wanders. She will seek revenge. She is not at rest. You do not know the things I have seen. You do not know what it is to be in the constant presence of these Moreau women who consistently seem to know things they should not."

"Perhaps, they found it in a book?" Severina quipped.

Basile's eyes flashed with anger.

"Save your temper, Basile, for it is I who should be furious. You would not so much as touch me last night, but sure as the snow upon the rocky face of Rocchetta Alta, I heard you murmuring her name as I woke this morning. And now, here you are, not only discussing the witch of a woman, but also, it would seem, regretting your actions and *threatening* me!"

"She haunts my dreams," Basile replied, a distant look creeping into his tired eyes. "It is the reason I cannot sleep at night. I cannot bear the thought of seeing her."

"And yet, when I tried to wake you, you slept quite soundly, husband!" She stood from the table. "I do not wish to hear another word about this woman, or one unfortunate night, you just may have an accidental fall from the bedroom balcony. And you can rest assured, I will not sit at breakfast regretting your clumsiness." With that, she left the room.

As darkness descended, he could feel the hand of fear taking hold of his heart. He had always esteemed himself to be a man of action, of courage. Few things ever troubled his nerves. And yet, as he saw the sunset fading into the blue-bathed night, a tremor crept into the hand holding his wine.

"Some fresh air might do you well," a small voice, suggested. Ines had entered the sitting room and had noticed his discomfort. "Papa often takes walks, when he wants to clear his head."

"A walk, in the dead of night?"

"Yes, *Signore!* I only just took a walk myself!" she volunteered with obvious excitement. "But please do not tell Mama. She would be furious! You will find the garden well lit. Papa lights the torches in the turf maze at sunset, as he says *Signora* loves to take walks there. The bushes are just brambles now in the winter, so you needn't worry about getting lost."

Basile's defensiveness was no match for her patience, and so he looked at the child with renewed respect. She had a common face, but uncommonly blue eyes, and a sweet demeanour. One would struggle indeed to remain angry in her presence.

"Would you like me to show you the way, *Signore?* It is best to take the back door and go up the garden path. There is a patch of ice close to the entrance of the maze, but you should be fine, I think. I left a walking stick by the door, if you should care to use it."

"Thank you," he found himself saying. "You are very kind." She fetched his hat and coat, then wished him a happy walk, and went to the kitchens to help her mother with supper.

As he strolled up the garden path, he passed her father, smoking quietly on the stump of a newly felled tree. The man acknowledged him with a slight bow of his head and continued to enjoy his pipe.

In the gardens, the scores of dancing lights marked the entrance to the courtyard maze. The pure white snow, bathed in the moonlight, shone like a thousand miniature diamonds in the night. The sheer beauty of it all put his heart at rest and reminded him that there were still small things to be grateful for.

As he wandered through the brambles and snow, he asked himself, *When did I begin to lose my heart to greed? When did I become a thief? A murderer?*

"Indeed, Basile, I oft' have wondered the very same thing!"

He spun around to face the direction from which the voice had come and would have lost his balance but for the brambles to hold on to. His heart raced; his breathing slowed. Surely, he had imagined the voice. So then, why had it sounded as though she were right beside him?

"Cha—Charlotte?" he called out.

Only the howling of the wind answered him, and yet, he sensed he was not alone. The very hairs on the back of his neck stood up, and the goose pimples on his skin had little to do with the wintry air about him.

"Are you afraid, Basile?"

He clutched the handful of brambles that had saved him from falling only moments earlier, his eyes never leaving the shadowy silhouette of a woman he now noticed up ahead. He crossed himself and offered up what prayers he could remember. "Get—get thee behind me, Satan!"

"With pleasure!" A heavy wind blew through the courtyard, putting out every torch that had been lit. And then he felt the coldness of her breath against his ear, behind him.

He took off into the darkness, driven by fear and guilt, and anger at his helplessness. Whether the shadowy silhouette continued to pursue him, he did not stop to see. Nor did he see the untrimmed branch snaking out just above the snow. It hooked the toe of his boot, and down into the snow he fell, his head smacking hard against the ice and stone.

As the wind continued to howl, he could almost swear he heard the loud cackling of an old woman.

CHAPTER XXV

The Wages of Sin

Severina rushed to his side, taking the cold rag from her servant's hands, and mopping his brow. She had only just returned from Rome, where she had visited with the lawyer who had seen to Basile's release.

It was Ines who met her at the door with the news. "It is entirely my fault," the poor girl had cried. "It was I who suggested he go for a walk! I had only just walked there myself and did not foresee any danger in him doing the same."

Severina had dropped all her things, and rushed up the stairs, with Ines behind her. What she had found was Basile laying feverish in bed, muttering and mumbling to himself.

"For how long has he been like this?"

"We found him this morning." It was Giu, her usually reticent manservant, who answered. "When he did not come for breakfast, the wife begged me to check the room. The bed was not slept in, but I remembered him walking by me in the night.

"It was a wonder he did not freeze to death. His face was resting on his hat, and he had worn his gloves—a lucky move, or his skin would have been black as a negro, I do not doubt."

"And no one checked that he had come in, safely?!" Severina shot at them.

"With all due respect, *Signora,*" Giu returned, "he is no boy, and we had no reason to suspect anything was amiss."

Severina ground her teeth, while a million maledictions went unsaid. He saw the hostility in her eyes and gruffly excused himself from the room.

Still in his feverish delirium, Basile reached up to touch her face, his eyes barely open. "Charlotte—is that you?"

Severina recoiled from him as though he had struck her, the cool rag falling with an impotent plop to the floor.

Wilma rushed to fetch it and resumed her nursing. "He is not well, *Signora,*" the old lady murmured, in hopes of soothing her fiery-tempered mistress. "He has been saying strange things all the morning."

"I imagine he has," said she, her voice colder than the snow he had lain in all night. "I trust there is still breakfast in the kitchen?"

"I will fetch it for you, *Signora,*" Ines offered, eager to make herself useful and offer recompense for the injury she believed she had caused.

Hours upon hours dragged on, until at last, Basile's fever broke. It was just before dusk. Wilma had fallen asleep by his side. The cold rag still rested on his forehead. The sunset threw lights and shadows about the room. It would have been beautiful, peaceful even, had it not been for the silhouette which drained the last bit of courage from him.

As the familiar figure stepped into the light, he saw the dark curls Charlotte had worn cropped to her neck, the silvery white nightgown she had worn to bed on the fateful night, and the knife still buried in her chest, where he had left it.

"Are you not happy to see me, husband?" this thing that looked so much like his wife, enquired.

He knew it was not her, could not be her. For where Charlotte had brought light into the darkest of rooms, this being brought only darkness. The black gloom seemed to descend upon the room faster than the sunset faded beyond the windows.

Basile tried desperately to move, to open his mouth, to do anything. But the words would not come, and his limbs lay useless, as though paralysed. The very warmth was being sucked out of the room, and the air from his lungs, as this thing fixed its black eyes upon him.

The dark spell was suddenly broken when young Ines burst into the room. *"Signor* Dubois!" she greeted him. "How pleased I am to see you awake!"

Her mother woke with a start, then. "Oh! Ines! You cannot come running into the *Signore's* bedchamber in such a manner."

"Signore?" Ines said, her eyes burning with curiosity and alarm. "You look as though you have seen a ghost!"

Basile shut his eyes tight, the last few threads of his sanity beginning to unravel. "Fetch me a priest!" he cried out. "I have looked into the very eyes of the devil; I have seen hell."

In the six-and-twenty years, since he had dedicated his life to Christ, Father Colombo had travelled from Rome to North Africa to Madrid to the West Indies and finally to Rocchetta Alta. In his time, he had listened to confessions from harlots and nobles, criminals and saints, Indians and soldiers, planters and slaves.

If only that had been preparation enough! In all his years, never had he heard such a tale as this one. Already, he had crossed himself a dozen times, and increasingly whispered more Hail Marys as the story unfolded.

"Worst of all is her ghost haunting me, seeking revenge!"

"Ghost? Haunting?" Father Colombo shook his head in disapproval. "The dead do not walk, Basile. It is ungodly to say such a thing: God forgive you!"

"Ungodly? Is the Bible ungodly then, Father? Does it speak falsehoods? Did Saul not converse with the ghost of Samuel on the brink of war, and did he not face the wrath of God for it? Is the Witch of Endor not writ on its very pages? And if this story is a lie, what else is?"

Father Colombo struggled to conjure up a coherent response, fearful of setting further astray his lost sheep. "There—there are other important reasons Saul fell out of favour with—"

"Charlotte was her mother's child, a witch's child!" Basile cut in. "And her daughter is every bit the same as her grandmother, and her mother before her, and on and on up the line. Witches, every last one of them. It is in their blood."

"With all due respect *Signor* Dubois, the Moreau Family has been a respected member of the Catholic Church, and some of our brothers' Faith, the Anglican Church, since the 1600s. Necromancy is a *very* serious charge to lay at the feet of such a family."

"I do not mean to lay any charge at their feet. I only mean to speak the truth as best as I know it," Basile professed. "I have been an unfaithful husband and a cruel father. Not a day goes by that I do not carry the heavy burden of guilt, not just from taking Charlotte's life, but attempting to put out the very light we brought into the world.

"At the very least, it soothes me to say I did try to save her in the end, for in time I saw my hatred of her was but a reflection of the resentment I felt for her mother. But she would not hear of going to her grandmother in Lamoreaux. For her own good, I implored her to take her leave, but she would not listen!

"Madeleine is such a wilful, disobedient, and *stubborn* child—and yet, were those not the very qualities I fell in love with, when I met her mother? The woman who did as she pleased, with little care for what society thought. The woman who was willing to marry beneath her rank, for love."

Father Colombo considered this for a moment before asking, "If you loved her, why did you take her life?"

"It is no easy thing to be a mere candle next to a roaring fire."

"And Madeleine? Perhaps you did try to save her in the end, but why-ever was she targeted at all? Your own child."

"Imagine being the candle sandwiched between *two* roaring fires. I did not covet my neighbour's wife; I coveted the very things that made my wife the woman she was."

"But you did covet your neighbour's wife. You married her," the priest said, before he could stop himself.

"And is that a greater sin than murder?"

"It is not for me to judge: only to listen and provide absolution, if you are truly repentant."

"And what of Charlotte, who died without seeking forgiveness for the murder she committed?"

"Murder?" Father Colombo repeated.

"Yes, murder. A life for a life," Basile replied. "You ask me why I should want her dead if I loved her so. There was one life I loved more than hers: my son's."

"Speak plainly, Basile," the priest urged him, now mopping nervous sweat from his brow.

"Madeleine is not our firstborn. She is our second. Our firstborn was Basile Dubois *fils,* or Basile Dubois Jr. as Charlotte sometimes called him, for she was as much an Englishwoman as she was French.

"He was born a happy, healthy boy a year into our marriage, the very image of his father. I loved him as I never knew I could love another. He was a part of me, my son, and he would be my legacy.

"And then one day, he fell ill. Dr. Frederik was called, and then a Dr. Martin, Dr. Thomas, and a Dr. Durand. One by one they passed through our doors, none leaving any wiser of what was amiss than the one before him. He could not be saved, they said. He would be gone in weeks, days even.

"Desperate, I begged Charlotte's mother to intervene on his behalf, to do whatever it is that witches do to heal people, to save lives. Charlotte was sceptical. I had never seen her sceptical of her mother's skills before; I could not understand it. Witch or no witch, I had seen with my own eyes as that cursed woman healed the lame and the sick coming into the back parlour she once used at the Barfleur Estate."

"That line of the Moreau women are talented healers, I have heard," the priest ventured, "but healing and witchcraft are not the same, Basile. You must take care with your words, for false accusation is a sin before God."

"Talented healers!" Basile repeated, now shaking with anger. "But she would not heal my son! Her own grandson! They left the poor, innocent boy to die. *My* boy! *My son!*"

He fell silent then, his face dark and brooding. "One day, not long after I had begged Mamie to do what she could for Little Bas, I heard them whispering in that back parlour. 'It will be like Olga and the son of *Seigneur* Boucher,' said the mother. 'History repeats itself.'

"'Then it is done,' said my wife, weeping. 'My son will die.' The words had barely left her lips when I took to running through the house to get to him, for I felt in that instant, they had damned him. I met Betha and the nurse upon the stairs, just as they began to raise the alarm. My son was dead.

"I wept when we buried him, watching as they put my heart and soul into the Earth, never to be seen again. Charlotte did not shed a tear, though I could see the emotion behind her cold exterior." He added with strong conviction, "It was guilt, guilt for what she had done, or rather, what she had refused to do for a boy she claimed to love."

"Basile, I confess I do not follow your line of reasoning. It seems clear to me that your son, bless his heart, was beyond the healing of any doctor, even your mother-in-law."

"How would they know that until they *tried?* They let him die!" A few moments of quiet seething passed before he reclaimed some semblance of control and continued his story. "My mother was distraught. She had overheard me asking Charlotte and her mother to intervene, but not their refusal. And when my son—when he died, she blamed Charlotte's mother for it.

"When Mamie could take the affront no longer, she packed her things and left for Lamoreaux. Not long after, I found my mother cold and stiff upon her bed. The death was ruled to be of natural causes, but there were whispers in the streets, and perhaps the whispers were true. As my own mother had told me many years before, 'hell hath no fury like witches scorned!'

"Still, I do not curse them for her passing, for I learned shortly afterwards that she had been stealing from me. Money that had gone missing over the course of a few months—for which I had punished one of Charlotte's *nègre* stable boys—were found in the drawers in her room, down to the very last cent. That is the only favour the witches ever granted me!"

The priest could not believe his ears. In his heart, he felt the old stirrings of his noble birth, the pride and haughtiness and disbelief that a man of low breeding, who would murder his own wife and daughter, would dare to speak ill of not one, but two noblewomen of the Church.

Father Colombo whispered a silent prayer and urged his prejudices to be still in his heart. He could not allow himself to forget that the kindest to him on his travels was often the man with the least to give, and that he had seen evil thrive in the wealthiest homes in Rome.

And yet, there was an even more dreadful kind of evil lying deep within the man before him. He sensed it as surely as he could feel the breeze sweeping in through the open window. It was the evil that rejoiced in the ill-faring of others. An evil that sought to punish, but never to be punished. It was an evil that knew no rank or race of man.

"Pray tell then, *Signor* Dubois, why would Charlotte and her mother refuse to save your son, if they could have spared him suffering and death? After all, he was no less their son and grandson."

"Is it not obvious?" Basile shot back at him, eyes wide as though a fit of madness had descended upon him. "To preserve the Moreau Matriarchy!"

"I see," the priest humoured him. "And did you ever confront your wife?"

"So she could lie to my face? I would have struck her down right where she stood!"

"And yet, you struck her down anyway, while she slept, without ever trying to learn the truth. What if you are wrong?"

Basile did not answer. Instead, he returned his attention to the window and the snow-covered world beyond. "Will you absolve me, Father, now that I have confessed all? God forgives he who repents and seeks His mercy."

"Are you truly sorry?"

"Of course, I am."

"Then, you must give yourself over to the authorities. You must face the law."

"The only law I bow to is the law of God."

"And yet, you have not," the priest returned. "This is not how forgiveness works, *Signor* Dubois. True repentance requires accepting accountability for our actions. The law of man, in this case, reflects the law of God. *Thou shalt not kill. Thou shalt not commit adultery. Thou shalt not covet thy neighbour's wife.*"

"Are you here to judge me, priest?!" Basile snapped.

"The Bible forbids me from judging," Father Colombo replied, "but I cannot allow a member of my flock to go astray in how he has interpreted the Word, and Will, and Grace of God. I can only absolve you from a prison cell, *Signor* Dubois. Until then, you are not truly repentant for your sins and crimes."

"Then, I am lost."

"I am truly sorry to hear it."

"Will you bless the house, at least? It might keep her—the spectre away."

The priest shook his head, his eyes filled with sorrow. "I cannot bless the home of a man and woman who wilfully live in sin. I am sorry, *Signor* Dubois."

"So you will alert the police then and betray my confidence?"

"I am bound by the sacred seal. Nothing you have told me will leave this room." After a moment of heavy silence, he added, "A man that strikes me as being of disreputable character came asking after you at the cathedral today—an Englishman. Could this be connected with—with what you did in London?"

Basile squared his shoulders, as though already preparing for the worst. "I would not be very much surprised if it were." When the priest said nothing more, he added, "May my death be upon your conscience, Father, for I fear it will be soon."

"My prayers shall be with you, then," the priest replied, as he turned to leave.

When he had reached the door, Basile arrested him with, "Will I burn for this, Father?"

"Only God can decide that." Father Colombo then disappeared out the door and fled Villa Martelli as though escaping through the very gates of hell.

Not long after he had gone, Severina burst into the room. "What did you tell the priest?"

"That...is between me and God."

"Did you tell him what we did? Do you truly think he will not act on the information you have provided? Are you mad!"

Basile helped himself to the wine Wilma had brought him earlier. "I daresay I am, wife."

"You are a fool!" She hurried from the room, her heart once again heavy with the task set before her. She could not let the priest live.

He watched from the window as her carriage sped from the court-yard, with snow rising like white smoke behind it. Severina had only just disappeared over the hill when he felt the spectre's icy breath upon his skin.

It was with half parts relief and frustration that she arrived at the cathedral to find Father Colombo had stopped only for a moment's notice, before leaving for an important trip.

"He said he would be gone for some days, yet," the unsuspecting nun told her.

"Did he say anything at all when he arrived?" Severina asked, sweetly.

"On the contrary, *Signora*," she answered. "He is usually quite the talker, but he spoke scarcely a word when he entered, and only because I accosted him about his plans. Are you certain we cannot be of service?"

"I am afraid not, but I do appreciate your kindness, Sister. I will let you return to God's work."

"God be with you, *Signora*."

It is just as well, she consoled herself. *He must have smelled trouble ahead and fled the town. Does he know about Father Castello? Surely, not even Basile knows. Still, something he said may have given me away.*

So lost was she in her ruminations that she hardly noticed when the carriage came to a stop before the villa, until Ines ripped the door open.

"Signora!" she greeted her, eyes wild with excitement. "It is the *Signore*. Mama sent me up to fetch him for dinner, but his door is locked, and he will not answer."

"Perhaps, he has fallen asleep. He has been over-tired of late and may have given in to exhaustion."

Ines did not look convinced. "I heard voices in the room before I knocked, *Signora*. And then, I heard a loud thud, and nothing more. I offered to climb up by the tree outside your window—a simple thing—but Mama would not allow it. I have been calling at the door, since."

"Do you have a spare key to the door?" Severina asked her driver, as she entered the villa.

He shook his head. "I gave the spare key to the *Signore* when you first arrived. Nevertheless, with a good axe, if you will forgive the damage, I could have the door open."

"Then, fetch the axe."

He left through the back door, while Ines hurried with her up the stairs, to the master suite. The door was locked, just as she had said, and no amount of knocking, pounding or pleas produced any movement or sound on the other side.

"Step back, please!" Giu warned, the axe already raised high above his head.

The door, made of thick, heavy oak, did not come away from the hinges with ease. Strike after strike Ines's father sent against it. On the seventh, the door finally gave way enough for him to force it open.

A loud scream rang throughout the air. Was it her, or the little girl? Severina could not tell. She could only stare with wide eyes at the horror before her, as her knees gave way, and the floor rushed up to meet her.

CHAPTER XXVI

A Message from the Church

"Betrothed!" Mamie exclaimed, as they sat together on the bench, admiring the sunset.

Madeleine looked at her with some surprise. "I see you and Mother have been discussing my private affairs, Mamie!"

"You will forgive her, I am sure. She asked me to make some enquiries after Sir Jacob Andrews, to ensure he is of good character, as we have always esteemed him to be. You understand, she would not wish for you to fall into the same incapable hands, she did."

"And what did you find?"

"He is an exemplary young man. There is one small matter he will need to clear up with you, but I am sure he will mention it."

"Is there another woman?" Madeleine asked, surprised at her own jealousy.

"There is not," Mamie assured her. Her keen eyes did not miss her granddaughter's reaction.

"Then, what is it? Is it gambling? Opium? Are there debts?"

"No, no, and no," Mamie answered. "He will tell you in good time, I am sure. And when you hear it, you will know immediately that it is what I speak of, now. It is nothing that should worry you, and if he never mentions it, it will be because he cannot, and then I will break the secret. I give him a year to tell it."

"A year!" Madeleine could already feel her patience wearing thin. "Grandmother, you cannot tell me this and then expect me to wait a year."

"A good wife is a patient wife, you will find," Mamie replied. "I was never a patient woman, and so I was not married long. If you truly love Sir Jacob, let that be the one path of mine in life you do not walk.

"Believe me, dear, I am truly happy with the news of the betrothal, especially following my enquiries. I could not have picked a better match for you, myself."

"I am glad to hear it, Mamie."

"As you very well should be. It is indeed time for another daughter, but perhaps time for another ship, as well?"

Now, Madeleine laughed. "I pray it will not be so, Mamie! But come, let us return to the house, for I can already smell Regina's famous *soup joumou!*"

Long after dinner was devoured, and the servants had cleared the tables, the Moreau women sat together with Regina in the back parlour that had been so long shut up.

Charlotte reclined on the chaise lounge, the colour returning to her cheeks, and the flesh to her bones. New streaks of grey had crept into her hair, but she wore them like badges of honour, for all she had suffered. Madeleine had taken her usual place on a cushion on the floor just before her, engrossed in one of Alexandre Dumas's latest works, *Le Maître d'armes.*

Mamie sat in an armchair by the window, focused intently on her knitting, while a kerosene lamp burned brightly beside her. Regina, who was also completing her needlework, sat at her right hand, humming a melancholic tune.

But for the crackling of the fire and Regina's melodic alto voice, the house was silent. The clink and clatter of pans and dishes had long since ended, and even Miss Harper had retired to bed after seeing to her patient. Not even a wind stirred outside, to goad the trees into any of their not uncommon smacking of branches into the roof and window panes.

Thus, it was all the more frightening when a loud knock sounded at the front door. Suddenly, the entire house was alive and alert.

"Could it be Basile?" Charlotte fretted. "Madeleine, you must hide while we distract him! We will get a message to Sir Jacob. Surely, he can not now be far from Barfleur."

"Madeleine, you will remain where you are," Mamie said calmly, from her seat by the window.

Regina ceased her singing and now looked from the eldest Moreau to her daughter and then to the youngest Moreau, with piqued curiosity. In the neighbouring rooms, they could hear hushed voices, followed by the shutting of a door, and footsteps leading into the anteroom.

When Betha entered the back parlour just moments later, she was trembling from head to toe. "I do not know the gentleman who delivered this," she avowed, while Madeleine seated her close to the fire.

"Indeed, it could have been a woman! His head was covered in a cloak and he said but a few words. Only, 'Compliments of the Catholic Church!' and then he handed me the envelope and disappeared into the night.

"Eli went out after him, but I daresay he will not find him. Like the very spectre of dark tidings, he was, all cloaked in black."

With still trembling hands, she handed the envelope to Madeleine, who was closest to her. The young heiress removed the note, one eyebrow climbing higher and higher the more she read.

A guilty Frenchman of some renown to the British and French police has taken his own life. God be with you.

— F.C.

"Poor fool!" Mamie said over her knitting, unmoved, though the rest of the room was in uproar.

Madeleine left the coven of women who had gathered round Charlotte and the note, and went to Mamie's side. Like a *tricoteuse* her grandmother sat, unperturbed by the head the guillotine of Fate had just rolled to her feet.

"Is this your work?" Madeleine asked, her voice barely a whisper.

"Me?" Mamie replied, barely suppressing the twitch of a satisfied smile tugging at the corners of her lips. "Why, I've been in France all this while! And after all, did you not tell me 'magic' was not real?"

"Mamie, can you believe it?" Charlotte exclaimed, flying from the sofa to her mother, while Miss Harper fussed behind her. "The threat is passed!"

"The threat is not yet passed," Mamie replied, lifting her eyes to meet her daughter's for only a second before spreading her masterpiece out about her legs.

It was a raven-black blanket embroidered with the amber and crimson of the Moreau House's family crest: a knight's black visor held by a lion and his lioness, above a plain black shield trimmed with crimson. She had only just begun to stitch the Latin words engraved in the Moreau crest: *Igni Ferroque*—with fire and iron.

It had once been the coat of arms of Pierre Moreau *fils* when he rode into battle alongside his uncle, a Moreau from the senior branch of Bourgogne, never dreaming he would be granted a *seigneurie* for his pains. Maria Moreau had made it the family crest of the Lamoreaux branch of the Moreaux, in honour of the man who made the matriarchy.

"The new wife lives still," Mamie continued to say, "but fret not. No weapon formed against this family has ever prospered."

Before Charlotte could interrogate her further, Eli burst into the room, perspiration upon his forehead. "It is Esther who delivered the message," he said, "but she will not name the man who gave it to her."

"Esther, the Myal woman?" Regina said with obvious surprise. "But she specifically said it came from the Catholic Church. And who is

F.C.?" Her eyes widened as a frightening idea dawned upon her. "Could it be Father Castello, bringing tidings from the grave?" she wondered aloud.

The room went quiet, but for Mamie laughing by the window. "That would be quite the tale, wouldn't it!"

CHAPTER XXVII

Shadowed Faces

The Daily Courant: *January* 28, 1840

LADY CHARLOTTE MOREAU FOUND ALIVE BUT GRAVELY INJURED IN FRANCE. HER FRIGHTENING TALE OF TREACHERY AND SURVIVAL.

by George Walker

In the early morning of last December 18, Lady Charlotte Moreau came face to face with death when her husband plunged a dagger into her chest.

Upon examining the murder weapon a few days ago, provided by the Lady Moreau herself, Dr. John Arthur remarked, "It is a miracle she survived, and that it missed all major organs and arteries.

"Nevertheless, I imagine the Lady suffered an immense amount of pain, and that she was in and out of consciousness for some time due to the loss of blood. The medical practitioner who tended to her must indeed be of great skill."

But, how did she survive this act of treachery? And, was it truly her husband who had committed the awful act?

While Scotland Yard and the *Gendarmerie Nationale* continue to maintain

a respectful silence, Lady Charlotte Moreau is ready to lend her own voice to the frightening tale of her attempted murder, disappearance, and survival.

The tale is not altogether a happy ending, as the Lady has a long road to recovery ahead of her and spends most of her days reclining on a couch in the sun room, while her daughter, Madeleine, and her servants, tend to her needs. She is often heavily sedated for the pain she still suffers and may sleep up to 20 hours in a day.

The medical practitioner "of great skill" who saved her life, an Englishwoman by the name of Sarah Harper, still tends to her today. Though trained as a nurse, Miss Harper first met our French-born playwright when she auditioned for a role in one of her productions, a role she has since set aside to nurse the Lady back to health.

The Daily Courant conducted the interview under Miss Harper's watchful eye. We were advised not to excite Lady Moreau and did our best to put the

Lady's health first, while helping her tell her story. Below is the transcript of our highly anticipated interview.

MR. WALKER: In the letter you entrusted to me, you were already quite sure of Basile's attempt on your life, days before it happened. Why did you not flee the house, to see to your safety?

LADY MOREAU: I knew if I went missing, Madeleine would be a target yet again. And if we ran, we would spend the rest of our lives running. Better to stay and fight, come what may.

MR. WALKER: Do you regret that decision?

LADY MOREAU: I do not. I am a free woman now. Yes; it nearly cost me my life, but at least all of England and France now see for themselves the monster I married in the folly of my youth.

MR. WALKER: Do you have any idea as to how your late husband met his end?

LADY MOREAU: I do not know the full story, but I do know God is not sleeping. He sees all and will rise us up or set us down as He sees best.

MR. WALKER: Well said. What are your plans for the future? There are talks that you have put up the London house and *The Lady's Playhouse* for sale.

LADY MOREAU: I have. I had an excellent time in London and met people I will cherish, always. Some, like Miss Harper, are the only reason I am alive today, but if I am honest, I fled to London to get away from my late husband. Now that he is gone, and I have witnessed first-hand how fragile our lives are, I wish to retire peacefully in Barfleur with my daughter.

MR. WALKER: I am not sure "retire" is the word I would use for your current occupations—if you will forgive my saying so! Many stages in London, Paris, and even Rome and Madrid, have requested the rights to air your plays.

LADY MOREAU: Yes; I am honoured that these requests were made. *Monsieur* Alexandre Dumas was kind enough to offer to see to the production of my plays in Paris, while my manager and (I can say now, my paternal half-brother) Eli Bernard, will handle production in London and Barfleur. He will also appoint worthy overseers for Madrid and Rome. I put my faith in his expertise.

MR. WALKER: Mister Eli Bernard is your brother? Why did you wait until just now to share this?

LADY MOREAU: We live in an era where human beings are still considered lesser because of the colour of their skin, and my late husband (and many others of the suitors who courted my attentions before him) would have forced me to cut all ties with my brother had he known of that familial connection. I would not, for anything, cast him away. When *Monsieur* Alexandre Dumas came to visit, being in his company and witnessing his successes in the flesh, reminded me that there is hope, yet.

Since this interview was conducted, *The Lady's Playhouse* was bought by none other than Eli Bernard, who will continue to show his sister's plays, alongside other notable acts. You may watch Lady Moreau's newest play, *A Love, Betrayed* at seven o'clock at The Lady's Playhouse, tomorrow evening, January 29th.

Her cheeks flushed with pleasure as she read the words he strung together of their last interview. He read hope in her smile, kindness in her eyes, but when he addressed the rift that stood between them, that smile evaporated like mist before his eyes.

He had prepared himself for this, and yet her words took the very wind out of him all the same. It brought him no comfort that she looked as torn as he felt, as broken, as hopeless.

"You are young, George," Charlotte said for what felt like the thousandth time since he had known her. "I cannot be the wife you deserve. I will never bear you a child. You are scarcely thirty, and in the very prime of your life, some ten years hence, perhaps, you will be burying a wife. Why would you want such a life?" Her voice broke, as she continued, "I love you too much to subject you to such dreary prospects. I cannot. I *will* not."

George took her in his arms, smoothed the hair back from her forehead and pressed his lips to hers. If this was good-bye, he would not go without knowing what it felt like to be in the arms of the woman he had all but worshipped for so many years.

"This is a happy time of triumph for your family, for your daughter," he said, when he released her. "Let us not mar it with our own heartbreak." He dried her tears, straightened his jacket, donned his hat and pressed his lips to her forehead. *"Adieu,* my love."

Pain intensified with every echo of his footsteps, taking him from the back parlour, down the hallway, and out the back door. Summoning all her strength, she clung to the arm of the chair she had sat in, pulled herself up, and forced one foot before the other until she had made it to the cushioned seats by the window.

Even in the fading twilight, she could see the sadness in his smile and the defeated droop of his shoulders, as he turned for a last look in her direction. Pity and selfishness stirred within her, urging her to but reach out and pluck his youth from the palm of his hand. And what would she give in return? A title, but no heir? Gold to warm his bed, after he had buried her?

It took every ounce of strength to do nothing but return his own sad smile with her own, as he tipped his hat in farewell. He then turned down the street with no company but his shadow, as the night descended.

"Are you certain?" Jacob enquired, straining every ounce of self-possession to keep the desperation from his voice.

"Yes," she answered. "I would bet my life upon it."

He could feel her sizing him up beneath her hood, calculating not just how much she should share for her own sake, but also his. "It was I who delivered the cryptic note."

Jacob's eyes widened. "From whence did it come?"

"From the Catholic Church, as I said. Put in my very hand by a man who travelled far to pass the news."

"Did he say anything else?"

"I pressed, but he could not tell me, for the Seal of Confession."

Jacob swore an oath under his breath, but quickly apologised for using such coarse language in the company of a lady.

"You needn't worry about the ears of a woman who married a sailor, and who works in a tavern," she returned. "And, I am sure your man will confirm the news in due time."

Jacob sighed. "And my chance at her hand slips like sand between my fingers."

Esther only smiled at that.

"Does my misfortune amuse you?" he said, with obvious irritation.

"I do not see a misfortune," she replied. "I see a gentleman who does not give the Lady he loves credit enough. Go and see her. I have it on good authority that she waits to hear from you, night and day."

The flame was instantly rekindled in his eyes. Then returned the playful upturn to his lips, as though they could break into a smile at any moment. "And pray tell, Esther, whose very good authority was this?"

"Priests are not the only ones bound by the Seal of Confession, even if mine is voluntary. I do not share matters of the heart, unrelated to our business."

"And, I respect that. Thank you, Esther. I will wait for Stanley, however. Better failure with precise answers, than failures and uncertainty."

When he returned to his apartments that night, he found that no wait was necessary. The smell of tobacco arrested his senses the second he entered the room. In his reading chair, there sat the shaggy-haired Englishman he had hired. As was his wont, the chair had been turned so that Jacob could only see the back of his head, while he smoked.

"You neglected to share your hand in the Lady's escape, Stan," Jacob greeted him with some impatience.

It did not sit well with him that news of his assassin's involvement in saving Charlotte's life had come from Esther, instead of from the man himself. Stan would have been hanged a dozen times over had it not been for his timely intervention. He was a scoundrel of the streets of London, but a useful scoundrel all the same.

"I did neglect to share that useful bit of information," Stan agreed with his usual nonchalance, "but perhaps now you understand why I did not charge my usual price." Blue smoke curled in the air, above his head. "And in any case, her party did ask for my confidence! *And...* it was not all for love that I refused Basile's price on his wife's head, or even respect for you."

Jacob felt his blood run cold in his veins. "Basile hired you to murder Charlotte?"

"He tried, and shortly thereafter, another fine gentleman hired me to return the favour, and then so did you."

"Stanley, you—"

"Neglected to mention that, yes. But you forget, your currency is knowledge, and mine is secrecy. In any case, you interrupt me, and now I lose my train of thought. Where was I? Ah, yes!

"Before all of these timely requests, months before, there was a colleague of mine (one of the best I know!) who accepted an offer (against my advice, might I add) to assassinate the woman who I expect will become your grandmother-in-law. He never returned.

"Why should I then accept a challenge for the younger one? And I imagine the youngest is thrice the tigress!"

"You would not dare lay a hand upon her."

"Have you not been listening, Jacob? Of course, I would not! That is the very point I was making. I know if I crossed you, all the forces of England and France would seek me out for it, but there is another power I fear far more than you."

"Oh? And what power is that?"

"Why, my wife, of course!" he laughed. "How she adores Lady Charlotte Moreau, and the Moreaux in general, really. She is a true tyrant, my wife, and so naturally idolises women who do not bow to the tyranny of men.

"She certainly never bows to mine! If ever I rose a hand against her, as Basile is said to have done, I could not but sleep with an eye open for the night!"

Jacob could not stifle the chuckle that rose within him. "Do you really have a wife, Stanley?"

"I mention her often enough, do I not? What are our lives but a compilation of the things we tell ourselves and others are true?"

However amusing the discourse, Jacob was in no mood to speak in riddles and philosophise about existence. "Tell me what happened in Rocchetta."

"Ah, yes! The business at hand. My, Jacob! Where did you get this tobacco? I was always under the impression you did not smoke, and I rather believe this is the best I have ever stolen!"

"Stanley. Rocchetta Alta."

"If you insist," he said, as though he felt Jacob was being a perfect bore. "The villa was easy to find, though there was not a soul who knew who lived there, aside from the old couple and a young daughter.

"There was talk, however, of a newly married couple who arrived in town not long before myself. It was said the wife was Italian and the husband French, though he spoke excellent Italian himself. I asked of one of the nuns if a wedding had been performed recently, but they suspected me, so I was forced to help myself to some of the Church records."

"You broke into the Church!"

"Well, it is not as if you're Catholic, so don't pretend to be offended. Or is it practice for your new wife? *That* is an excellent idea!

"So, as I was saying (before I was unnecessarily interrupted for trifles), I chose the time, the tools, and the day. I waited until the visitors had left the room, and even the wife had gone (as you had not asked me to do away with her, nor had the other gentleman who put me up to the task, though it appears to me, she is no less guilty).

"I made my way up to the roof, down the side of the villa, and onto the balcony (in very much the same manner I made my way into your apartments!) and what should I find, but the Lord hanging by a noose? He was almost naked and there was a whip beneath his swinging feet, and the peaceful drip, drip, drip of blood from his back, presumably from self-flagellation. Morbid thing. Why-ever would I wish to whip myself?"

"It is considered penance, to show remorse for one's sins," Jacob explained, his mind in a daze.

"Remorse? Dreadful little of that I've got. It explains why my back is as smooth as a baby's bottom!—but we digress.

"I stayed an extra day to hear the news. It was ruled a suicide, forbidding him a proper Catholic burial to the dismay of his new wife (if we can indeed count her as a wife, since Lady Charlotte is very much alive, and she technically has not, and cannot divorce her husband, being Catholic! An excellent case for an Anglican conversion, I think. Did you know-)"

"Stanley!" cried Jacob, for he could bear the suspense no longer.

"Yes, yes, back to the story, because we cannot just speak as friends. I suppose Sirs do not condescend to make friends with criminals.

"Well, I hurried back to tell you what had happened, for I believe this new wife meant Charlotte harm, and much as I would like to witness such a standoff, I believed the best thing the Lady and her family could arm themselves with is knowledge."

"And here I was, thinking you did not have a conscience."

"Every man has a conscience, and every man his line that once drawn in the sand, cannot be crossed. Even a man like Basile. Even a man like me."

"What are you owed?"

"I find I am much compensated already. The mountain air was splendid, and I have bought a trinket or two I know my wife will be most grateful for!"

"Bought or stole, Stanley?"

"Let us not concern ourselves with mere trivialities. Was it not you who wished me to get to the point, when I wanted to have a friendly chit-chat?" He put out the pipe, emptied the ash, and pocketed it.

"I will be taking my leave now, Sir. It was a pleasure doing business with you, as always. I am sure, should you or Baby Vickie and her *Teuton* husband have need of my indispensable services yet again, you know how to find me, however much I oft' wish it were otherwise."

The crook then pulled his hood over his head and disappeared through the open window into the night.

CHAPTER XXVIII

A Lover's Confession

The sight of the widowed Moreau relaxing in the sun room was bitter-sweet. Yet, when he saw the look in her eyes, that pleasant curiosity mingled with expectancy, he knew she suspected his reason for coming, and approved.

Did mothers truly always know when a man meant to make a claim on her daughter's hand? He seemed to recall his own mother making such an assertion, once upon a time.

"Madeleine has been watching that door with eager eyes for some time now," Charlotte said, as though guessing his train of thought. "I should have known it was for you."

She meant to say more, but he never heard it. There was the sound of fast-approaching footsteps, followed by the sweeping of black chiffon into the room.

"Jacob!"

Charlotte looked at her daughter with some alarm. The young heiress was still wearing her nightclothes, dyed black instead of the customary off-white, and covered by a crimson, chiffon *peignoir*; the braid Gaëlle had begun and lost the chance to finish, just moments before, coming loose.

"Madeleine!" She turned to Jacob. "I am sure she is only just on her way up to properly dress to receive you."

Madeleine laughed, her curls bouncing as she did. "Nonsense, Mother!" She slipped an arm through the crook of Jacob's elbow. "Come! You have kept me waiting for long enough. We'll take a walk through the gardens, if you do not also feel inclined to make me go get pretty."

"Why would I, when you are already beautiful?"

Madeleine stopped in her tracks, her cheeks aflame. "You flatter me, Jacob, but come, before Regina and Gaëlle get to gossiping about us."

She threw a knowing look at her chief companions, as she led him along the garden's wooded path.

"It embarrasses me to say I have failed you, Madeleine, but alas it is the truth. Your father got to himself before my man could."

"Perhaps for the best. I should never have asked you to soil your hand on such a mission. I confess, though the deed itself brought me no unease, that it may later rest upon your own conscience, if you were successful—this stole many a wink of sleep from me, at night."

"I am no fiery-tempered *chevalier*, 'tis true, but there is no blackened conscience for me in avenging my betrothed, if you still intend to be such."

"I do have the intention."

He stopped then and slipped a hand about her waist. "But, is it because you want to, or because you feel you must? I would never breathe a word of what transpired between us; I have not.

"If this is not what you truly want, then I would sooner return to pursuing you in the fashion I always have. To call you mine, but have you never truly love me, would break my heart far more than your refusal, for I could not bear to see you unhappy, and worse, know myself to be the cause of it!"

She pressed a gentle hand against his unshaven cheek, now growing rough with a dark beard for the winter cold. "I am a stubborn woman, Jacob. I do as I like, and never otherwise. I said I would marry you, and I shall. I could not choose a better husband, I think. I pray you never give me reason to regret that estimation of you."

The boyish smile returned to his face. Her reassurance was more than he had hoped for. "My aunt was visiting in England when I returned to attend the Queen's wedding."

"The *Marchesa del Schiavone*?"

"Yes, the same. I had written to her, telling her I meant to ask for the hand of the beautiful Heiress at Barfleur. She admires your family, as I suppose most women do, and came all the way to England to present me with a gift to mark our engagement, in person."

He took from his pocket a tiny wooden box, and from its depths, a ring certainly fit for a *Marchesa* in Italy. It was not elaborate in design but made a statement with the polished gold band and a large oval-shaped diamond that showed a thousand Madeleines looking into it.

"Am I to wear an estate upon my finger?" Madeleine teased, though he could see she was obviously impressed with the gift, which was indeed worth an estate and the household to manage it.

"It would bring me immense pleasure, if you did," he replied. "But first, there is something I must tell you. I trust that we are alone, and that your woods do not have ears?"

Madeleine's heart skipped a beat. Was this the secret Mamie had warned her of? "We are safe here, Jake. Only Mamie and I ever brave the cold in the gardens at this time of year, our servants being from warmer climes, and Mother now being indisposed. I left Mamie asleep upstairs when I came down to see you."

"Then, I must confess that though I have never done you the dishonour of lying, I have not been entirely honest with you. Most men die with this secret, their wives never knowing who and what they have married, but am I mistaken in presuming there is a... a stronger understanding between us, now?"

Madeleine took his hands in hers, her eyes fixed on his. "I believe there is, Jake; speak freely." She could feel the tremor of his hands in hers.

"What I say may make you regret your earlier estimation of me, Madeleine, though I pray it does not. I must preface my confession to say this does not affect you in the least, that you need not fret for your safety, or for your country."

"My country?"

"Yes; I belong to a Society of gentlemen, Englishmen, with unwavering loyalty to the British monarchy. The Society was first formed by King William IV for fear that the French Revolution should spread to Britain, that our legacy would be destroyed. In short, I am an agent of the British crown."

For a moment, Madeleine could not find the words. "I fear I am not sure I understand you. Are you a spy?"

"It is not the word I prefer, but it would not be out of place for my profession," he replied, with obvious anxiety. "But I swear to you, Madeleine, my Order has never interfered with French affairs—especially not now when your monarchy is restored and we enjoy such excellent diplomacy after years of fighting, so much so that the daughter of your king is married to the uncle of our queen.

"Yet, it remains a common saying in France that for the shooting of kings, there is no closed season. Thus, we watch, we listen, we protect the young queen. That is our only task, our only focus. I have never, and will never, be a threat to you or your country."

"And I suppose this is how you were knighted," she guessed.

"Yes." He squeezed her palms, as if in fear she would walk away at any second. "It will come as no surprise to you that there are many who still refuse to see a girl sit upon a throne and be called a queen. I uncovered a French plot to assassinate Victoria, and have been stationed here, since.

"I was glad for it, since it meant being ever-closer to the French beauty I had met at a certain ball in London, who was in the heat of a debate with the brilliant Ada, who could not graciously concede that she had met her match, and perhaps, for the first time in her life, been outsmarted!"

There was a flush of colour in Madeleine's cheeks at the memory of the first night they had lain eyes upon each other. "I daresay you have surprised me, Jake!" said she. "I find you are living a far more exciting life than I originally imagined!"

"I am sorry I could not tell you sooner, Madeleine. Indeed, I am forbidden to tell you at all, but a woman of your intelligence would no doubt learn the truth by some small slip of mine once we were married. And, if you could trust me with the knowledge and task that you have, surely, I can trust you with this."

"Indeed! Better this than finding out I have some pretty rival in Rome, I suppose." The smile she threw him was full of mischief.

Jacob cupped her face in his hands. "There isn't a woman in all the world, that ever lived, who could rival your place in my heart, Madeleine." He pressed his lips to hers, then forcing himself away, presented her with the ring once more. "Now that you know the truth, do you still accept me? Am I still to be your husband?"

With the question now put to her, so direct, Madeleine saw all her doubts rear their ugly heads, yet again. "Do you promise not to interfere with my education? Not to attempt to induce me to change my name? That you will treat me as an equal, for as long as I behave as such?"

"I am aware of your family's customs, and respect them," he assured her. "You shall keep your name, and I, mine. And I shall take pride in having an educated woman at my side. I would not be very surprised if my Order recruited your talent. You would not be the first woman, or wife, who found herself among us."

Her fears once again soothed, she offered him her hand in acceptance. "A perfect fit," she noted as he slid the ring onto her finger.

"I had Gaëlle give me your measurements nigh upon a year now," he confessed. "I am surprised she managed to keep the secret, anxious as she was about not telling you my intentions, as though they were not obvious to every man for leagues."

She laughed.

"There is one more thing, I must ask of you," he said, now boldly taking her hand in his, as they walked back to the manor. "I should rather like to be a marked man myself, you know, so women can also know I am not a man for the chasing."

"I think I rather like this idea of yours. I should not like to employ your assassin to dispose of any fair beauties in France or England, for lack of it."

"Indeed, it would be a pity! So, to its effect, I am sure the Moreaux are not short of heirlooms they can part with, to make a present to me on my wedding day, which I rather say is far more a mark of accomplishment for me, than it is for you. Lord knows, you have dragged this courtship on for long enough."

"Tut-tut, Jacob! Do not now begin to complain when you have me. And was it not your English playwright who said that all is fair in love and war?"

CHAPTER XXIX

Dead Woman Walking

As winter merged into spring, the darkness that haunted their lives from the colder months seemed to fade into the unseen shadows. Under Miss Harper's care, and with the help of Mamie's remedies, Charlotte soon regained her strength.

By the time the first flowers bloomed in the early spring, she was able to walk about the garden unaided, and often wandered to the front yard to watch the comings and goings of the people of Barfleur. Many stopped to talk with her, and a few, to ask after Mamie who had done them a kindness or two in the past.

Eli and Gaëlle had also finally settled down together in London. Not a week went by that Madeleine did not receive letters of her friend's adventures and misadventures as the wife of a wealthy theatre manager in the city.

And with her own nuptials creeping ever closer, Madeleine found it was no easy walk down the aisle. Before *I do*, there was the matter of purchasing a home, and the ever more complicated one of finding a house that suited both the soon-to-be bride and groom. Not to mention hiring a household who would tend to this home, while the woman of the house tended to her education, and the man to the matters of the British crown.

These tasks presented such a challenge that it was mid-spring before a date for the wedding was set, at which point they gladly left the rest of the wedding particulars up to their families.

"Who knew marriage could be such a complicated affair?" Madeleine said with a heavy sigh. She rested her head against his chest as they sat together on a garden chair, enjoying their first quiet evening together in quite some time.

"Oh, come now, darling! I rather think you enjoyed shopping for a new home."

"You barely gave an ounce of input," she complained.

"My mother died when I was young, but not before passing on a wealth of wisdom: one bit of which was never to come between a woman and the home she desires. A man's job is only to pay for it, and hers to fill it with love."

"Your mother is wise, but she neglected to tell you what to do with a woman who is quite used to fending for herself."

"You needn't worry. For that, I have the *Marchesa*, my mother's youngest sister. You will find she is as strong-minded as you are. I am sure you two will get on famously!"

"I would love to get on famously with my bed at present, tired as I am."

"And I look forward to getting on quite famously in bed with *you*."

"You really must do better, Jacob. These past few days, I daresay you forget you are a gentleman. The things you say!" She tried not to let him see the smile tugging at her lips, but it was much too late for that.

She could feel his breath on her neck, warmer than the afternoon sun. She bolted from the garden chair, unwilling now, to fall under his spell any sooner than before she had said *I do* before God and man.

"You, terrible little scoundrel," said she, obviously flustered and trying to ignore his ever-widening smile. "I think it is time we meet the others inside for tea and coffee. And did Regina not promise us some of her delicious *dous beniyè?*"

"I am sure she did not."

"Well, we will go all the same," she said, leading the way as fast as her feet could carry her.

"They are outside trimming the front hedges," Betha said, as she entered the house.

Madeleine made for the door, moving quickly through the rooms, while Jacob lingered behind her. When she made it to the front garden, she found Mamie standing before the hedges with clippers in her hand, while Charlotte stood at the gate. They were both looking across the street at a haggard woman, who was twice the scandal she had been just months before.

"I know what you did!" the woman shouted as loudly as she could, for all to hear. "You murdered my husband! You and your mother and your daughter and all your witchcraft—you, Moreau witches!"

Charlotte did not reply. Instead, she sent the elderly woman, who had stopped to speak with her just moments before, on her way. The old lady almost tripped over her feet in her rush to get to safety.

"He went mad, and it was *you*—*you* he kept running from, *your* name that he shouted out in fear, while he slept! It was not suicide; it was murder!" She brandished a gun then and pointed it at Charlotte.

Jacob pushed past Madeleine and brandished his own. *"Madame* Anglais, put away your pistol!"

"My name is *Signora* Dubois! And I will not rest until her blood is spilt upon the streets!" she declared.

Mamie appeared beside Jacob, and put a gentle hand on his, as he cocked the barrel. Her eyes were shut, her lips moving as though uttering a silent prayer.

Emboldened by her rage and determination, Severina stepped out into the streets, the pistol still pointed at the woman she had so long abhorred. With all eyes fixed on the drama unfolding, no one saw the carriage coming up the street, until it struck her—four horses, carriage man, empty carriage, and all.

Passers-by and neighbours rushed into the street to see what had become of the driver and the unfortunate Severina. Charlotte never budged from the gate, and Madeleine remained transfixed in the doorway.

With trembling hands, Jacob lowered his gun, noticing only then that Mamie had long left his side. Screams rang out. Calls for the doctor, the police, and the priest, echoed up and down the street. And in the bushes, ignoring them all, Mamie continued to snip, and snip, and snip at the hedges; unperturbed.

Severina did not recover from her injuries, and Charlotte soon found the injured driver and splintered carriage belonged to none other than *Monsieur* Pierre Anglais. All around Barfleur, there was talk of witchcraft and that old gipsy blood in the family. But no one dared accuse them to their faces.

After all, hell hath no fury like witches scorned.

THE END

GLOSSARY

1. **Alexandre Dumas, père** was a popular French playwright and novelist in the 1800s. Today, **Dumas** is still considered one of the most widely read French writers of all time. He was born to the highest-ranking officer of Mixed ancestry in the French military and a White innkeeper's daughter. He is most well-known for penning *The Three Musketeers* and *The Count of Monte Cristo.* See https://www.britannica.com/biography/Alexandre-Dumas-pere.

2. Augusta Ada King-Noel, Countess of Lovelace, sometimes referred to as just "**Ada Lovelace**", is the mother of computer programming. She was an English mathematician and writer who created a programme for the prototype of a digital computer invented by Charles Babbage. Her husband, William King, 1st Earl of Lovelace, was also a scientist. Her father, Lord Byron, was friend to Percy Shelley and the soon-to-be **Mary Shelley**. See https://www.britannica.com/biography/Ada-Lovelace.

3. *Adieu* is a Late Middle English word inherited from Old French. It means "goodbye". See https://en.oxforddictionaries.com/definition/adieu.

4. **Barfleur** is a small, coastal town located in the Normandy region of France. The town was bustling in the Middle Ages as one of the main ports with ships disembarking for England. However, at the time in which the novel is set, there were less than 2000 people living in Barfleur. See http://en.normandie-tourisme.fr/barfleur-214-2.html.

5. **Bloody Mary** is the nickname often given to Queen Mary I, England's first female monarch. This was due to her persecution of Protestants in an attempt to restore Roman Catholicism in England and Ireland. The Marian Persecutions led to the deaths, imprisonments and fleeing of more than a thousand Protestants during her five-year reign. Many were also burned at the stake

for heresy. In addition to this, Queen Mary I executed the 1st Duke of Northumberland for supporting Lady Jane Grey's claim to the throne. Lady Jane and her husband were also executed. See https://www.history.com/topics/british-history/mary-i.

6. The **bourgeoisie** was not synonymous with the **nobility**. The bourgeoisie referred to the usually wealthy middle and upper middle strata of society, while the **nobles** were titled members of society. Not all nobles were wealthy. In fact, many were poor. See *The Oxford History of the French Revolution* by William Doyle.

7. **Bread riots** have occurred in many different countries at various points in time. However, the 1789 bread riots in France, which led to the French Revolution, are arguably the most talked about in historical circles. Bread constituted roughly 75 percent of the average person's diet in 1700s France, and the poor spent about 33 percent to 55 percent of their income on bread alone. So, naturally, when the prices soared in Paris, riots became widespread. This precipitated the storming of the Bastille and the French Revolution on a whole. See *The Oxford History of the French Revolution* by William Doyle.

8. *Brioche* is an enriched type of French bread-type pastry which uses more egg and butter than regular bread. It is considered a part of a traditional French breakfast, but not a regular breakfast. It was most often eaten as a treat on the weekends or on holidays. See http://www.myrecipes.com/extracrispy/what-the-french-know-about-breakfast-that-americans-dont.

9. *Café au lait* is coffee made with hot instead of cold milk. It is considered part of a traditional French breakfast. The French have historically brewed and drunk more—and some would say better—coffee than anywhere else in the Western Hemisphere, and that boom started around the 18th and 19th centuries. See http://www.myrecipes.com/extracrispy/what-the-french-know-about-breakfast-that-americans-dont.

10. In Vodou, a ***caplata*** is a female witch-for-hire who serves both good and evil. They are, however, more frequently painted as the evil alternative to a ***mambo***, which is a Haitian Vodou Priestess. The male equivalent of a ***caplata*** is the ***bokor*** and the male equivalent of a ***mambo*** is the ***houngan***.
    See https://web.archive.org/web/20111006144910/http://www.webster.edu/~corbetre/haiti/voodoo/overview.htm.

11. **Charles Darwin** was an English naturalist and scientist. In 1859, some 19 years after the book is set, he published *Origin of the Species* to illustrate his theories of evolution and natural selection. During the time in which the novel is set, Darwin is in the early stages of researching and developing this theory. His circle of friends included the programmer Charles Babbage and, by extension, **Ada Lovelace**.
    See *Darwin* by Adrian Desmond and James R. Moore.

12. **Charles Dickens** was a celebrity writer in his time, known from the shores of London to New York. He was born into a poor family and first entered the workforce at just 10 years old. He later worked in law, politics, and journalism. Heartbreak and disappointment from a failed romantic pursuit of Maria Beadnell, a banker's daughter, is said to have fuelled his determination, influenced his writing, and spurred his taste for the company of strong, intellectual women. Along with being a writer, he was a philanthropist who helped raise awareness about the plight of the poor and the harsh conditions under which they laboured.
    See *The Victorian Era: A Very Short History* by Tristan Clark.

13. A ***château*** is the French equivalent of a castle, palace, manor, or large countryside residence usually owned or inhabited by members of the royal family, nobility, or the gentry.
    See https://www.britannica.com/technology/chateau-architecture.

14. A ***chevalier*** was the French equivalent of an English knight or soldier. In many of **Alexandre Dumas's** stories, *chevaliers* were

characterised by chivalry and a near obsession with defending the honour of their lady loves.

See *The Chevalier D'Harmental* by Alexandre Dumas.

15. A **coat of arms** can now be used by organisations and states for a number of reasons. However, in the context of this novel and the era in which it is set, it is an insignia usually borne by an individual member of a noble family. It was especially used by knights or **chevaliers** to display their achievements in battles and competitions. This is often confused with the **crest**, which represents the noble family as a whole and is incorporated into the design at the top of the coat of arms. However, in France, not all noble families used crests or coat of arms. Also, many bourgeoisie families created and registered their own arms.
See: https://ancestralfindings.com/real-truth-behind-coats-arms-family-crests/.

16. In the 16th century, the big cities of the Ottoman Empire were the first to see **coffee houses** spring up. Thereafter, they spread to London, Paris, and the rest of Europe, and played a major role in the spread of ideas of enlightenment from as early as the Renaissance era. Not unlike coffee houses of today, patrons conducted business, played board games, engaged in intellectual debates, and read newspapers and magazines.
See *World History, Volume I: To 1800* by William J. Duiker and Jackson J. Spielvogel.

17. The *cravat* is the predecessor of the modern necktie. During the Victorian era it was a piece of fabric, often elaborately tied and tucked into the neck of a shirt.
See image at https://en.wikipedia.org/wiki/File:Louis1667.jpg.

18. The term **Creole French**, especially in the 1600s to 1900s, was used to distinguish between the mainland French and Francophones who were born abroad in French territories like Haiti and Louisiana. Some people also referred to Black and Mixed-Race Francophones as being Creole French.

See *Toussaint L'Ouverture, The Haitian Revolution* by Toussaint Louverture (presented by Jean-Bertrand Aristide).

19. *Curé* is the French word for priests. In *The Oxford History of the French Revolution* by William Doyle, it was specifically used to refer to parish priests who lived less glamorous lives than the nobles who occupied the upper echelons of the clergy.

20. A **dandy** is the Victorian era equivalent of a metrosexual. The word dandy denotes a man who pays excessive attention to his appearance and often spends heavily on fashionable clothes. **Charles Dickens** was described as quite the dandy in his youth. See https://en.oxforddictionaries.com/definition/dandy.

21. *Dous beniyè* is Haitian sweet fritters made with flour, sugar, fruits, and milk. They are very similar to the banana fritters made in Jamaica.
Find the recipe here: https://www.glahaiti.org/haitian-recipes/.

22. Dubbed the "Virgin Queen," **Elizabeth I** was Queen of England from 1558 to 1603. Under her rule, England emerged as a force to be reckoned with in matters of economics, political power, and the arts. This period in history, especially as it relates to England, is called the Elizabethan Age.
See https://www.britannica.com/biography/Elizabeth-I.

23. At the time in which the novel is set, a **family seat** referred to the principal place of residence for the head of a noble family or a family that belongs to the landed gentry. Ruling families often took the name of their dynasty or house from the name of the family seat.
See *The Oxford History of the French Revolution* by William Doyle.

24. A **fortnight** describes a period of time lasting for two weeks or fourteen days.
See https://en.oxforddictionaries.com/definition/fortnight.

25. In Saint-Domingue, the term *grand blanc* referred to the wealthy Whites who occupied the uppermost echelon of the social hierarchy. These were politicians, planters, and others who held and exercised great power on the island.

26. ***Gros Fermiers*** were farmers in France who leased or rented land for farming. They were not well-liked, since they often received the most fertile plots of land and disregarded community practices, such as gleaning and open grazing. See *The Oxford History of the French Revolution* by William Doyle.

27. The **hackney** is a two-horse carriage for hire that first took to the streets in the 17th century. In the 19th century, on the brink of the Victorian era, a smaller, lighter, faster, safer carriage that only required one horse began to replace the traditional hackney carriages. This was the hansom safety cab, sometimes just called a **hansom.** In colloquial Victorian English, it appears that even though hansom and hackney were two different types of vehicles, they were sometimes used interchangeably to mean "taxi" or "cab".
See https://janeaustensworld.wordpress.com/tag/hackney-cab/ and the *Sherlock Holmes* series of stories by Sir Arthur Conan Doyle.

28. ***Itemba alibulali*** is a Zulu African proverb used by former Haitian President, Jean-Bertrand Aristide, while writing about the Haitian struggle for economic and political emancipation. It means "hope is not dead".
See *Toussaint L'Ouverture, The Haitian Revolution* by Toussaint Louverture (presented by Jean-Bertrand Aristide).

29. **Jean-Jacques Dessalines** was a West-African born slave who joined the slave rebellion in 1791 in **Saint-Domingue**. He later rose to the ranks of lieutenant under **Toussaint L'Ouverture**. When **Toussaint** was taken by the French, and Napoleon announced that slavery would be reinstated, **Dessalines** fought to preserve freedom. This culminated in the declaration of independence and the returning of Saint-Domingue's name to **Haiti**. Dessalines later declared himself Emperor Jacques I of Haiti and began a ruthless rule of forced labour for Blacks and hostility towards Whites and Mulattoes. This lasted until he was

killed during a revolt led by Alexandre Sabès Pétion in 1806. See https://www.britannica.com/biography/Jean-Jacques-Dessalines.

30. **King William IV** was the predecessor of **Queen Victoria** and ruled from 1830 to 1837. He had many scandalous affairs during his time as a sailor, producing ten illegitimate children along the way. However, neither of his two legitimate daughters survived infancy, causing the throne to pass to his niece, Victoria. See https://www.britannica.com/biography/William-IV-king-of-Great-Britain.

31. *Kreyol* is the French-based creole language spoken in Haiti. Linguists also believe there are influences from West African languages, Spanish, and English. Though French is also recognised as an official language, for some Haitians *Kreyol* is the only language they know.
    See *History of Haitian-Creole: From Pidgin to Lingua Franca and English Influence on the Language* by J. L. Bonenfant

32. Historians believe **La Guinaudée** (sometimes Guinodée) was the name of the plantation where Marie-Cessette Dumas, the enslaved grandmother of **Alexandre Dumas**, lived with the *Marquis* Alexandre-Antoine Davy de la Pailleterie. She has been called a "great matriarch to a saga of distinguished men". In the novel, Maria Moreau, the mother of the Moreau Matriarchy, was named in her honour and lives with her mother, Olga, on "...a quarter acre of land bordering Les Bouchers and La Guinaudée".

33. The *Kreyol* words *Liv Lanmò* means "Book of Death" in English.

34. **Louis Philippe I,** *King of the French,* was the last king of France before the French abolished the monarchical system for the second time. During his reign, there was a common saying that "...for shooting kings, there is no closed season". Ironically, he had fought in support of the French Revolution, which first dismantled the monarchical system. His daughter, Marie-Louise,

sometimes called Louise-Marie, was married to the uncle of **Queen Victoria**, Leopold I.

See https://www.britannica.com/biography/Louis-Philippe.

35. The act of **lynching** refers to the hanging of an alleged criminal without fair or legal trial. While this has happened numerous times throughout history, for people of African heritage, and perhaps for everyone in the New World, lynching is most strongly tied to the cruel hanging of slaves and freed Blacks—often by planters, angry mobs, and White supremacists.

See https://www.pbs.org/wgbh/americanexperience/features/ emmett-lynching-america/ .

36. The French phrase ***ma chérie*** is a term of endearment. It translates to "my darling" or "my sweetheart" in English.

37. According to former President of Haiti, Jean-Bertrand Aristide, ***machotara*** is "a Kiswahili word meaning 'coloured people'." See *Toussaint L'Ouverture, The Haitian Revolution* by Toussaint Louverture (presented by Jean-Bertrand Aristide).

38. The French word ***maman*** translates to "mom", "mum", or "mummy" in English.

39. The ***mambo***, ***mambo asogwe***, and ***mambo si pwen*** refer to various hierarchies in Haitian Vodou. A ***mambo*** or a ***mambo asogwe*** is a high priestess, while a ***mambo si pwen*** is a junior priestess. *Mambos* serve **Bondye,** the Supreme Creator, whose name is believed to have come from the French phrase *"Bon Dieu"*, meaning "Good God".

40. ***Mamie*** is French for "grandmother" or "granny".

41. A ***Marquis*** is the French equivalent of an English Marquess, though they occupied different levels of nobility at the time of the novel. Originally, a *Marquis* was in possession of a *marquisat* from which his title came. However, especially after the French Revolution, it became a *titre de courtoisie* (courtesy title), often used by French children of noble parents, or other members of noble families who did not have official titles. In the novel, the

Moreau Family adopt the male title of *Marquis* and the female title of **Marquise** because the family's original titles of **Seigneur** and **Seigneuresse** died out after the abolition of feudalism due to the French Revolution of 1789.

See https://www.britannica.com/place/France/The-abolition-of-feudalism.

42. **Mary Shelley** was the English author behind *Frankenstein*, which is also known as *The Modern Prometheus.* She was the daughter of liberal political journalist, William Godwin and his feminist wife, Mary Wollstonecraft Godwin.

43. The French words **nègre** and **négresse** may look like the translations of the English words "negro" and "negress". However, in late 1700s France leading into the 1800s, these were much closer to the word "nigger". The word *nègre* is used in Napoleon's angry retort regarding Toussaint's victories in Haiti. Translated to English, it says, "I will not rest until I have torn the epaulettes off every nigger in the colonies."

See *Tracing War in British Enlightenment and Romantic Culture* by Neil Ramsey and Gillian Russell.

44. The French word **papa** translates to "dad" or "daddy" in English.

45. The **peasantry** were subsistence farmers who made up the lower class in the countryside.

See https://en.oxforddictionaries.com/definition/peasantry.

46. A **peignoir** is an outer garment made from a sheer fabric, usually chiffon, worn by Victorian women. The garment was worn when brushing out a woman's hair, and also as dressing gowns or bath robes.

See image at http://farm1.staticflickr.com/496/31175067144_1 49173ef74_o.jpg.

47. **Penny dreadfuls** were sensational graphic stories sold for a penny a piece in Victorian era London. The stories covered murder fiction, gothic fantasy, and other sensational genres. They were primarily aimed at the working class, who could not

afford more expensive publications.

See https://www.bl.uk/romantics-and-victorians/articles/ penny-dreadfuls.

48. The *Pickwick Papers* were serialised adventure stories published by **Charles Dickens** between 1836 and 1837. They were then made available as a full novel in 1837.

You may read a free eBook copy courtesy of The Project Gutenberg here https://www.gutenberg.org/files/580/580-h/580-h.htm.

49. The saying **"prescription without possession availeth nothing"** was the English quip for Spain's claim to the Americas in the 1600s, as the English ignored the Spanish claim to unoccupied areas of the New World and established their own colonies. In the novel, Sir Jacob uses it ironically to mean that the prescribed term of "courting" means nothing if Madeleine does not acknowledge his efforts, and if she continues to deny him her hand.

See *A Short History of Europe, 1600-1815: Search for a Reasonable World* by Lisa Rosner and John Theibault.

50. A *quadroon* is an archaic term for a person who is one-quarter Black ancestry, and otherwise of European descent. It seems to have been a matter-of-fact term used in the 1700s, and perhaps a matter of pride for Haitian Mulattoes who were granted rights Black citizens were not, but it is now considered offensive in most circles.

See https://en.oxforddictionaries.com/definition/quadroon.

51. The Victorian era is named after **Queen Victoria**, who was queen of the United Kingdom of Great Britain and Ireland from 1837 to 1901, and later also Empress of India from 1876 to 1901. Queen Victoria was the longest reigning monarch before she was outdone by Queen Elizabeth II. She died at the ripe old age of 81. However, at the time of the novel she is only two or three years into her reign.

See https://www.britannica.com/biography/Victoria-queen-of-United-Kingdom.

52. The **Roma** are people of Indo-Aryan descent often called "gypsies" (sometimes spelled **gipsies**, as it is in the novel) though this term is sometimes considered offensive. In the novel, they are also referred to as **Tzigane**, which was the name given to them by the French.

53. A **seigneurie** is a plot of feudal land which grants the title of **Seigneur** or **Seigneuresse** to its owners. Feudal rights were abolished after the French Revolution in 1789 and these titles disappeared with it.
See https://www.britannica.com/place/France/The-abolition-of-feudalism.

54. The **Kreyol** word **Sekré** means "secrets" in English. Its use as the name of a book of Vodou rituals is entirely fictitious and invented by the author for the purpose of this story.

55. The word **shrew** is perhaps best popularised in the Shakespearean play, *The Taming of the Shrew*. It was often used to imply that a woman was bad-tempered, ill-mannered, proud, and was not accepting of her lesser place in society.
See https://en.oxforddictionaries.com/definition/shrew.

56. At the time of the novel, **Signor** was the formal address in Italy for a man of noble birth or who was a member of the gentry. **Signore** was used when the title is not followed by a name. The female equivalent was **Signora**.
See https://www.merriam-webster.com/dictionary/signor.

57. **Sos pwa** is a delicious Haitian sauce made from garlic, scallions, beans and other delicious ingredients. Some recipes use chicken bouillon, but there are vegetarian alternatives. This sauce is great for pouring over plain rice and can be eaten with a side of meat.
See here for recipe https://www.glahaiti.org/haitian-recipes/.

58. **Soup Joumou** is a rich pumpkin soup, often made in celebration of **Haitian Independence** in January. During slavery, this was a delicacy reserved for planters and other members of the upper

strata of society. After **Dessalines** declared Haitian Independence, it became a symbol of Haitian freedom.

Recipes vary, but you may find one here https://www.glahaiti.org/haitian-recipes/.

59. A **swallowtail coat** or **dress coat** is a special coat worn by gentlemen of the Victorian era as formal evening wear. It is considered the precursor to the tuxedo.

See image at https://en.wikipedia.org/wiki/File:BrummellDighton1805.jpg.

60. *Teuton* is a somewhat poetic reference to Germans, which is believed to have first come into use during the Victorian era. The word is an allusion to an ancient Germanic tribe, known as the Teutons.

See https://www.merriam-webster.com/dictionary/Teuton.

61. **Toussaint L'Ouverture** was the primary force behind the success of the slave rebellion which grew into the **Haitian Revolution**, though he was himself a free and wealthy Black who owned slaves. Toussaint not only helped to rid Haiti of slavery, but is also considered one of the toughest opponents Napoleon ever faced. He was nicknamed "Black Spartacus". Toussaint and Thomas-Alexandre Dumas Davy de la Pailleterie were the two highest-ranking soldiers of sub-Saharan African ancestry in Europe and the Americas until 1975. If the name **Dumas** sounds familiar to you, that would be because he is the father of the celebrated author, **Alexandre Dumas, père**.

See *Toussaint L'Ouverture, The Haitian Revolution* by Toussaint Louverture (presented by Jean-Bertrand Aristide).

62. The word **trap** was commonly used in the way the word "car" is used today. It was a two-wheeled carriage that was light enough to be drawn by either a horse or pony.

See https://en.oxforddictionaries.com/definition/trap.

63. A *tricoteuse* is a woman who knits, but the term mostly refers to women who knitted by the guillotine during public executions in the French Revolution.

See https://en.oxforddictionaries.com/definition/tricoteuse.

64. Until 1859, *Wallachia* was an independent principality in Eastern Europe. It was not until 1859 that it joined with Moldavia to create what would be called Romania from 1866 onwards. People of *Wallachia* were often referred to as *Wallachian* or *Wallacks*.

See https://www.britannica.com/place/Walachia.

65. **West Indian** is the demonym for the people of the **West Indies** (also known as the Caribbean). People of Caribbean ancestry are for more likely to refer to themselves and the diaspora as West Indian than Caribbean, especially in English-speaking countries like Jamaica, Barbados, and Trinidad and Tobago. The term was commonly employed in Britain in the time the novel is set, and is still used there, today.

ACKNOWLEDGEMENTS

This book is dedicated to the family, friends, and followers who have been a constant source of support on the long, hard road of publishing.

To Topaz and Tracy, who saw potential in my earlier works and pushed me to publish. To Anne J and Vanessa who refused to give up, until I caved and wrote the witches' tale in full. To Elizabeth, who was the first to offer the use of her magical red ink to polish up my novel. To Rosetta, who added the British authenticity I needed. To Shadow, my beloved miniature black panther, who reminded me to take breaks by head-butting the keyboard and who graciously published my book under the **black CATastrophy** division of our firm. To Google, who knows all the things.

To my Haitian father who first encouraged me to quit my corporate job to travel and write; and to my Jamaican mother who shed tears in fear for the risks I took but supported me nonetheless. To *Mama,* the retired matriarch and fellow bookworm of our family, who first inspired me to write a period piece.

And to my own "Basile" who assured me I would amount to nothing.

~Merci~

THE AUTHOR OF THE MOREAU WITCHES

Alexis Chateau is a Jamaican author of mystery, paranormal, and crime fiction. Follow her non-fictional tales of trials and triumphs at **www.alexischateau.com.**

Is *The Moreau Witches* your first novel? If not, what is?

I think of this as my debut novel, since it's the first one I've published, but this is probably the 39th novel I ever wrote. My first novel was written in 2002 and was entitled *The Family*. Many people thought it was a cry for help—it was.

Who is your favourite character in *The Moreau Witches?*

Stanley, the assassin, is my favourite character. Not the answer you were expecting, eh? I don't play favourites with my leading ladies. Sorry, not sorry.

Why did you choose the Victorian era for *The Moreau Witches?*

I have always preferred to read antiquarian novels and plays, and mostly watch movies and TV shows with sweaty long-haired men wielding swords and old pistols. However, I've also always been terrified of writing in an era I never lived in. In 2016, I found the courage and published the original *Moreau Witches* short story series on my blog. And well—here I am!

Near the end of the novel, Basile made some strong allegations against Charlotte and her mother. Are they true?
Are they? That depends on who the reader wants to believe and was a question deliberately left unanswered. I believe in the duality of nature. After all, if God truly created everything and there was nothing before He came into the world, we must accept that evil exists because He created it. Even Lucifer was once the right-hand man of God, *the morning star, the bringer of light.*

The book cover also reflects this: showing Madeleine when she ignores the black abyss of her family's legacy, and then Madeleine when she looks into that black abyss and it seeps back into her. Likewise, whether Basile's allegations are wrong or right, he laboured under the belief that it was so, which begs the question of where we draw the line between pure evil and justifiable vengeance—all left up to the reader and their own code of morality.

Is there a significance to the ship Mamie proposes to Madeleine as a gift, when she learns of her engagement?
Indeed. Throughout the story, Madeleine is frequently compared to her grandmother, Mamie. When Mamie was a young wife, she tired of her husband, and as she could not divorce him, she sent him off to Saint-Domingue to manage the old plantation inherited, perhaps, from Maria Moreau's planter father upon his death.

When she learns that Madeleine is to be married, she offers the same escape route to Madeleine, just in case she ever feels compelled to rid herself of Sir Jacob.

Will there be a sequel to *The Moreau Witches?*
I have a few ideas I'm toying with for a sequel. A few readers asked to learn more about the assassin, and many others want to read Mamie's story, especially as it relates to her role in the French Revolution and the blackened castle she kept in thanks. But ultimately, my readers will decide. If they love the witches' tale enough to ask for another, I might oblige.

What else have you been working on?
As soon as I typed "THE END" on the first draft of the witches' tale, I started working on completing a vampire novel I first started in 2005. I hope to publish it by 2019.

What is your ultimate goal as a writer?
I would really, really, really love to have at least one book banned by the Catholic Church. That's when I'll know I have truly arrived.

www.ingramcontent.com/pod-product-compliance
Lightning Source LLC
Chambersburg PA
CBHW021424110726
47901CB00008B/2291